To, Em,

Happy reading!

Jayne May x

18 months ago

I remember the day quite clearly…the day that my happy married life as I knew it changed forever. I was walking home from the train station, I'd popped into the local supermarket on my way past, realising I hadn't got an onion to make the lasagne with and as I walked past the local pub…bam, there it was. A sight I never in a million years expected to see was just there...in front of me. That was the day my whole world fell apart.

It was like somebody had knocked all the air out of my body. I felt like I was on another planet. There he was - Mark, my husband, sitting in the window at a local pub with a group of his colleagues, paying close personal attention to someone in particular, well one woman in particular to be more exact.

I was shocked, traumatised, I just completely froze to the spot. My legs felt like lead and my mouth must've dropped open bigger than the channel tunnel. Do I confront him? Do I go home and wait to confront him there? Hot angry tears erupted from my eyes and I knew if I confronted him there and then, my humiliation would only be worse.

After what felt like an hour had passed I managed to get home, but how…I don't know, that part seems such a blur now looking back. Hearing his key in the lock when he finally arrived home that night made my stomach flip, the nerves were like nothing I'd ever experienced before. Nerves of confronting him, nerves of knowing that this was it, things would never be the same again. There was no way I could forget what I'd seen, there was no way I wanted to forget. I couldn't just ignore it, although part of me wanted to. Stupid I know, but I thought we were so happy I just didn't want things to change, but I knew they had to after that.

What if he denied it? how could he? I saw it with my own eyes! What other possible reason could there be for seeing your husband running his hands through another woman's hair as she straddles his lap?

What made it worse is the fact that other people he worked with were there, standing right next to them, they must've been aware of what was going on, how could they not be? It was our local pub close to our home which made it even worse in a way. Our neighbours could have been in that pub, people that we knew, so it just shows even more the total lack of respect he had for me.

I was sitting in the dark upright on the sofa in a daze when Mark finally came into the living room that night.

He leaned to kiss me on the cheek. "There you are…"

Smelling the drink on his breath straightaway I could say nothing at first, it just hadn't sunk in. As his lips lingered on my cheek, they felt cold and misplaced. He switched on one of the lamps as I sat staring at the charcoal coloured carpet and was transported back to the day we had it fitted.

I pictured the carpet fitter who worked like a trojan on his own for three hours solid, even refusing numerous offers of a drink. Maybe it was my mind trying to block things out, but I remember how normal things seemed and how happy I thought we were as we put the finishing touches to our newly decorated living room.

Mark flung his black trench coat onto the arm of the sofa. "Meeting went on a bit longer than I thought, sorry. Shall we order takeaway or have you cooked?"

All I could think was 'is this the kind of meeting you've been having four times a week for the last six months?'

I continued to sit and stare at the floor, at the wall - anywhere, as long as it meant my eyes didn't have to focus on him. He finally realised something wasn't right as he lowered himself onto the sofa next to me, reaching desperately for my hand.

"Luisa, has something happened?"

I think he began to get worried from the look on my face and the fact that after all of that crying, I must've looked like someone had scrubbed at my face with sandpaper.

I spent the next two hours trying to get a confession out of him. He told me what I'd seen was innocent and I was paranoid and then at last, when I felt like I was close to collapsing with exhaustion, he cracked.

"Her name's Fiona, she's a temp that started earlier this year."

There they were, the words that were fatal to our marriage. Hearing him say those words, despite already having seen them together with my own eyes that day, it was like finding out all over again. I felt like someone had kicked me in the stomach whilst tearing out my heart.

"I don't care what her name is or whether she's the office bike, which she clearly is…have you been having an affair with her, yes or no?" I couldn't bear it any longer, I was drained of every tear, there couldn't possibly be any more.

At least now I knew. They'd been having an affair for three months, or so he says. How had I not known, am I stupid? Mark promised me faithfully it was over. He begged me to stay, begged me to forgive him, told me he loved me more than anything in the world and he'd do anything to put things right. But what could I say? If he loved me that much we wouldn't be having this conversation.

I packed a bag straightaway and went to stay at my best friend Jodie's where I stayed for the next six months, give or take a weekend here and there that I spent with my parents to give Jodie and her boyfriend Darren some space.

To cut a long story short I moved back in after months of phone calls, bouquets of flowers and constant begging to give things another try. I didn't want things to end and I know Mark isn't a bad person, temptation got the better of him it's as simple as that. Constant reminders from my Spanish mother of how divorce isn't an option also pushed me into reconciliation so, I agreed to give things another try.

It took a long time and I slept in the spare room for the first five months. Mark seemed to have changed. He was more attentive, sometimes to the point of annoying, but I just wanted back what we had. Things have never been the same since and I could cry when I think back to how we used to be before. The year we were together before we got married and of course after we got married, were perfect…but I doubt they will ever be right again.

If I'm speaking honestly from the heart, I don't feel the same way about Mark that I used to. I think that once something like that happens a part of the relationship dies, it never comes back - no matter how hard you try. Slowly over time, things are starting to seem more like a chore than a relationship and I wish we could turn back the clock and I know Mark does too. I'm trying my hardest, but it shouldn't really be this hard if we're meant to be together. His long working hours continue but I'm trying to learn to trust him again, very slowly. There are times though when I feel trapped, isolated even, but maybe I just need to give it more time.

Chapter 1 – Present day

The loud familiar shrill of his mobile phone pierces the silence, waking me from a deep sleep. It's not unusual but it certainly is infuriating. It never seems to wake Mark always me, which means I have to continually nudge him to wake him up. Ironic really as whoever's waking me doesn't want to speak to me - they want to speak to him.

Mark groggily leans out of the bed managing to knock his mobile from his bedside table onto the floor. I prise my eyes open once more to check the time, 5:47 a.m. as Mark grumbles his apology to me.

"Sorry Lu, got an early meeting so they're chasing me for the agenda."

I can't help but think if the meeting is that early maybe the agenda should have been done the night before, but that's not even worth voicing.

He snuggles back in beside me, making me wince at the feel of his body in close contact with mine. I try my hardest to allow myself to relax, closing my eyes and forcing my mind to drift off elsewhere, somewhere where we're happy - where I'm happy and I don't have to pretend. Gradually, it begins to work. We're in Mexico on our honeymoon on the most beautiful tropical beach but then, it seems that the culprit can sense my relaxation levels are creeping up and so, decides now would be a good time to call again.

Mark leans over to his phone once more. "Sorry…"

I slowly climb out of bed and move back the heavy grey blackout curtains to see that once again, it's raining. I close my eyes and begin to imagine how brilliant it will be to feel the sun on my skin tomorrow and instantly feel myself calming down. Closing the curtain back I turn to look at Mark still in bed, his salt and pepper hair in complete disarray, but already working - checking emails on his phone as he rubs his eyes in an attempt to wake up. I wouldn't mind but this is my wake-up call almost every day now.

Tonight we're going on holiday for two weeks to Croatia, I'm hoping that this is what we need, time together to reconnect. I'm trying to stay positive, but in some ways I feel like spending two weeks with Mark and Mark alone isn't going to be easy. In fact…I think it will be anything but.

Mark works hard, too hard. We rarely get to see each other which in some ways, and I know I sound awful now, isn't always a bad thing. When we do see each other, he has his phone constantly glued to his hand or his ear. He's quite often with me but his minds at work, which leaves me feeling like he's a distinct case of the lights are on but there's no one home when he's around.

Although I don't sound it, I do try to be a really supportive wife. I work meals around his long unsociable hours, help him prepare for presentations and in turn, he's fairly supportive of my work too. I write novels, well when I say novels I mean singular - just one novel so far, the second one is a work in progress.

Things with Mark started to change in a big way a couple of years ago, a while before his affair. When he first got his promotion at the bank to director level, he started to work longer and longer hours until sometimes, we'd go two days without seeing each other. I did my best not to complain, I knew Mark was extremely ambitious when I met him, I knew he always worked hard and I was so pleased that he'd achieved what he'd strived for. Admittedly with the longer hours, we started to drift apart slightly so I made every effort I could to make sure we didn't crumble.

We met for lunch once each week, if a quick coffee was all he could manage, then a quick coffee it would be. On the occasion when he was home at a reasonable hour we'd sit together and catch up over a bottle of wine or sometimes even go out for food to our favourite Indian restaurant a few streets away. We'd sit in a cosy corner and just be us...Luisa and Mark, with no interruptions other than a waiter bringing us delicious food.

Mark and I met around four years ago when I was 23 and working as a travel agent in Birmingham city centre. For as long as I can remember, I've had such a passion for travel that a job in a travel agent seemed an obvious career choice for me. I worked there for eight years, was promoted to branch manager and was lucky enough to visit some fantastic places and even better, at heavily discounted prices. Travelling was something I'd always wanted to do and this in turn, was helping me to travel and to help others do the same. Whether I was booking a weekend away snowboarding for a customer, a two week holiday in the sun, a city break taking in lots of culture or just a flight booking...I loved doing it.

There are still so many more places I would love to see in the world and I'd planned to take six months off at some point to go and see more of those places, but then I met Mark.

I remember the day we met vividly. Mark came in on his lunch hour to book a flight to visit his friend working in Canada. I immediately thought he was attractive. A slight hint of a tan with blue eyes and black hair - slowly starting to mix with grey but it really suited him. I guessed he was a few years older than me, he had a certain maturity about him and I fell for his charms. When he asked if he could take me out one night, I didn't have to think twice.

A week later, he took me for a drink at my local pub. Mark came to pick me up pulling up in his sleek black hatchback outside the house I was sharing at the time with Jodie - my best friend. As I got into the car, she texted me her approval of his attire and his car...obviously snooping through the window.

Me and Mark became inseparable after that night and after just a year together, he proposed to me and I immediately said yes. I was ecstatic. A year to the day later on 22nd July, we got married in the same church I was christened in. I didn't want a church wedding I was desperate to get married abroad but for various reasons, we didn't.

Mark's parents couldn't understand why I could possibly want to get married outside of the UK. The clear choice for me would have been to get married in Spain like my parents did with my mother being a born and bred Spaniard. It would've been great to get married there with both of our families, but it just seemed too hard, offending people is something we really didn't want to do.

We had a lovely wedding, despite the fact that our mothers fought for most of the time leading up to our special day. I had a Catholic upbringing, although not particularly strict and it meant a lot to my Mom for us to get married in a church. Mark's Mom Tina thought we should have a Civil Ceremony as their family aren't religious, followed by a reception at their golf club. Mark and I felt we couldn't even have the wedding day we really wanted. To keep the peace, we decided on marrying in church, followed by the golf club reception, so there you go fulfilling everyone's wishes, except ours.

I was never one of those little girls that dreamt about their wedding day when I was growing up. I didn't spend time picturing the dress, flowers and horse and carriage. I was painfully shy and never really thought about getting married, certainly not to that much detail. I wasn't quite sure how I'd ever talk to a boy with my shyness let alone marry one.

When hunting for my wedding dress Mom, Jodie and I spent one Saturday afternoon in two shops. I think I tried on around six different dresses before deciding on the first one from the first shop we went to. So back we went to *'All Things Bridal'*, where I chose a strapless ivory A-line dress with stunning diamantes which fitted my curves in all of the right places, along with a beautiful sparkly tiara and some ivory peep-toe shoes.

On the big day itself, Shelly my hairdresser arrived and styled my hair as requested into a chignon towards the crown of my head. Jodie did my make-up as she's always been an expert in that department, before slipping into her champagne coloured bridesmaid dress, ready to walk down the aisle behind me.

From the doors of the church as I entered I could see Mark looked so handsome in his grey suit, white shirt and champagne coloured tie to match Jodie's dress. He actually looked like he was fighting back the tears as I walked down the aisle towards him, which amazed me as he always portrays himself as a bit of a macho man.

As I reached the altar and stood next to him he took my hand, looked deep into my eyes and told me I looked sensational. I remember feeling like I was walking on air, like I could explode with happiness and excitement. The wedding went without a hitch, even both sets of parents managed to stay talking to each other for the whole day.

I remember looking around the room at all of our friends and family at the wedding breakfast and I felt so content. That feeling is miles away from how I feel now. It feels like on our wedding day, the bride - me was a character in a chick-flick movie, and now I'm just 'a somebody' watching it back on TV, with no connection to the 'character' on screen at all.

My mother is originally from Córdoba, Andalusia. Her sister Nina and her family still live there and until six years ago, until he died, so did my grandfather...*Tito* as we called him. We visited him a couple of times a year when I was growing up, I've got so many happy memories of holidays spent with him and the family.

My brother Ben and I would travel to Spain when we were teenagers to visit *Tito*, we had some real adventures together. We'd travel out to cities such as Barcelona, Malaga and Granada. I really miss my *Tito* he was the warmest person I've ever met. I still can't believe it's been six years since he was taken from us.

As well as travelling, as a child I loved writing stories and our visits to *Tito's* house would often inspire me to write. My parents always said I had an overactive imagination so I had no problem making up stories and characters. I would sit night after night writing stories, but I never did let anyone read them, I suppose I thought they'd laugh at me. It was almost like if they could see how my imagination worked, they could see through me and know every minute detail about me which was something that my shyness simply could not allow. Writing has always been my way of expressing myself.

Last year on my train journey home from work one night, I noticed a competition in a magazine to win the chance to have a book published. I thought what have I got to lose?

That night I got started on my book which I then worked on every single night after work. The words were just flowing out from my brain through my fingers onto the page and it was like I couldn't stop.

Some months later, I had a phone call from '*Fletcher's Publishers*' who were running the competition, congratulating me on winning first prize. I couldn't believe it, I was gobsmacked.

The next two months were a whirlwind of meetings with publishers and editors, a magazine interview and the excitement of *my* book coming out in the shops to buy with *my* name on the front. Now that was the icing on the cake, seeing my name on the cover – *Forever, by Luisa-Maria Paz*. I toyed with the idea of publishing in my maiden name, or perhaps even in my mother's maiden name, but Mark seemed almost offended when we discussed it. In the end, as my *Tito* had helped and inspired me so much in my teens, I settled on using his name as my surname, which Mark eventually agreed would be a fitting tribute to him.

My book did relatively well and Mark encouraged me to write a follow-up, but insisted that I needed to give up my job to devote more time to do this. I can still hear him now when he told me he thought I should give up my job…

"Just imagine how it will sound telling people you're a writer rather than a travel agent…"

There was something about the way he said travel agent, almost belittling what I love. *"…you'll get further believe me."*

I remember thinking I don't really care what people think, I love my job but I really did want to give writing a serious shot so after persuasion, I listened to Mark and left the travel agency in March of this year. It's a decision I've since regretted. I know I probably sound really ungrateful, my husband was telling me to give up my job so I could write full-time and his wages would more than suffice for both of us, but I couldn't help but feel I was losing a part of me. I knew I could have happily done both, especially considering how much time I spent alone whilst Mark was working.

Chapter 2 – Present Day

Struggling to close my suitcase with one hand and with my mobile in the other, I've been chatting to Jodie for almost half an hour. Jodie has always been so perceptive of my mood, but if you're good friends…as we are, I suppose it's bound to happen.

"You sound really down…" she tells me. "…are things okay, only you're going on holiday tonight shouldn't you be more upbeat?"

"I'm fine…it's just…"

"Luisa, shall I come over?"

20 minutes later I'm opening the front door to my best friend, who stands at five-feet-five with the most beautiful figure you've ever seen, long brown hair and emerald green eyes.

She walks into the hallway and closes the front door behind her. "Before you say anything I've taken an early lunch."

Jodie knows I worry about her, she's like my younger sister and the last thing she needs is to keep running to me every time I'm in crisis.

I'd been at the travel agency for two years when Jodie started. Being quite a small firm of only five staff members we used to have some hilarious girls nights out after work, most Saturday nights were spent in the various bars and nightclubs in Birmingham. Jodie still works at the agency with the girls, so at least I still get invited on the work nights out.

Jodie and I shared a rented house after just a few months of working together. My housemate Freya was moving to Edinburgh and Jodie was looking to move out of her parents' house so it seemed ideal. I didn't actually realise at the time that Jodie would be moving in with her two King Charles Spaniels – Zack and Belle, and her new puppy Yorkshire Terrier, Molly.

I knew her beloved dogs were show dogs and she and her Mom did all manner of grooming them every weekend without fail and getting them ready for different competitions. However, I didn't realise they would also be moving in with us, assuming they would stay with her parents. Luckily the landlord didn't mind and neither did I. She did junior dog handling growing up so she's become quite the expert over the years. They are the most adorable well-behaved dogs and I really miss living with them.

No sooner has she sat down in the living room, my bottom lip starts wobbling and I'm struggling to fight back tears. Why is it when you're trying to be strong and you're doing well even though you feel like you could cry at any minute, as soon as someone asks if you're okay, the tears you've tried so hard to hold in suddenly decide to make an appearance?

"I knew it, what's wrong? It's not Mark is it?"

I try desperately to wipe my eyes on my sleeve - the classy woman that I am, as Jodie produces tissues. I take a deep breath.

"I'm sorry, it's nothing. I just….don't know if I can do this anymore."

"I know it must be hard Lu, but just think this holiday is exactly what you need - the two of you together like old times."

"But what if nothing changes, what if I still feel like this next month or next year?"

"Then no one can say you haven't tried. Forget what your Mom says about divorce, not that I'm saying you'll get divorced but you need to look after *you*. Nobody wants you to be unhappy you know that." She rubs my knee in comfort.

"I've tried to speak to Mark but he just keeps telling me to give it time, but how much time will it take?"

I'm sobbing by this point, fighting hard to control my breath. I blow my nose and pull myself together, Jodie's right. I need to just relax, enjoy the holiday and we'll take it from there. Perhaps it's me, maybe I'm being melodramatic, Mark's my husband and I owe it to him to try…even harder it would seem.

After a cup of tea and putting the world to rights, I follow Jodie to the front door and as I glance down I see a horrendous ladder in the back of her black tights.

"Jode…your tights…"

She turns around feeling the backs of her legs, finding the snag. "Oh, that would've been Zack this morning. I was trying to leave the house and he was jumping up my legs."

I laugh as I can picture the image so clearly. "I'd better get you a fresh pair."

As Jodie heads back to work in her snag free black tights I paint on a brave face, but the reality is…I feel like I'm drowning, desperate for someone to rescue me.

***

Mark gets home from work, undoing his navy blue tie as he walks into the living room.

16

"Are you all packed?" He looks tired, I notice. Dark bags sit underneath his eyes, making him look pale despite his natural olive skin tone.

I walk towards him, kissing him lightly on the cheek like I'm supposed to.

"Yeah you know me, everything but the kitchen sink."

I continue to pack my hand luggage on the sofa whilst Mark hovers in the doorway. Passports, boarding passes and travel insurance checked at least a dozen times.

I try my best to sound chirpy. "You'd better finish your packing, only an hour until the taxi."

I'm really looking forward to the holiday and seeing Dubrovnik, I have to concentrate on that.

He heads towards the sofa and encourages me to sit down. For some reason I immediately feel uncomfortable.

He takes a deep breath. "Something's come up, I'm really really sorry but there's a chance I'll have to do some work whilst we're away."

Half of me isn't surprised but the other half of me can't help but be immensely pissed off, and my face obviously more than shows this but he carries on.

"…I promise, it won't ruin our holiday and it won't stop us spending time together." he speeds up his sentence as I stand up in annoyance. "I know how much we need this holiday, Lu. We'll still have a great time."

"Mark, this is our holiday!"

He looks desperate as he tries to pull me back down to sit beside him.

"Please I'm sorry, it won't be much…honestly…I do this job for us for heavens sake!"

Not completely true I feel, but I don't want to sound like an ungrateful cow.

I exhale. "Okay fine you've got to do what you've got to do."

"It does mean it'll be me you and the laptop..." I think he's actually trying to make a joke of it.

"… but I'll make it up to you I promise."

The taxi arrives right on time marking the start of our holiday. It's a strange feeling as I glance up at our house as we drive off, it's like I know things won't be the same even more so when we get home. I can't really explain that feeling of detachment.

We check in at the airport before heading to the *'Corner Bar'* for dinner and then it's time to board the flight. Once on board the plane I feel more relaxed and positive about our holiday despite Mark's surprise he dropped on me earlier. I was just having a wobble this afternoon with Jodie, perhaps.

As I switch my phone to flight mode I see a picture message from Jodie of Zack, Molly and Belle all sitting on the sofa *'wishing their Auntie Luisa a good holiday'* which makes me giggle. I relax back into my seat, closing my eyes and listening to the sound of the engines increasing noise as we slowly start to lift up and take off.

***

The two hours 20 minutes flight goes by in a heartbeat, the fact I slept for most of the journey certainly helped and before we know it, we're waiting for our luggage to appear on the carousel before we board the coach to our hotel in Lapad, Dubrovnik.

From the coach windows it's difficult to get a real feel of Croatia because it's so dark outside and everything always looks so different in the dark. The roads from the airport at first are along the coast with hills on the right-hand side, occasionally giving way to small white houses which seem to stand out in the darkness of the night. The closer we get to Lapad, the coach passes by groups of people in good spirits, seemingly on their way home, or back to their hotel from a night out.

Even in the dark, there's no hiding from the fact that our first impressions of our hotel - *The Sun Elegance* are just that, simply elegant. The foyer is large, bright, spacious and full of sophisticated cream marble. A huge crystal chandelier is hung in the centre with tiny spotlights at the outer edges of the ceiling. A black grand piano dominates one corner and enormous potted plants are dotted around sparingly, bringing some greenery inside. I can hear the gentle trickle of running water as I notice the water feature to the left of the reception desk.

Tired from the travelling, we head straight to bed and I fall into an exhausted sleep, waking suddenly at 7:15 a.m. Feeling confused by my surroundings and desperate for water, I slowly sit up in bed and study the room before my eyes.

A beautiful light and open room stands before me, bathed in sunlight. Cream walls with cleverly hung mirrors reflecting the light, elegant pine furnishings and three marble steps leading up to what I'm assuming is the bathroom, which barely registered with me earlier this morning when we arrived.

Getting out of bed and opening the mini fridge in the corner of the room hunting for water, I quench my thirst with a satisfied sigh. I slowly peel back one of the biscuit coloured curtains, just enough to open the door leading to the large balcony without waking Mark. Stepping outside I immediately feel the welcome heat of the sun on my skin, already so deliciously warm even this early.

The vista before me from our second-floor view is beautifully landscaped gardens with palm trees, prettily grown flowers in striking yellows, oranges and vibrant pinks are visible, leading out to the perfect sea view. A smile takes over my face naturally as I lean on the rail of the balcony to study every inch of our outdoor surroundings.

Mark suddenly appears behind me wearing nothing but his boxer shorts and a smile, putting both arms around me, resting his chin on my shoulder, making me tense up as he joins me in admiring the outlook.

I can't take my eyes away from the scene in front of me. "It feels like it goes on forever, don't you think?"

Mark agrees, squeezing his arms around me…I can tell he wants more than an early morning cuddle. I turn to face him and kiss him on the cheek but as I go to pull away and head indoors, Mark pulls me back towards him with his hands on my hips. Sensing his urgency, a feeling of weariness begins to take hold of me and as I try to relax into his kiss, I force myself into the moment.

Mark's kisses become more passionate as he slowly peels one of the shoulder straps on my nightie down. Not wanting to provide a peepshow for my fellow holidaymakers, I motion with my eyes to head back inside. Closing the balcony door behind us, Mark thrusts himself in my direction, gently tugging at my nightie. Everything about this situation feels completely wrong and alien to me.

Since his affair, every time we do anything, all I can see is him in bed with that other woman. I wonder if he's thinking of her. Is he wishing I was her? Every time, it's as though I'm just going through the motions with Mark whilst my head is on another planet, desperately trying to block everything out.

I tell myself to stop thinking about it and I try to respond to his advances and kiss him back.

Mark lowers me to the bed and lies down beside me, his hands working their way up my body. I feel myself begin to tense once again beneath his touch, until I can take it no more and I grasp at his wrist.

"I can't… Mark, I'm sorry…I…."

"Is everything okay?"

"Sorry, I'm just tired…not enough sleep."

He smiles at me before kissing me on the lips and rolling onto his back. I continue to lie next to him, unsure if I should speak or not. I roll onto my right-hand side to face him before looking up at his face to check his expression, but he's impossible to read.

Sometime later I wake up with my head on Mark's shoulder and his arm around me, I notice he's awake and seems deep in thought.

"What are you thinking?"

He jolts slightly at the sound of my voice. "Nothing, just daydreaming." He jumps out of bed and checks his watch. "What do you say we unpack and head to breakfast? I'm starving."

I watch him for a moment, something about him doesn't seem right, it's almost like he's covering something up.

I make a start of hanging up my various dresses, skirts, tops and adding to the large dressing table, my multitude of toiletries. Mark's mobile begins to ring and he looks at me awkwardly, wondering what my reaction will be. I just glance in his direction and half smile before announcing my intention of having a shower, feeling I'd better leave him to it.

As I look at my reflection in the bathroom mirror once I'm dry, I decide it would be silly giving Mark a hard time about working on holiday. If it's got to be done, there's no point in letting it ruin our break…it could be difficult enough between us as it is.

Heading back out to the bedroom in my towel, I see Mark sitting on the bed dressed in his navy blue shorts and crisp white T-shirt hastily closing his laptop.

"Everything okay?" I check.

"All fine." he smirks pushing his laptop aside and relaxing back onto the bed with his hands behind his head.

I opt for my emerald green summery dress for breakfast and I leave my long dark chestnut hair to hang loose. With my stomach growling for food we head downstairs to the restaurant where the aromas of fresh bread begin to surround us. I always say I could live on bread alone if I had to, it's one of my weaknesses.

The restaurant all seems very inviting, with floor to ceiling windows that overlook a huge swimming pool and even more gardens. There are pine tables and comfortable high back cream leather chairs in the dining room with a small display of delicate purple/blue flowers in the middle of each table.

As we look around there seems to be a large array of options to eat including a full English, cereal, fruit, a variety of meats and of course, pancakes. Those with no self-control could be in trouble here.

The maître d' greets us with his upbeat mood. "Good morning Sir, Madam…your first time with us here at the *Sun Elegance*?"

"Sorry?" Mark enquires, struggling to understand his strong local accent.

The maître d' sees the funny side and begins to chuckle to himself, breaking the awkwardness in the atmosphere before he resumes his welcoming.

"Welcome to Croatia, I am Franjo, let me show you to a table."

We follow Franjo, a portly man with a thick moustache, through the busy restaurant and are seated near to the hot buffet section. The restaurant itself is painted a warm terracotta colour and now as we sit down I notice the soft cream drapes hanging from the huge floor-to-ceiling windows. Franjo pulls a chair out for me gesturing for me to sit down.

I smile to him as I take my seat. "Puno hvala."

"Nema na cemu." he grins as he walks away.

"I'm impressed." Mark declares as he takes his seat opposite me. "I think he was too. Speaking a few words goes a long way."

"Shame you couldn't even understand his English." I giggle. "Come on, let's get some food."

We make our way over to the food stations, with so much choice I don't know where to start first. Opting to check out the hot food on offer whilst Mark heads straight for the freshly squeezed fruit juices, I take a plate and join the queue of people at the hot food counter.

I've never been the sort of person who can miss breakfast, I tend to wake up absolutely famished every day, no matter what time I eat dinner the night before. I spot freshly cooked pancakes at the end of the row, so I linger in the short queue until I reach them. Looking around to find Mark, I notice he's sitting back at our table with his back to the buffet with two glasses of orange juice and a plate of fruit. Reaching the pancakes, I pick up two using the tongs and as I do, I notice from the corner of my eye, a figure to my right-hand side from behind the buffet station.

For some reason, I feel an intensity in the air and as I look up, I meet the gaze of the chef behind the counter. As our eyes meet for just a few seconds, I immediately feel my face start to flush and my stomach feels as though I have thousands of butterflies darting around, demanding attention. He has the most amazing dark eyes, brown hair and a small goatee.

Feeling almost shaken by the intensity of the situation, I completely forget the maple syrup to go with my pancakes and join Mark back at the table.

Sliding my chair in closer once I've sat down, I can feel that he's still watching me. It's like there's a heavy presence in the atmosphere, almost a feeling of familiarity with some kind of magnetic force, drawing me, pulling me to look over at him again. As I slowly look up, taking a sip of my orange juice, our eyes meet again. I look away quickly and try to carry on with my breakfast, wondering what that was all about.

After orange juice, tea, pancakes and cereal, my fizzy stomach seems to calm down. Mark seems really enthusiastic about booking an excursion or three at the welcome meeting and it's almost uplifting to feel he's making a real effort. Exchanging more pleasantries with Franjo as we leave the restaurant, we take a look at the various posters, leaflets and general hotel information in reception. I notice a poster advertising the day trip to Montenegro, just as Mark's mobile begins to ring.

"Five minutes, I promise." Mark kisses me firmly on the lips apologetically as he holds up his mobile. Whilst he talks to the office, I sit on a sofa in reception and relax whilst I wait for him. He reappears a few minutes later holding his mobile down by his side.

"Sorry, sorry, I need to go back to the room and get the laptop on. I can't do what I need to do over the phone."

I roll my eyes in annoyance. "How long will you be?"
Mark reaches in his pocket and takes out his wallet, giving me his credit card. "Here, you go to the welcome meeting book us in for however many

trips you fancy, we'll do them all If you want, I'll leave it totally with you. Sorry babe." He squeezes my hand and turns to run back to the room.

"Great." I mutter under my breath.

I go outside, following the signs for the conference room where the meeting will take place and when I arrive, I take a seat on the second row of chairs that have been laid out for our welcome meeting. A handful of people are already seated and waiting for the meeting to start, more people soon begin to float in, including the rep who waits patiently at the front for the rest of the group to arrive.

Kristina the rep looks no older than around 24 years old with quite an English rose complexion, despite her being a local guide, with jet black hair cut into a sharp bob with a fringe which really accentuates her eyes. After a 30 minute presentation giving us more information on Croatia than the whole of the internet, Kristina declares the meeting over. People begin to look through the leaflets explaining the various excursions on offer and head towards Kristina with excitement.

The couple in their 60's next to me are discussing the Konavle Wine Tour with anticipation. I smile at them as I consider this trip myself.

"Is this your first time to Dubrovnik?"

"Oh no, this is our third year in a row at the same hotel." The lady laughs before going on to introduce herself as Pam, and her husband Pete.

Pam appears to be a very glamorous woman with heavy eyeshadow on her eyes, even in this heat and very smartly dressed in a cream blouse and flowing blue skirt. She has fairly short white grey hair and I notice as she speaks the multitude of bangles that clatter about up and down her arm with every movement. I wonder how long they've been married. They're very touchy-feely with each other but at the same time, seem like best friend's the way they're joking around together.

"I'm Luisa, maybe you can give me some tips? I've never been to Dubrovnik before."

Pam and Pete exchange glances making me feel paranoid that I've asked the wrong thing.

Pete laughs. "Don't get us started love, we could talk about it for hours. Are you here alone?"

"No, my husband is erm…working upstairs…don't ask."

The three of us join the queue to book some excursions and they continue to fill me in on what they love about Dubrovnik.

"Get yourself down to the old town a few times." Pam stresses. "You must go on the cable car at sunset - it's breath taking. We first visited Dubrovnik years ago on a cruise, we loved it and came back the following year for a week and like I say, three years on, we're still coming back for more. Although one week isn't long enough now, so we always do two."

Just hearing Pam talking about the sunset gives me goosebumps, I love the feeling of being in the dark, seeing anything lit with a million lights. The feeling I get, it's indescribable.

When I reach the front of the queue, Kristina is really friendly offering me more help in deciding what to choose. Despite not knowing much about her at all, I envy her. I wonder what her life is like here working in the travel industry and helping people make the best of their holiday every single day. She seems to really love her job and I can't help but think about my old job at the travel agent and how much I miss it.

I decide on the Elaphiti Islands cruise and the day trip to Montenegro. Handing over Mark's credit card, I wonder if this is actually really his thing, coming here with me.

I walk back up the stairs to our room, my head full of confusion, to see Mark working on his laptop.

"Hey, sorry, still going…why don't you carry on to the pool and I'll meet you there when I'm done?"

Grabbing my lilac beach bag, I fill it with my earphones, notebook, pen and sun lotion. I always carry a notebook and pen in the hope that ideas for my book will pop into my head. I decided against bringing my laptop with me, hoping the break will do me good by awakening my imagination a little. I managed to pick up a second-hand dictaphone online and with that and my good old notebook, at least any ideas I do get I can record.

Chapter 3

I don't mind my own company, in fact, I like it. I've had a lot of my own company the last couple of years of our marriage, probably more than most married couples. For some reason, I just can't get rid of this feeling that things aren't how they're supposed to be for me. Thinking back to all of those couples at the welcome meeting and how excited they were to be on holiday together and discovering new things together…that's what I want from a marriage and it's certainly how I thought it would be for us. Self-pitying over, I take the gentle walk through reception and outside to the pool.

The enormous lagoon pool is surrounded by very modern looking wooden sun loungers, with thick white cushions on top, which actually look more comfortable than our bed back at home. Despite it being well after 11:00 a.m. there are still plenty of sun loungers vacant, unlike some hotels we've stayed at in the past. I choose two loungers next to each other with a parasol in the middle in what looks like a quiet spot away from the small poolside bar. I lay the towels down, remove my green dress to reveal my bright purple bikini and apply my sun lotion, desperate to lie down and let the sun work its soothing magic on me.

As soon as I get settled on the lounger, a feeling of peacefulness begins to wash over me. It feels too long since I really let myself relax and I decide there and then that I'll definitely treat myself to a massage whilst we're here. I make a mental note to pick up a leaflet from the spa later.

It seems to be mostly couples of all different ages here with some groups of friends thrown in to the mix. My mind starts to wonder and I find myself realising that although it appears I'm the only person on my own around the pool, I still feel comfortable, and not so long ago that wouldn't have been the case. Like I said I think the amount of time I've spent on my own and the emotional stress I've been through has made me stronger and certainly more self-sufficient and resilient.

It's lunchtime before Mark tears himself away from his laptop and joins me around the pool. I'm midway singing along in my head to a 90's dance anthem when I feel something ice cold on my leg. I'm startled and open my eyes to see Mark holding an enormous cocktail on my leg with a goofy grin.

"Your face..." He laughs. "You were completely away with the fairies..."

"You scared me!" I reach over and take a huge swig from my well-deserved cocktail. "Mmm, that's good. Thanks."

"No problem, sorry I took so long. I'm here now."

"Everything sorted?"

Mark takes a gulp from his beer. "For now. Did you plan any trips?"
I reach in my bag and pull out the list of excursions I picked up at the meeting this morning. As I go to pass this to him, I see he's playing around with his work phone again, so I just sit and look at him. It's a good few seconds before he's back with me.

I hand him the leaflet. "I've only booked two at the moment, see if there's any you fancy on here..." He scours the pages as I continue to fill him in. "We're going to Montenegro on Friday and then a cruise around the Elaphiti Islands on Sunday."

Mark studies the list, nodding his head in agreement. "Good choices, we'll stick with those."

I feel slightly pissed off by his statement '*stick with those*', how patronising does he want to be?

He looks up at me, frowning. "You know what I mean. Now, how about you rub some sun lotion into your husband's back so he doesn't burn?"

Guilt washes over me as I think to myself perhaps it would serve him right if he did get a touch of sunburn.

Sometime later, one of the pool bar waiters approaches us tray in hand. "Sir, Madam, can I get you any drinks from the bar?"

Mark sits up. "Are we too late for food?"

The waiter produces two menus. "Not at all sir. I will give you a few minutes to decide."

Mark looks awestruck as he takes the menu from the waiter. "Really good service here, don't you think?"

Sitting up on my lounger, leaning back on my elbows I have to agree. "Well, this hotel was recommended by my old agency, what do you expect?"

Mark stops reading the menu and looks up at me. "You miss working there, don't you?"

Slightly taken aback by the fact that he has actually realised this and comprehending just how true his observation is, I find myself wondering whether I should be honest with him, but I know I should be.

"I do miss it….more than I thought I would."

I don't know why, but I feel like I shouldn't miss my old job. Maybe because it was Mark's idea for me to leave and when he suggested it, I really did want it to be the right choice, the right thing for me and for us.

After lunch I try to make some notes for my book, whilst Mark begins to doze off. I don't feel like I've actually done much writing since I left my job and its been four months now. I've started writing, but I feel like I'm struggling for inspiration at the moment.

Needing a break from the sun, I pull my dress on over my head and attempt to find my flip-flops underneath the lounger. With Mark clearly asleep, I decide not to wake him and head back to the room to give my parents a quick call.

Back in our room I'm distracted by an intermittent beeping noise which seems to be coming from Mark's laptop. Looking over at the computer, I can tell it's switched on and wonder whether I should maybe turn it off. Deciding not to just in case I cock something up, I continue with my phone call.

It's Wednesday, which is one of my Mom's two days off per week from her job as a dental receptionist. The line seems to ring out for a while and I'm just considering putting the phone down when she answers.

"Hi Mom, it's me."

"Luisa-Maria, how are you? How's the holiday?"

"Yeah, I'm okay thanks. It's good."

"*Cariño*, are you sure? I worry about you." I can always tell when Mom's worrying about me. Ever since I was a little girl, when she's worrying, she always calls me *cariño*.

I sit myself down on the bed as I listen to her voice and stare out onto the balcony with the overwhelmingly striking view and immediately wish I was outside. I get up from the bed and open the door and take a seat on one of the plush chairs.

"No need to worry about me. You'd love it here, the hotel's wonderful."

"You know I want you to be happy Luisa, don't you?"

"I know you do." I reply, wondering where this conversation is leading.

"You and Mark - if you put the work in will be as happy as your dad and I…we have had our ups and downs through the years but we are happy."

I can't help but feel she should be more on my side after what's happened in my marriage. I know she means well, and I understand her point of view, but in the nicest possible way, I wish she wouldn't keep telling me about it and I can't help but question why she would want me to stay with someone who has treated me with so little respect.

My parents actually met in the UK in the early 1980s. Ria Fernandez Molina met Andrew Summers in May 1984 in a London nightclub. Dad was living and working in London back then and always tells the story of how he asked her to dance, but soon regretted it when he saw how good she was.

When Mom went home to Spain three days later, they wrote to each other for eight months before finally seeing each other again the following January, when my Dad went to stay with her and her family. Dad went home two weeks later, leaving her with the extra weight of an engagement ring sitting proudly on her finger.

When my parents got married as my mother was losing her Spanish surname, she managed to persuade my Dad when my brother and I were born, to let her choose our names, being desperate to hold on to some of her Spanish heritage. She named my brother Benito and three years later, Luisa-Maria was born.

Mom could be quite pushy at times when I was a teenager and I no doubt needed that. I think that's what actually helped me to be quite resilient growing up and gave me independence, but somewhere along the way, my confidence dwindled again over the last couple of years but it's definitely building back up again, I haven't really had much choice in the matter. Had to just try and get on with things.

After a few more minutes of chatting with Mom about Dubrovnik, the weather and the hotel, she passes on some good news.

"I'm sure they won't mind me telling you, if Benito hasn't already? Benito and Georgia have set a date for their wedding."

My big brother getting married, I feel really proud. "Oh really? That's lovely. Where and when?"

"Next April in Córdoba." I can hear the smile in my Mom's voice as she tells me the happy news.

My brother Ben and his girlfriend Georgia have been engaged for around a year now and I know they've talked about getting married in Spain, so I'm really pleased they've set a date at last and that they're going for what they want for their wedding day.

When we were teenagers, Ben was always so popular with the girls. He definitely has Mom's mediterranean looks with his dark hair and dark brown eyes. I got Mom's hair colour too, but somewhere along the way, I picked up my Dad's blue eyes and pallid skin tone.

I actually remember one occasion after a night out, when Ben must've been around 20 years old, when two girls sat outside of our house in the early hours of the morning, trying to coax Ben to come back outside. I remember teasing him about it the next day, he loved the fact they'd followed him home from a nightclub and tried to get his phone number.

"What can I say, I have to fight them off." Ben announced, shrugging his shoulders with a smirk on his face.

Despite how he sounds, he's grown up to be a really caring and trustworthy guy, even though his looks certainly went to his head in his younger days.

Mom finally stops gushing about the wedding...allowing me to get a word in.

"Are you and Dad okay?"

"We're fine, Luisa. Don't forget, if Ben gets in touch, you don't know anything about the wedding..."

"Mom's the Word." I laugh. "Speak to you soon."

"Have a holiday to remember, Luisa."

I end the call and decide to send Jodie a quick message before sliding back into my flip-flops and making my way back down stairs.

Reaching the pool, I stop in the doorway leading outside to read a poster on the window advertising a mediterranean massage. I pick up a leaflet from the display holder and stroll back over to our loungers.

Mark watches me walk towards him, and lifts his sunglasses as I reach his side and I can see he doesn't look too happy.

"I wondered where you'd got to."

I take a seat back down on my lounger next to him and remove my dress again.

"I just went to give my Mom a quick call, that's all. Good sleep?"

"Very…." Mark eyes my spa leaflet. "What you got there?"

"Thought we might treat ourselves to a massage?"

Mark looks at me like I've gone criminally insane. Anyone would think I'd suggested abseiling down the side of the hotel, naked and in broad daylight from the look he gave me.

He pulls his T-shirt on over his head. "Another drink? I need to stretch my legs."

"Just water for me please."

As he walks away towards the bar I note Mark certainly seems quite shifty, and I've no idea why. It's then I notice his mobile on the floor next to his lounger, so I assume work have been in contact again.

Several snoozes later, I wake to find the pool area almost empty. Mark seems engrossed in reading a book which is nice to see, rather than being constantly glued to his phone.

I tentatively approach him. "Fancy a walk before dinner?"

He sits up, seemingly less tense than earlier. "Yeah, why not."

We gather up all of the mess that is our belongings and pile it all into my bag. Beach bag bulging at the seams, we head back through the hotel and out through the front entrance.

I'm not sure if it's my imagination, but there seems to be a slight awkward atmosphere between us. I try to ignore it and continue walking beside Mark. I notice he's somewhat agitated, he can't keep his hands still they're in and out of his pockets, then running through his hair.

He notices my curiosity of his tension. "Sorry, I think I put my phone in your bag, I won't hear it if it rings."

"Mark, I'm sure you'll hear it. I know I will…just relax."

I tentatively, reach for his hand in an effort to calm him down. He gives me an appreciative smile and exhales sharply. I focus my attention on the view that stands before us.

Leaving the hotel and walking just a few metres, we follow the pretty cobbled promenade down towards the shore line. A walkway opens up ahead of us, curving around along the sea wall, offering an inviting walk along a coastal path. The walkway is dotted with tables and chairs alongside the sea wall, tempting people to sit, eat and gaze out at the wonderful view that is the Adriatic Sea. Just imagining myself sitting at one of those lovely tables by candlelight makes me feel out of this world. As I smile to myself, I notice Mark's staring at me.

"You love this don't you?"

"What's not to love?" I take a deep breath, breathing in the sea air. It feels so fresh and cleansing.

Mark lures me over to the sea wall, we sit down and turn our heads to get a closer look at the view.

"Let's get a picture of us together." He gestures to my bag for one of our phones.

I purposely pass him my phone rather than his and as I hand it over, Mark wastes no time in asking a passer-by to help us out. With his arm around my shoulders, he pulls me in closer to him.

For a split second before the photo I find myself looking up at the expression on his face. To strangers, to the person about to take our picture - we must look the image of happiness. Only we know different. I know different.

One month ago…

I slid forward on my comfortable seat on the soft grey sofa, reaching for the remote and in one swift movement the television was off. Silence crept into the room, filling the void between us.

"Mark, I need to know…" I began steadily. "How do you think things are between us? How do you feel?"

Mark looked on edge as he placed both feet flat on the floor from their original position on the pouffe and turned to face me. "What, w-what do you mean?"

I gave my words some more thought before I continued with my questions, which only seemed to frustrate him more. "Just, us…do you think it's working?"

As I spoke about my uncertainty, Mark rose to his feet with his hands on his head in distress. "Oh, not this again…"

This wasn't the reaction I was expecting, my heart began to race with dread, with anticipation with wondering of how our marriage became this complete and utter mess in the first place.

He starred up at the ceiling, he couldn't even look at me as he replied in anguish. "How many more times do I have to tell you I'm sorry? What more do you want?!"

"It's not about whether you're sorry, I'm asking about how you feel things are between us now!"

There it was again, that alarming quietness, the calm before the storm no doubt.

"…are you happy, Mark?"

"I'm happy with you Luisa, just tell me you're happy with me?" He threw his arms around in frenzy as he finished his sentence. I suddenly felt sick.

Mark sat back down next to me on the sofa, took a deep breath and he reached for my left hand as he changed his tone to calm and controlled.

"I know I ruined everything, but I'm putting it right aren't I?" He didn't give me chance to respond.

"...look, just give it more time you know we can make it work, you *know* we can. Don't give up on me, you know I love you."

As he spoke, I felt like screaming at him...telling him how I felt, except I couldn't find the words, not the words I felt I needed to say.

I hesitated. "It's hard Mark, I don't think things will ever feel like they did before. I'm trying..."

He rose to his feet. "What more can I do? I tell you to leave your job, so you can concentrate on your writing and this is how you repay me?"

I struggled not to burst into sobs of frustration and as my eyes met his, I saw his eyes were filled with tears, he really looked hurt. I immediately felt awful, the fact it was me making him feel like this in that moment. I was lost. He slumped down to his knees beside me and I instinctively reached up to his right eye and wiped away the stray tear trickling down his cheek with my thumb. It was something I did without even thinking about it and almost immediately after, I regretted it. It was an act more out of compassion than love, but I knew how Mark would read it.

"I'm sorry." I whispered, trying not to meet his eyes.

Mark slowly leaned in towards my lips and I surprised myself by returning his kiss, going through the motions just for a moment before I pulled away a second later.

He shook his head. "It's me who should be sorry…I wish I'd never set eyes on that woman."

I felt uncomfortable straightaway at the mention of *her* but he didn't even notice that, he just kept talking, pleading his case.

"…I know I need to make more of an effort, I need to make you realise we're worth fighting for. Don't give up, please." He pleaded, leaving me in turmoil and feeling utterly shattered knowing that no matter how hard I try, I can't change the fact that I don't think I love him any more in the way that a wife is supposed to.

Chapter 4 – Present Day

Trying to decide what to wear for dinner each night on holiday is something I love doing. I normally let my mind wander through my wardrobe during the day so I can step more or less straight out of the shower and into my outfit. Tonight, I decide on my blue, white and yellow tropical print maxi dress, with my black sparkly gladiator sandals. Again, I leave my hair to hang loose and go for natural make-up, but with plenty of bronzer to give me some colour, yep, I definitely have my Dads' skin tone as opposed to my Moms'.

Before we leave the room, I notice a text reply from Jodie.

"Hope everything is okay? It's my interview tomorrow, wish me luck XXX"

I type a quick good luck message in response telling her that things are okay, but Mark's working a lot, and promise to call her tomorrow to get the lowdown on the interview.

Last week at the agency, the manager and the part-time assistant manager both left after being headhunted by a rival firm. Jodie has been temporary manager since then, but tomorrow she has her official interview. Jodie will be perfect for the job as well she knows, the interview is just a formality.

Mark and I leave our room, taking the stairs down to the restaurant to the most delicious smells of freshly cooked food. I can definitely smell something spicy, maybe chilli, I can't really put my finger on what exactly but it smells divine.

Downstairs in the restaurant, we're warmly greeted once again by Franjo. "Doblar vecer....good evening."

Franjo escorts us to a table for two in the middle and I leave my bag on the table so no one takes our seats, as we make our way to the buffet. Mark heads to the salad station to start, whilst I go straight to the main course area.

Taking a plate from the pile I weigh up the different options of chicken, freshly grilled steaks, chilli con carne or swordfish. I settle on a grilled steak and mashed potato. I round the corner to the vegetable section and feel like I've been hit with a stun gun as I spot in front of me - the same chef from breakfast. I stop in my tracks as a sudden pang of nerves takes over my body. We briefly make eye contact and to my surprise, he speaks to me.

"Hello." he utters confidently, encouraging me to avert my gaze back to him.

Trying to remember how to speak as my mouth has rapidly become drier than the desert, I say hello back, but it seems to come out of my mouth making me sound more nervous than I feel.

A moment of awkwardness follows, where I don't know if I should speak more or just continue on the vegetable hunt. How has this mysterious man managed to make me feel this way? I've never been so glad to see carrots in my life for the want of having something to do with my hands. I spoon some carrots on to my plate and instantly hear shouting from a couple of metres away as someone who I can only assume is the manager, comes rushing towards the chef. Whatever it is he's shouting as he motions towards the beef steaks that the chef is now piling on top of the chicken, as he looks in my direction, it doesn't sound good.

"Concentrate!" The manager grunts as he walks away.

I can't help but smirk to myself and I notice from the corner of my eye that the chef is doing the same as he looks up and we make eye contact again and smile at each other.

I walk over to the table and take my seat. Mark eyes my plate suspiciously. "I thought you didn't like broccoli."

I look down at my plate and it's only then I notice that I've picked up about five florets of broccoli, even though as Mark pointed out, I don't like it. I was obviously distracted. "Oh, I thought I'd try it…it's been a while."

We make small talk as we eat our meals, but I can't help but feel the need to look over in the chef's direction. As I do so, he appears to be concentrating on grilling more steaks. I hear a mobile begin to ring. Straight away I look up at Mark in disbelief that he's brought his mobile out with him tonight, then even more annoyance as he takes it from his pocket and answers it whilst sitting at the table. I feel mortified as he sits talking about work whilst people are trying to eat their evening meal.

I can see people looking in his direction, then at me. I put down my knife and fork and sip my wine several times, hoping to disguise the embarrassment on my face. Looking over at the grilling station, as I again sense the chef's eyes on me, he's there, watching me.

We observe each other for what must only be about five seconds, but it feels more like five minutes. Him turning the steaks on the grill as he cooks them and me nervously chugging back my wine. Feeling brave I smile in his direction, but this time I hold his gaze as I do so. He returns my smile, but I immediately feel guilty.

Mark covers the mouthpiece on his phone as he apologises to me. "Sorry, need to pop back upstairs, come up when you're done with the food."

He casually walks out of the restaurant and back to the room, leaving a practically full plate of untouched food to go to waste.

Well, at least now I don't need to pretend to be enjoying the broccoli, I push my plate aside leaving the broccoli left-overs. I decide to go to the dessert cart to see what's on offer and take a bowl of strawberry sundae. When I begin to eat the sundae I realise I couldn't have picked anything messier to eat and find myself constantly wiping my mouth with my napkin, actually hoping the chef isn't looking my way.

Dessert eaten and wine now finished, I guess I don't really have a reason to linger any longer so I stand up and tuck my chair under the table. I find myself taking double the time to sign a receipt to charge the drinks to the room and double the time to put my bag on my shoulder, just so I get a couple of extra seconds in close proximity of the chef that I mysteriously seem to be attracted to.

Turning to walk away from the table, I fight the urge to look in his direction, that is until I hear him call out 'good night' with an almost embarrassed looking wave.

I can't help but smile as I reply. "Good night."

Reaching the door to our room, I realise Mark has the key card so I have to knock but as I do so, I notice he's left the door slightly ajar for me. He's sitting on the balcony still using his laptop with his back to me as I enter the room. Arriving at the sliding door, I reach for the handle and see Mark grasp the laptop screen and pull it sharply down towards the keypad in what looks like pure panic.

He jumps to his feet....guilt written all over his face. "Luisa you scared the crap out of me! Did you get a spare key card?"

"W-what.."

Placing his hands on my waist, he steers me away from the balcony and back into the bedroom. He obviously realises from the look of bewilderment on my face I'm wondering why he did that.

"Sorry, it was a reflex reaction.".

"You left the door open for me, so I thought."

Mark laughs nervously. "Of course I did. Now, shall we get a drink?"

***

Arriving at one of the bars located alongside the beach, we sit down and pick up a menu. Seconds later, the waiter arrives to light a candle on our table before swiftly walking away again to take the drinks orders on the next table.

Mark clasps his hands together enthusiastically. "Champagne?"

There's something about him tonight. He seems to be over compensating for something.

"Erm...I was thinking more along the lines of a Tequila Sunrise."

He appears almost hurt as he orders a Tequila Sunrise for me and a glass of red for himself.

I try to put the earlier laptop situation to the back of my mind as I enjoy the beautiful sea view. The sea looks a dark inky blue, little boats are floating gently on the water in the distance with lights twinkling in harmony with the waves. I find myself lost in the vista before me, watching the sea and listening to other peoples gentle chatter.

The drinks arrive and we raise our glasses in cheers. The cocktail smells really strong and one sip tells me that my observation is right, but boy does it taste good.

"Mom said Ben and Georgia have set a date for the wedding." I take another long swig of my drink.

"Oh, about time." Nothing else is asked or said about the matter on his part.

"That's exactly what I said." We look at each other and exchange a smile as to say *'look at us, we do still have things in common after all.'*

"I can't help but think this view is wasted on us tonight." Mark blurts out to my surprise.

I put my almost empty glass down on the table in front of me. "You seem distracted."

"It's just work, that's all. Don't worry." He rests his hand on my leg in an act of reassurance.

"That's the problem, it's always work." The drink has definitely loosened my tongue tonight. I tried to hold it in, but why should I?

Waiting for a reaction I see Mark knock back the last half of his glass of wine, before ordering the same drinks again from the waiter and staring back out to sea, clearly avoiding what would be a confrontation between us.

I let my mind wander and find myself replaying in my mind the events at dinner. I'm really surprised at the level of attraction I clearly felt when I saw the chef again tonight, I've never felt that lure with anyone else before in my life. It was like some kind of addiction, I had to keep looking over, had to see his face, his gorgeous face. This is crazy! I felt so guilty sitting opposite my husband and the whole time, I just wanted to be making more awkward-or not so awkward chitchat with another man. This man…the chef he paid me attention, made me feel like I was in the room and worth spending time with and talking to.

Guilty, I wish I didn't feel guilty and maybe I shouldn't, it's not like I jumped over the table and leapt on this man, but god knows I thought about it. At the end of the day Mark and I are still married, although not happily and not in the way that a marriage should be.

"Now who's distracted?" Mark nudges me. "Shall we head back? I don't think our hearts are in it tonight are they?"

I actually can't wait to get back to the room and into bed to be alone with my thoughts.

Back at the hotel whilst Mark uses the bathroom I change into my nightie, remove my make up and get into bed. He gets into bed beside me, and I'm filled with dread as Mark lies on his side to spoon me, pressing himself against me. He moves my hair away from my neck and begins to lightly kiss my neck as he fumbles with the bottom of my nightie. How can he think I want this? He's barely spent any time with me again today, he doesn't even try to make conversation with me it's just work. All he wants to do and think about is work. Then we get to bed and he thinks I'll do whatever he wants.

"I'm tired Mark." I tell him, but still he tries to force the issue. "Mark!" I shout meaningfully and he backs away mumbling under his breath.

As I close my eyes, all I can see is my mystery man's face and suddenly I begin to very much look forward to breakfast tomorrow morning.

Chapter 5

Waking the next day, I see Mark's sitting up in bed next to me reading his book.

I begin to sit up, clearing my throat. "Have you been awake long?"

He closes his book, putting it on the bed beside him. "About half an hour, its' gone nine you know." I get the impression he's back to his normal self this morning.

Sitting up I detect a hangover kicking in and suddenly feel a desperate need for my morning cuppa so we both get dressed and make the mad dash to breakfast before it closes.

When we walk through the doors to the buffet, anticipation kicks in and I begin smoothing my hair down as casually as possible. Franjo seems to be in deep discussion at the other side of the restaurant, so we help ourselves to the same table as last night. I scan the food areas frantically but with no luck, I feel crushed as I realise, he's not here.

I pick at my food of a bacon sandwich and drink two cups of tea, feeling stupid about the excitement I felt about coming to breakfast.

Mark touches his hand to mine as it rests on the table. "You look like you have the weight of the world on your shoulders, Lu."

I push my plate away, unable to manage any more. "Just hung over, that's all." I glance at the door, unwilling to give up hope that he might be around somewhere. "Shall we go to the pool again today? I noticed they have Croatian lessons on Wednesday mornings."

Mark wipes his mouth with a napkin. "Not really my thing, but you do it. I'm happy enough just relaxing around the pool."

***

Feeling slightly more exhilarated after my Croatian lesson, I walk back outside with Pam.

Pam exhales as we approach the pool area. "I don't know how people sit sunbathing all day…I find I need to be exploring or doing something like that lesson."

"It was great, didn't Pete fancy it either?"

She laughs as she takes her mirror from her bag to check her mascara. Her bangles of choice today being wooden with green, yellow and blue stripes to match her green floaty blouse and pale blue trousers.

"He much prefers drinking his body weight in beer!" She gestures toward the pool bar area as Pete lifts his pint in a greeting to me and I wave back.

Pam tells me how she prefers to stay covered in the sun, opting for light and airy clothing.

She takes my arm. "Where is this elusive husband of yours?"

"He's just over there." I point. "…come over and meet him." *God I hope he's in a good mood.* Mark lifts his sunglasses as we approach him.

"Mark, this is Pam, Pam, meet Mark." I introduce them wearily, waiting for his response as he takes Pam's hand in his and kisses it captivatingly.

"Pleasure to meet you, Pam."

I see Pam fluttering her eyelashes and her skin begin to flush ever so slightly as she takes in the full image of Mark. He is a good-looking man. Today he's just wearing his navy blue board shorts and his sunglasses now sit stylishly in his salt-and-pepper hair. He certainly has that twinkle in his eye as he watches Pam fall for his charms. I begin to see part of the old Mark that I once knew and loved.

"Erm…..Niceto vas zadovoljiti." Pam stammers as she laughs nervously. "Was that right, do you think?"

"It sounded right to me, you've got a good memory."

Mark shakes his head. "I have no idea what you just said to me."

"I said it was nice to meet you, or at least I hope I did…" She guffaws some more before calling Pete over from the bar.

"You must be Mark?" Pete advances towards us with his one hand outstretched in readiness to shake Mark's, the other clutching a beer.

Mark shakes his hand. "Pete is it? Good to meet you."

Pam and Pete join us for a drink at the poolside as they regale us with stories about their children, previous holidays and drinking stories. The best one being the night Pete got so drunk he lost his front door key and so came home through the back garden via the pond and couldn't quite make it up the stairs, so he slept on the kitchen floor.

Observing Pam and Pete, I can't help but realise how different they are. As Pam tells us these stories, she's shaking her head in irritation at the state he gets in, but at the same time she's laughing her head off with the rest of us. Two very different people, yet they're clearly very much in love and very happy together. A thought then hits me that as with us, things aren't always as they seem from the outset.

Drinks turn into lunch of tuna baguettes for Mark and I, whilst Pam and Pete share a cheese and pineapple pizza and a plate of chips. I notice Mark begins to look uncomfortable in his seat so I check if he's okay.

He gulps his beer. "Just really hot, think I need a swim."

I swear I see Pam's eyes light up and I smile to myself.

He stands to cast an eye over the pool. "You coming in?"

"No, I think I'll just sit under the parasol for a while."

Pam and Pete decide on an afternoon nap and so gather their things and go up to their room, whilst I make myself comfortable sunbathing.

Mark slips his feet into his flip-flops to walk to the pool side. "They linger a bit don't they?"

I glance behind me, wondering who he's talking about. "Wh-what Pam and Pete?"

He nods. "Well, yes."

I'm surprised to hear him talk like this. "What? No, they're really nice. Do you not like them?"

"Not really our kind of people are they, Luisa?" he raises his eyebrows and walks off to the water.

I stay resting back on my elbows on the lounger in shock at his self-importance.

"Arrogant little…" I mumble under my breath.

Sometime later, when Mark has dried off we decide to head indoors for a *siesta* ourselves.

The extreme coolness of the room hits me like a slap in the face. I rush over to the air-conditioning controller and turn it up a few degrees.

"I'll give Jodie a quick call first to see how her interview went." I slip out onto the balcony with my mobile, whilst Mark gets into bed. Jodie answers after the first ring.

"Hi, how did it go?"

"It went really well, they told me I've got the job!" I can tell she's buzzing with excitement from the tone of her voice.

"Oh, Jodie well done, I knew you would."

"Thanks Lu, I'm so excited. It feels a bit weird though having your old job. I feel a bit bad actually, I know how much you loved it."

"Feel bad? Don't be silly, you're perfect for the job."

"My first job as official branch manager is to hire a part-time assistant manager, know anyone who'd be interested? You know, I'd take you back like a shot."

I hear the dogs suddenly start to bark in the background and Jodie shushes them…it's like even *they're* telling me to say yes.

I'm beyond tempted, maybe I could go back on a part-time basis. I really miss the job and the girls and I wouldn't be so restricted with my writing time working just part-time.

Jodie continues with her persuading. "I know you want to, you can't tell me you're not interested Luisa, I know you are. Just think it would be perfect, you'd still have two and a half days a week to write."

I giggle with excitement, glancing back into the bedroom at Mark in bed hoping he hasn't heard me. "Can I say yes, in principle?"

"That's a yes!" She says excitedly. "Anyway, how's the holiday, are you having a good time?"

"I love it here Jodie, the place is great."

"Oh good, you had me worried when you said Mark was working a lot."

"Well, he is but I'm enjoying the holiday anyway."

"How's the situation with the two of you...or can't you speak now?"

I quieten my voice, so he doesn't hear as I glance around me. "Not the best. Most of the time, it feels really false between us. It's definitely over, it's just..."

"I know...well, you've given it everything you've got, he's lucky you did that after what he did to you...I'm just sorry you're there by yourself, it's only your second day."

"It's difficult, I mean what do I do seen as we're away? He tried it on last night, he wasn't happy when I knocked him back. It's probably my own fault."

I casually lean slightly over the balcony rail in the hope that I don't see any of our neighbours, so hopefully they aren't able to hear my conversation.

Jodie momentarily panics. "He didn't try to force himself on you did he?"

"No, no, he didn't...it's just...normally the easy option to get on with it. Do you think that's bad?" I rub my head.

"No...but if you're feeling like that, what makes you think he wouldn't force himself on you?"

"Mark may be many things, but I know he wouldn't do that."

Explaining to Jodie makes me comprehend the situation more so. Maybe I'd be better off checking into another room or hotel and ending things with him sooner rather than later. The quicker I do, the quicker we can both get on with our lives.

"I'd better go, thanks for listening I really appreciate it. Congratulations again! Is Darren pleased for you?"

"Yeah, he's chuffed. He said he's taking me out tonight to celebrate. Look, stay strong and ring me if you need me."

What would I do without Jodie? Ending the call, I spend a couple of minutes enjoying the view of the sea. Feeling at peace with my final decision now made, taking a deep breath I quietly open the balcony door back into the bedroom. I lower myself as quietly as possible onto my side of the bed. With all of these questions swirling around in my head I doubt I'll get any sleep, but at least I can do some thinking.

I must drop off to sleep just for a few minutes until I'm woken by Mark pacing the room in front of me and clutching his stomach.

"I feel a little sick…hope it wasn't the lunch."

I sit up slowly. "Well, we had the same and I feel okay. Maybe it was the beer? Here have some water." I pass him a litre bottle of water half-heartedly from the fridge and he slowly begins to sip it. It's then that I notice he seems to be shaking.

Mark slams down the bottle of water and heads to the bathroom where I hear the clunk of the toilet seat being lifted and the thud of Mark dropping to the floor beside it. I stand at the bathroom doorway to see him leaning over the toilet bowl, still shaking.

I have a sudden realisation. "It could be sunstroke, you didn't go in the shade today."

There's no way I can talk to him about us now, I need to make sure he's okay. I rush back to the bedroom to retrieve the water.

"...you need to drink and get back into bed, maybe I should get a doctor?"

Mark slowly begins to stand up from the floor. "No! No need, I'll just sleep it off."

He slowly begins to walk back to bedroom before falling into bed. Again I fetch the water, this time pouring him a glass. I sit on the bed next to him and insist that he drinks it.

"Mark, drink!" I hold the glass towards him. He seems almost childlike as he tentatively takes the water, still shaking and begins to drink. His phone begins to ring from the other side of the room, snatching Mark's attention. He tries to get out of bed to answer it.

"You have got to be joking. Leave it, look at the state of you!"

"I can't, can I?" We glare at each other for a couple of seconds.

"Are you asking me, or telling me?" But I already know the answer.

He crawls across the bed away from me over to his phone. I feel more and more convinced that my decision about our marriage is the right one as the minutes go by. I just need to find the right time to broach the subject again. It won't be easy with us being away, but I've got to do it and this time will be the last time. There'll be no turning back.

Mark finishes his call and edges back into bed with an expectant look on his face. "I thought you'd start complaining as soon as I was off the phone."

I sit back down next to him on the bed. "What would be the point?"

"Do you really think I could have sunstroke?"

"Could be, how's your stomach now?" I ask as I touch his forehead to check for a temperature.

"Still the same, I just feel so tired." He checks his watch. "You must be starving, get ready for dinner…don't worry about me, I'll be fine."

I shake my head. "I can't leave you here feeling ill. I'll order room service."

"Don't you dare do that…it's bad enough I have to stay in, I'm not ruining your night too. Honestly I'll just get some sleep, you go…have dinner and a few drinks."

I feel guilty leaving him alone, despite our current circumstances, but Mark keeps pushing me. In the end I decide to eat and then come back to the room so I can't feel any worse than I already do.

After showering, I dry my hair and pull on my royal blue vest dress. I check on Mark again before leaving the room, he seems to be asleep so I reach for another bottle of water from the fridge and leave it next to the bed for him.

Walking into the restaurant for dinner alone makes me feel a little self-conscious at first, until I see Franjo.

"Dobra vecer, Madam."

"Dobra vecer, Franjo."

"Alone tonight?" He glances behind me.

"He's not well." I feel unable to bring myself to call him my husband.

"I will look after you." He promises, leading me to a table. "Are you enjoying your holiday? I hope your husband is alright."

"Erm…. Odmor je veliko hvala." I tell him the holiday's great in a nervous tone, wondering if I should have attempted that or not.

"Very good, have you been taking lessons?"

"I tried one this morning around the pool and really enjoyed it."

"That is my sister Jelena, she is the teacher." He boasts proudly. "Your usual drink, Madam?"

"Call me Luisa, please. I think I'll have a rosé tonight, thanks."

Franjo walks over to the bar to collect my drink whilst I slowly begin to people watch. There's no sign of Pam and Pete, although I'm quite late in coming down to dinner. I see Kristina the rep over at the salad bar and she waves in acknowledgement, as she takes her seat with her plate piled high of what looks like the healthiest meal I've ever seen, with crisp green lettuce and red tomatoes almost falling from the plate.

Franjo delivers my glass of rosé and I wait until he walks away before taking a mouthful. It's delicious, really fruity and very easy to drink. Oh how I needed that.

I'm still yet to see the chef tonight and can't help but feel slightly saddened that it doesn't look like I'll get to see him today at all. I know it's pathetic, but just seeing him makes me feel my self-esteem creep up a notch and makes my nerve-endings spark like never before.

I arrive at the meat section and begin to help myself to some chargrilled chicken, as I turn the corner to the vegetable section there he is, coming through the doorway from the back kitchen area. He sees me right away and I get that extreme jolt of nerves that makes my legs almost begin to shake.

This time he's not wearing his chef's hat at first meaning I get a closer and unrestricted view of his gorgeous dark hair and eyes, with his hair lightly gelled to perfection. He gives me an extremely alluring side grin as he puts on his chef's hat, walks past me and over to the grilling station.

I pick up some cauliflower, green beans and a small slice of fresh crusty bread and purposely walk past him en-route back to my table which tonight, is further towards the windows at the back. Sitting down, I pick up my knife and fork and cut into my delicious looking chicken. I steal another glimpse in his direction and for a split second I think he's coming over to me, but then I see he's heading for the bar. Moments later he returns with two bottles of beer and disappears back through that doorway to the kitchen. I really must stop this I'm technically still a married woman, but I can't help myself. There's just something about him.

I wish I could sit here all night, but after finishing my dinner and my wine, I should think about getting back upstairs to check on Mark. I have a thought that maybe I should take him back some food, just in case. I go back over to the bread section and wrap a couple of slices in a serviette and pick up a few slices of Dalmatian ham and tuck those in the parcel too.

"How are you?" I'm startled to hear a man's voice from beside me.

I turn to my right to see the chef, carrying what looks like a tray of freshly washed glasses underneath a tea towel. He catches me off guard.

"Hi…" I clear my throat. "Good…thanks. How are you?"

As I speak to him, I notice his smile slowly spreads from his mouth and seems to reach his eyes, which makes me feel an excitement inside like I haven't felt in years.

"Good." he looks around. "You are alone tonight?"

"Erm, yes. He's erm…not well." I'm completely lost in his eyes and wishing I wasn't currently attempting to smuggle food from the restaurant.

"Well, if…" Now it's his turn to clear his throat, and I begin to wonder what he's going to ask. "…Erm, have a good evening." he finishes, our eyes still connecting as he walks back towards the kitchen, facing me at first, before turning his back to me and walking away. *What was he going to say??*

Chapter 6

A feeling of disappointment washes over me and I decide to take the lift up to the second floor to our room. I slide the key card into the door handle and creep into the pitch dark room. The distinct chill from the earlier air conditioning still hangs in the air.

I put the key card into the slot on the wall to activate the lights, just switching on the bathroom light with the door open so I can see my way around the room without waking Mark. I tip toe over to the bed and am taken aback to see Mark's not there. I switch the full light on still clutching the sandwich I've made and walk to the balcony door, flinging back the curtains expecting to see him sitting on the balcony, but he's not there.

"Mark?" I call out, maybe he's in the bathroom after all and I didn't notice him.

Popping my head around the bathroom door, it's obvious he's gone out. I stroll back towards the bed in disbelief and fling the sandwich across the room in anger. Momentarily calming down, I reach for my phone and try to call him believing he'll definitely answer, as he normally can't keep away from his phone. Voicemail, great.

I decide to leave a message. "Mark, it's me…I'm back in our room, where are you?"

I toss my phone onto the bed and lie down next to it in aggravation. I begin to hear that intermittent beeping again from Mark's laptop and see that it's still switched on, with the lid partially down. I reach for the laptop, dragging it towards me on the bed and pull up the screen.

On the task bar at the bottom of the screen sits a blue flashing icon with *"SL"* on it. Intrigued, I double click on this icon and I'm completely dumbfounded with what I see.

A dating website opens up. I feel like I'm reading about another person's life as I click on the inbox that tells me there are three new messages waiting to be read, from three different women, one of whom is thanking Mark for *'the best night of her life last Wednesday.'*

My mouth falls open. I feel sickened that I've been such a fool, where is he now? Is he meeting up with one of these women here?

I think back to last Wednesday night, and distinctly remember Mark working, he didn't get home until gone midnight. I continue reading the messages including the ones Mark has sent to each of them where he takes pleasure in describing how his wife doesn't understand him and isn't fulfilling his needs. I'm flabbergasted.

Everything seems to make sense now, as when I check Mark's profile he has the box ticked to receive an automated telephone call each time he receives a new message. This would explain how even when he feels ill, he still breaks his neck to answer his phone.

From his profile I see he's been active on this site since 2nd June. I wrack my brains and check my calendar on my phone, I'm sure this is just a couple of days after the last time I tried to talk to Mark about our marriage, the one where he cried and pleaded with me not to give up on us. I think I've seen enough as I shut the laptop down and put it back where it was.

I need some air, I need a drink, but not necessarily in that order. I open the fridge and pick up the first miniature bottle I find - whiskey and throw it straight back. A violent coughing episode follows, as it burns the back of my throat. I don't even like whiskey…wow, that was strong. I go out onto the balcony and breathe in some sea air to clear my head, what now?

After a few minutes of letting my mind wander aimlessly and as the after effects from the alcohol start to relax me, I watch the world continuing around me from the balcony. I surprisingly feel like I begin to think straight - perhaps for the first time in months.

Yes, I feel sickened by what he's been up to, but deep down I'm not entirely surprised. I realised I didn't love Mark anymore quite some time ago and I think he knows that considering that chat we had. Maybe this has made things easier for me, I'll just tell him I know what he has been doing and that we're finished, something I think we both realised a long time ago. Should I confront him tonight or shall I wait? So many questions, but I wish I knew the answers.

I march back inside over to Mark's side of the bed, pick up the phone and dial "0" for reception.

"Hi, I'm calling from room 206, I'm staying here for two weeks until 8th July. I wondered if you had another room available until then? Any room is fine."

"I am sorry, madam but we are fully booked. Is there a problem with your room?"

I'm beginning to feel desperate now. "No, there's no problem. Do you happen to know if any other hotels in the area may have a room?"

"It is a busy time of year for us in Dubrovnik, there may be rooms in apartments near the old town. Do you not like our hotel, madam?"

"No, it's not that, this hotel is perfect…it's…don't worry, sorry to trouble you. Good night." I put the receiver down.

I eye my suitcase in the corner of the room and have a vision of me going from apartment to apartment in the old town lugging my suitcase over what I imagine is miles of little cobbled streets, desperate to find a room. I'll have to stay here, I'll sleep on the floor if I have to. Maybe Jodie can help with getting a room in another hotel tomorrow if I don't have any luck online. I pick up my phone and open a browser and start to search for somewhere to stay but a desperate need to get out of the room takes over and so I stop.

I decide to try Mark one more time but again I get voicemail. I'm not letting him ruin another moment of my holiday. I pick up the key card, my bag and some cash from the room safe and head back downstairs, maybe he's having a drink in the bar.

I enter the bar next to reception named *Opustiti*, I'm told by the sign on the bar that *Opustiti* means relax. You can tell that whoever designed the bar wanted you to do just that, the bar is full of wicker sofas covered in large cream cushions inviting you to sit down and unwind. The walls are painted a beautiful soft relaxing green and the whole bar is lit by just a couple of standing lamps and candlelight. A relaxing scent that reminds me of lavender fills the air and the soft music being played only adds to the ambience. There's no sign of Mark and I doubt he's stayed at the hotel anyway, so I decide to go out for a walk.

I step out onto the front steps of the hotel and into the dark, walking around to the right, through the car park and around towards the pool area. I see a familiar face walking towards me and my heart rate begins to quicken as I recognise through the darkness - it's the chef.

"Hello again." He smiles.

I'm now really glad I had that whiskey. "Hi, just finished for the night?"

"Just finished." he nods. "Where is your husband? You are always alone… sorry, that is none of my business."

"That's okay…I'm not sure where he is." I have to remember I'm talking to a stranger, although he doesn't feel like one, so I don't want to say too much.

He looks concerned. "Are you fighting?"

"Not fighting as such, no. We're not really together anymore." I realise I've told him before I've even told Mark aaaand there's that pang of guilt. I sense that he begins to feels awkward.

His slides his hands into his pockets. "Sorry to hear that."

"It's okay, I've had a lot of time to get used to it." For some reason I'm finding it really easy to talk to this man. I only hope he doesn't think I'm one of those over sharers - telling him everything.

"I am Luka." he extends his hand towards me, stepping closer.

"I'm Luisa." I take his hand in greeting. My hand begins to heat immediately from his touch and sends a shiver through the whole of my body.

We seem to hold onto each other's hand in greeting a little longer than is normal as we exchange a knowing smile. It's a smile that says that we both feel the same attraction to each other.

"Louisa, I like that name."

"It's Luisa…sorry." I feel awful correcting him.

He smiles. "Would you like some company, *Luisa*? We could go for a drink?"

My heart is screaming yes the top of its voice, but my head is telling me to be cautious. I take too long to answer and Luka seems to think he's offended me and looks mortified.

"I am sorry …" he holds up his hand as to say to forget it. "I thought that we…"

"I'd love some company. I was just going for a walk but a drink would be good."

We walk through the hotel grounds together, following the path leading around the back of the hotel and through the pool area, which looks really beautiful at night. Little lanterns are strung from the palm trees, uplighters light the water in the pool from below making the water glow a dazzling aqua blue. I feel awestruck, like I've been set alight from the inside taking in the lovely scene in front of me.

The chemistry I feel with Luka I simply can't put into words, I wonder if he feels it too. He looks strikingly attractive in that sexy casual kind of way, wearing a fitted white shirt with the sleeves rolled up, khaki green cut-off trousers and black toe-post flip-flops.

"So, are you enjoying your holiday so far, or is that stupid question considering…"

His accent…his voice, I could listen to it all night.

"I wouldn't say I'm not enjoying it, I suppose I'm hoping it can get started now." We walk on.

"You will have a great time…there is a lot to see in the area."

"Well Croatia is such a beautiful country from what I've seen so far."

Luka leads me from the promenade and around to the right and up along a passageway that I hadn't noticed before. I see lighting shining out onto the dark pathway before us as we arrive outside a bar called '*Baldo's*'. We walk up the three steps that take us inside, towards a table at the back. Two waiters call out to Luka and signal their hellos, he promptly walks over and shakes their hands in turn. I have no idea what they're saying, but find it fascinating all the same just listening to them.

"Sorry I haven't been here for a while, they were asking me why."

We sit down at a table in the corner, I notice a large TV screen on the wall playing a football match with the sound muted, but Luka opts for the seat with his back to the screen. A couple of minutes menu reading later and one of the waiters appears in front of us, addressing us both in Croatian.

"Baldo, this is Luisa. Luisa, this is the owner of the bar, Baldo."

We chat for a couple of minutes about how I'm on holiday and it's my first time in Croatia before ordering our drinks, which Baldo insists are on him.

I look around the bar, taking in the juke box in the corner as it plays gentle background music, the pool table on the left as a guy puts a coin on the side, signalling to the current players he wants to use the table next.

"Do you come in here a lot then?" I wonder out loud.

"Couple of times a week but, not so much anymore really. You do not see many tourists in here… it is mostly local people."

"Well it's pretty hidden away back here."

He laughs before holding eye contact with me. "I cannot believe what has happened to you with your husband, tell me to mind my own business if you want to forget about it tonight."

I feel slightly embarrassed, not that he's asking but embarrassed about what *has* happened. Telling him that my husband has not only already had an affair and I've taken him back, but now he's carrying on with who knows how many other women that he's met online won't exactly make me look good.

I pick the short version telling him about the affair, me taking him back, the constant trying to make things work. The always coming second best, with his work taking the trophy of first place and the realisation of my feelings for him, or lack thereof. Then the situation of him, I'm assuming feigning illness and disappearing tonight.

I don't think he quite knows what to say on the matter, but he seems sympathetic.

"That is terrible. Well at least you tried to forgive him, you did not decide to end it there and then, and wonder for the rest of your life if you had done the right thing. Have you been married long time?"

"For three years…not long really, but long enough. If I'm being honest, I still find it difficult to believe that I ended up in a relationship with someone who tried to be so controlling."

I turn the conversation back to him to take some of the heat off me and of course, I'm curious to learn more about him.

"Do you live locally?"

He puts his beer down on the table and leans forward in his seat, closer towards me.

"A few minutes away, just around the corner from the hotel."

"You're so lucky, seeing these views that you have here. The beautiful scenery…"

"Beautiful…" he reiterates, staring deep into my eyes just as his knee touches mine under the table. I yet again feel the hint of colour beginning in my cheeks, how does he manage to do this to me so easily?

He pulls my attention back. "What else have you done so far on your holiday?"

"Not much yet really, we're going to Montenegro tomorrow…well, *I* am, then the Elaphiti islands on Sunday. I want to see as much as possible."

"Montenegro, you will love. Will you go alone?"

"I'll be fine, I won't be alone there'll be a coach full of people with me." It's then it dawns on me that I will be alone tomorrow, and for the next 11 days. But I'd rather that than be with Mark anymore, no contest.

We order another drink but I sensibly order water, and Luka excuses himself to use the toilet. As I watch him walk away, I begin to notice his physique. He seems to have quite broad shoulders, the perfect inverted triangle shape leading down to a slim waist and gorgeous bum. Again, I have to restrain my thoughts. It's such a long time since anybody made me feel attractive, and here I am now with this very good looking man, and all I can think of doing is kissing him, and I'm wondering what he looks like underneath that shirt. Even though I know it's wrong and I shouldn't be thinking like this.

I see Luka returning to the table and I get that tingle low down in my abdomen, purely from just looking at him.

He tells me how he's worked at the hotel for two years, and he loves to cook but his other passion is photography. I learn that he has two DSLR cameras, both of which are second-hand and took him the best part of a year to save up for each one. When he talks about photography I notice a spark from inside of him, he seems to light up. He wasn't exaggerating when he said it's his passion.

Without thinking I put my hand on Luka's wrist to tilt his watch towards me, feeling so comfortable around him that it didn't feel strange in the slightest to do that. I see Luka's eyes try to find my own. It's 11:50 p.m. I wonder if Mark's back yet? I get the sudden urge to run back to our room, thrash things out with him and put an end to it all, but that means calling it a night with Luka.

He lightly touches my hand. "You have to go?"

"I wish I didn't, but I should. Need to sort things out."

"Sort things out, you mean…"

I panic, I hope he doesn't think I mean I want to make up with Mark. "No…" I interrupt harshly, before realising how I sound and soften my voice. "Just finish things once and for all."

I slide my seat from underneath the table and stand to leave. "Thanks for the drink, it's been great."

"My pleasure. Let me walk you back to the hotel."

Leaving the bar with Luka, I wonder what Mark would think if he saw me now. He'd definitely get the wrong idea, but then I couldn't really blame him if he did. A thought comes to my mind on the walk back, what if Mark's still not there? There's only one way to find out.

Luka and I stroll back down the alleyway and I can't deny feeling a touch of excitement at being with him in this confined space in the dark. My mind briefly plays out a scenario where he pushes me up against the wall and kisses me with such passion…

"Luisa?" He questions, snapping me out of my daydream as he stands still waiting for me to answer.

"Sorry? I was miles away."

"I asked if you are okay? You were breathing heavily…"

"I erm…I'm fine, sorry. I just suddenly felt rather hot but I'm okay now." That was embarrassing.

Seconds later we meet the promenade and for some reason, I was expecting it to be quieter now but the sound of laughter can still be heard amongst the gentle rhythm of music as it seeps out of every restaurant and bar that we pass. When we reach the gates to the hotel I feel the need to stop.

"I should probably leave you here…" *although I don't want to* "…if he sees us together…"

Luka understands immediately. "Of course, I do not want to make it any more difficult for you. I also should not really be seen with any guest…"

"Oh I'm sorry, I didn't even think of that. I was too wrapped up in…"

"No that is okay. I hope you enjoy Montenegro tomorrow, but do not forget us Croatian's." he gives me a slow sexy smile.

I return his smile with pleasure. "No chance of that." *Did I really say that out loud?*

I break out in laughter and he laughs along with me, momentarily taking my hand before letting it go again.

He lowers his voice. "I hope it goes okay…"

"Thanks Luka, and thanks again for tonight."

It's at this point I imagine him kissing me good night, but I know that would be wrong, and so does he…or would it? He walks away casually, hands in his pockets.

"Good night, Luisa."

Did I imagine that? Have I actually spent the last couple of hours in his company? I take a deep breath and turn to look up at the hotel, trying to work out which is our balcony. I think the lights are on, he must be there. My walking speed increases as I rush back through the grounds of the hotel, round into the car park and through reception. I think I'll get the lift, I need to steady my breathing and collect my thoughts before I confront him.

Chapter 7

Walking into our room, I see Mark on the balcony drinking what looks like vodka from a glass tumbler. He eyes me suspiciously as I throw my bag onto the bed, he knocks back the last of his drink and slams the glass down on the table, his face a look of contempt.

"I wondered where you'd got to." He stands up, moving back into the room.

"Funny, I could say the same about you. I take it you're feeling better?"

I can see the guilt written all over his face. "I, erm….yes, I went for some fresh air." He opens the door to the fridge to retrieve another miniature.

I watch him for a second, choosing my words carefully. "I was only out for half an hour if that, I came back and you were gone. I did call you a couple of times." I wonder how he'll try to cover his tracks this time.

"Sorry, I didn't hear my phone." He won't even look at me as he replies.

I sit on the end of the bed, and begin take off my jewellery. "Mark, I don't believe you. How come you were so ill when I went to dinner and yet half an hour later you make a miraculous recovery? And now what, a couple of hours later you're working your way through the contents of the mini bar?" *Calm down Luisa, don't lose control.*

He raises his eyebrows in apparent surprise. "I told you…I. WENT. FOR. SOME. AIR!"

I raise my hands to my head in absolute exasperation. "You know what Mark, I really don't care anymore. For some reason, I was genuinely concerned about you tonight. You'd think I'd have learnt my lesson by now where you're concerned." *Confess, come on…*

"Learned your lesson? Who the hell do you think you're talking to?"

I stand up to help me project my fury. "Where were you?"

I stay firmly rooted to the spot as he steps closer towards me. "Are you deaf, or are you choosing just to not listen to me?!"

My pulse is on overload at this point. "I know the truth Mark, why the hell can't you just be a man and admit it?"

He sniggers and finishes yet another drink. "The truth, what are you talking about?"

That's it, I'm done. "Your account on that website, Mark, I know…so don't even bother trying to deny it!"

Judging by the look on his face, the penny finally drops. "What website? You're going insane, Luisa…"

"For god's sake. Just admit it, you've been found out. It's over, that's it!" I feel like I'm going to explode, I'm so angry.

"I don't know what you've been drinking, but you need to sleep it off…"

I clench my fists and dig them into my thighs and breathe an exasperated breath. The laptop, the laptop. I begin to scour the room, there it is, I drag the laptop towards me from the other side of the bed and lift the lid, pressing the on button.

"Right it's me, is it?"

"Okay…okay….I can explain." he admits defeat.

I push the laptop towards him. "Explain away…"

"I, I…felt lonely, I need…" He's flabbergasted, the look on his face.

"No more lies! I know how long this has been going on for. I've seen your sordid little messages, a month ago that account was opened."

He looks down at the floor. "I only did it because after that talk we had I knew I was losing you, I panicked. I needed something, someone…anyone."

"Don't you dare try to turn this around on to me." I should have known this would be his reaction.

"If you hadn't have said those things to me that night…"

"You're telling me that the night I tried to explain that I felt it wasn't working between us, the night you begged me in tears not to leave you…that's when you thought I know, I'll join an online dating website?"

"I knew you didn't love me anymore, I could see it in your eyes. The way you looked at me and the way you still look at me now. Tell me I'm wrong?"

I fall silent, he knows I won't lie. "You're not wrong, no."

Mark puts his hands to his head in frustration.

I pace back and forth trying to burn off some of my anger. "This is ridiculous, if you knew, why didn't we just call it a day then? I could have moved out, leaving you free to do whatever it is you want to do with whoever it is you want to do it with! But instead…more lies!"

"Luisa, you're my wife, I didn't want to lose you…"

"You lost me that night I saw you with another woman, it just took me time to realise that myself."

I walk out onto the balcony, lord I hope nobody's heard us arguing. I make the most of the couple of minute's silence and realise the 10 tonne weight I've been carrying around with me for months has finally lifted. I hear Mark opening the fridge again and he appears behind me, holding out a drink. I try to read his expression on his face, he looks worn down. I look at the drink, and snatch it from his hand.

"What now?" He asks calmly.

I go back into the bedroom, he follows me and closes the balcony door behind us.

I exhale. "Well that's it, I'll move out when we get home."

"And in the meantime, let's just try to enjoy the holiday."

I almost jump out of my skin. "Enjoy the holiday? I intend to Mark, but not with you."

"Ha! What are you going to do? Pretend not to notice me on the other side of the bed?"

"I checked at reception earlier, but they don't have any more rooms. I'll sleep on the floor if I have to."

"No, we'll go home together and sort this out properly." He reaches under the bed for his case.

"What?"

T-shirts, shorts, shirts all begin to make their way into his suitcase. "Come on, we'll head to the airport, the sooner we get home, the sooner we can sort this out and save our marriage."

My blood begins to boil. "We haven't even been here for 48 hours yet, there's no way I'm going home and certainly not with you…there's nothing left to save."

His voice goes up a notch. "You're not staying here on your own."

"Try and stop me!"

"Don't tempt me…" He rushes forward grabbing my wrists, pulling me towards him. The look on his face is harrowing. I know I've been drinking but he smells like he's drank a brewery dry. I struggle to release his grip.

"Stop it…it's over…just let me go!" On that I use every ounce of strength to push him away from me, he falls on the bed and looks up at me in realisation.

My emotions begin to take over as someone turns on the taps behind my eyes. I hear the noise of sobs rising from my throat and they sound like they're coming from someone else but no, it's definitely me.

He picks up his laptop and switches it on as peace descends on the room, whilst I wonder what will happen next. I slump into the armchair in the corner, my head swirling with confusion as I rest my head in my hands. This can't be happening…how on earth am I in this mess?

He takes his wallet from his back pocket setting it down on the dresser next to his laptop.

"I'll check the flight situation, see when I can get home."

He begins searching on the internet whilst I get ready for bed, removing my makeup. I try to compose myself in the mirror, what did I do wrong? What did I do wrong that pushed my husband into the arms of someone else in the first place? Almost two years have gone by and I still don't understand why this happened. I refuse to let him knock me back down. It took me a long time to come to terms with his affair and even longer to build myself back up. He's not taking away my confidence again.

He interrupts me from my thoughts. "There's a flight to Manchester tomorrow morning, I've booked that. I can combine it with going to the Manchester office to sort a few things out. I'll get the train back from there." He closes the computer down, leaving the air feeling filled with tension.

"Okay." I whisper.

Work would never be anything below number one for Mark, well that and shagging his way around as many women as possible. We never should've got married, I really don't think he's the marrying kind, even if he doesn't realise it.

He points at the armchair in the corner of the room and tells me he'll sleep there.

I feel overwhelmed by what's happened tonight, I'm exhausted. He continues throwing his clothes into his suitcase and is fully packed ready for home within five minutes.

Chapter 8

I feel like I've been wide awake for most of the night, but take a little pleasure in knowing Mark has been too. If he'd been snoring all night, I can only imagine feeling even more annoyed this morning.

It was after 1:00 a.m. by the time I was in bed and Mark settled in on the chair. I did feel bad at one point during the night when I could see he was restless and told him to get into the bed, but he refused.

I'm not sure how long he's been up, but I definitely heard him in the shower a while ago. Now fully dressed in jeans and a black T-shirt, he emerges from the bathroom. That awkwardness rears its ugly head once again.

"Morning." he sounds very subdued. "I've booked a taxi with reception, it'll be here soon." He throws his shaver and toothbrush into his case and signals the finality of it all with the sound of the last zip of the case and the thud of his packed luggage hitting the floor.

I climb out of bed and feel uneasy in my nightie around him, which is really silly considering he's seen me wear that and a lot less a million times before, but somehow it just doesn't feel right any longer. I pick up my thin green robe and pull it around me.

"Well…safe flight." I fidget uncomfortably with my hands, picking at my pink nail varnish.

Mark retrieves his luggage with one hand and leans in to kiss me on my cheek, making me wince.

"Enjoy the trip today. I'll see you in a couple of weeks, we'll sort everything then?"

"We will." I nod.

He slowly wheels his luggage out of the room and closes the door behind him.

It's a peculiar feeling watching him leave, a strange sense of loss washes over me again even though I've had more than enough time to get used to my marriage being over, but I feel lighter. I glance down at my wedding and engagement ring and remove them in one swoop and see the un-weathered band around my finger where they sat. I can't continue to wear them so I place them in my jewellery roll until I get home. They were both Mark's grandmother's rings, so I can't contemplate not giving them back once he's got used to the idea of us being apart properly.

I take a quick shower and dress speedily as I realise it's only an hour until the coach leaves for Montenegro and have a fleeting feeling that maybe I shouldn't go. I pace the room up and down trying to persuade myself. For the best part of a year, I've felt so trapped but not anymore…Montenegro, here I come. I throw the necessities for the day into my beach bag, not forgetting to take my mobile along with me - maybe I'll call Jodie later.

When I reach reception on the way to breakfast, I spy Kristina updating posters of the excursion adverts.

"Doble dan, Kristina."

She turns around, poster in hand. "Doble dan. How are you?"

"Okay, thanks. Montenegro today."

She holds the poster out in front of me. "I was just updating the display with a beautiful new picture of Kotor."

"Ohhh, it looks fantastic." To think I almost considered not going on the trip just minutes ago.

Finishing my chat with Kristina I edge closer to the restaurant for breakfast.

After spending the evening with Luka last night, and the events that happened afterwards with Mark, I'm concerned I might seem flighty. I haven't been in love with Mark for a really long time, which I hope I've portrayed to Luka. Why I'm fretting about it, I'm not sure. It's not like anything has happened with Luka or will happen, but I just don't want him to get the wrong impression of me.

Franjo's pushing a trolley full of clean plates towards the door as I enter. "Jutros gospodo, good morning Madam."

"Dobro jutro."

I see Luka turning to look in my direction. He raises his eyebrows to me, making my stomach lurch with excitement. I put my bag down on a free table and move slowly to join the queue around the buffet he's stationed at. He's busy cooking an omelette for a lady as she waits patiently, meaning I'm almost at the other end of the buffet when he's free.

I see the concern on his face. "Are you okay?"

I dribble the maple syrup onto my pancakes and manage to cover most of my hand during the process and attempt to wipe it off. "I think so…"

Luka reaches behind him for a wet cloth and passes this to me as I grimace at the stickiness on my hand.

"Thanks." I pass the cloth back. "How are you?"

"Better now I have seen you. I was wondering how things were going last night…"

He thought of me last night. "It was hard, but we sorted things out…"

His face seems to fall slightly. "Oh, oh, you are trying again?"

I hear someone clear their throat next to me and notice I'm holding up the queue, so I try to step around to the side to continue my conversation with Luka, as one of the waiters shouts to warn him that his boss is coming this way.

"Sorry, I will speak to you later." he rushes as he makes himself look busy at the omelette station.

I spend the rest of breakfast dreading that Luka thinks I meant Mark and I are trying again, I didn't get chance to finish my sentence. If I go back over to try and explain the rest of the story I'll risk him realising just how much what he thinks bothers me. As much as it pains me, I only really get a chance to wave to him as I leave the restaurant as his boss is around, so I don't think going over to talk to him will be a good idea.

The coach arrives right on time for the excursion and as I reach the front of the queue I tell the guide my surname when he asks and then I have to explain there will only be one person now, rather than two. I take a window seat and make myself comfortable for what I'm told is just over half an hour's journey to the border of Montenegro.

Pam appears in the walkway of the coach. "Fancy seeing you here…where's that gorgeous husband of yours?"

I take in her beautiful multi coloured kaftan style long dress of pinks, turquoise and yellow.

"He erm…isn't feeling too well."

"Oh what a shame. Well, at least he didn't want you to stay and mop his brow."

The coach is rather packed now so Pam and Pete head to the back of the coach for the last two seats, Pams' bracelets of choice for the day jangling as they go.

Our guide for today is a local man named Tony and so far, has had the coach in fits of laughter. Considering we've only been on the coach for five minutes, I'm hoping that means we're in for plenty of laughs today.

I can't get my conversation with Luka this morning out of my head and keep hearing him saying *'you are trying again?'* I want to scream at the top of my lungs that no, there is no way Mark and I are trying again. Hopefully as I was still alone at breakfast he'll realise that. I pull my mobile out from my bag to text Jodie asking the best time to call her later but, a message from Mark comes through which I promptly delete before I can stew over it. I type a short text to Jodie, before throwing my phone back in my bag on the seat next to me and closing my eyes.

When I wake up, we've reached the Croatia and Montenego border, where we're told we may need to show our passports to immigration officials. After sitting for 10 minutes on the coach waiting, Tony our guide bounds back on board to tell us we can drive straight through. When he informs us that the currency in Montenegro is the Euro, there are some disgruntled passengers on board who complain no one has told them this before the trip. Luckily our rep told us this in the welcome meeting so I've come armed with my debit card to withdraw some money when I get there.

Another half an hour later after some people watching from the coach window and stunning views of the village of Perast with its mountainous backdrop, we all pile off the coach. We do the five-minute walk around the bay to catch a small boat over to the islet of Our Lady of the Rocks.

The water looks so peaceful and it's almost a shame to be getting on a boat and disturbing it. Once we're on the small boat, in the distance we see a tiny islet with a small red roofed church, with the spectacular scenery of mountains all around us. Combined with the beautiful blue sky and the sun beaming down, everyone on the boat is quiet and in awe at what we see, it's like we can't believe it. The sight really is something special.

A few minutes later, we're led from the boat and inside the church on the island. It's quite dark inside, and offers a welcome reprieve from the intense heat. There's a really calming atmosphere as I glance around at all of the beautiful pictures of history on the walls, the statues and the small chapel where hundreds of brides over the years have left their bouquets, now dried from age and heat.

We follow Tony upstairs to the museum where we see a famous tapestry which we're told that the lady used her hair and other threads to create, taking her over 25 years to complete whilst she waited for the love of her life to return from his long journey. She eventually became blind. Imagine waiting that long for someone you love. I spend a couple of minutes just looking at this piece of history and trying to imagine how the lady was feeling.

Moments later I see Pam absorbing the sight of the tapestry and she seems to be dabbing her eyes with a tissue, clearly feeling the emotion.

We learn that the island was built by local men by sinking fishing boats loaded with rocks. This went on for centuries until the islet appeared at sea level. I really begin to loose myself in the history of this fascinating country.

Back outside we allow our eyes to adjust to the bright sunshine once again and after a quick toilet stop, we catch the same boat back over to the coach on the mainland and onward to Kotor. Checking my phone again, I see Jodie has replied and tells me to ring her whenever I can.

The coach then parks up a couple of minutes' walk from the entrance to the walled city of Kotor. Kotor is bustling with people and traffic as we follow Tony on foot to the gate entrance. The temperature on the coach read 30°C, but it feels even hotter than that as we wait at the gate for our Montenegrin guide. People are fanning themselves down with maps and reapplying sun lotion as our local guide Tomas arrives. Tomas has the size of a bodybuilder hidden under his white T-shirt and instantly reminds me of a wrestler, but he seems to have a very gentle nature in the way that he speaks.

He gives us a brief history of Kotor telling us how the city became part of Yugoslavia in 1918 and that the city walls, whilst looking very similar to Dubrovnik city walls are actually smaller, apparently taking around an hour and a half to walk around. I suddenly become annoyed that I still haven't been to Dubrovnik city walls or even into the main town, but then it's only day three of my holiday, plenty of time yet.

Tomas gives us a short walking tour around the city, taking in the small cobbled streets, the Venetian looking buildings and even takes us inside a church for a few moments, which is huge in comparison to the church of Our Lady of the Rocks. Kotor is so picturesque I feel like I've already taken hundreds of photos. Tomas then takes us back to the main square to meet with Tony before our two hours of free time.

The main square is busy with pavement cafés and restaurants, people eating, drinking and chatting. I can see people consulting guide books, others examining maps and looking around them wondering which street to take next. Local people do their best to walk around in between the tourists, smartly dressed and going about their day. There's a real buzz about the place and so many places to get ice cream that I really wouldn't know which one to choose.

Pam appears next to me with a hand-held fan. "Do you fancy joining us for lunch, Luisa?"

"That would be lovely, thanks." I hadn't even thought about lunch…only ice cream.

The three of us amble around the side streets, which although are quieter than the main square are still busy with tourists and locals alike. We come across a smaller square with another host of eateries and choose a table under a parasol at a restaurant called 'Plava'.

As one of the specialities of Montenegro is Dalmatian smoked ham, I order the ham and cheese toasted flatbread with a side salad. Despite the heat, Pete goes for the *rastan* which is cabbage soup, and Pam decides on a green salad with a side of freshly baked bread.

My toasted flatbread is so simple but it looks like a work of art when it arrives. The thin slices of ham are really tasty with just a gentle salty flavour and they're delicately rolled into almost like cone shapes on the top of the bread. Then they're drizzled with oil and sprinkled with basil, the melted cheese and tomatoes underneath are equally as scrumptious. Pete seems to be sweating profusely with his soup but he refuses to give up telling us the taste is definitely worth it.

We all wash down our food with a bottle of ice cold water each and sit back and relax to take in the scenery. Pete excuses himself to the toilet so Pam and I sit people watching for a couple of minutes before she breaks the silence.

"Is everything okay, dear? I can't help but think you look tired today."

I really wasn't expecting that question, I begin to fiddle with my hands in my lap. "What do you mean? I'm fine."

Pam looks over her shoulder in the direction that Pete went before leaning slightly closer to me.

"I wanted to wait until it was just me and you. Mark's not really ill, is he?" She purses her lips together.

I hate lying to people and I can see Pam's concern, I don't really feel like we're strangers now anyway. "No, he's not… he's gone home."

She rubs my knee gently in a mothering kind of way. "Did you have a fight? Tell me to mind my own business if you like, I won't take offence."

"More than a fight really, I've finished with him."

"Oh, Luisa…"

"It's fine, don't worry. It's been on the cards for some time, I tried to do it sooner, but…well, it's done now, that's the main thing." I smile at Pam, grateful for her listening ear. It feels good to talk about it.

"I hope you don't mind me saying, but there was something about the two of you together, I could tell something wasn't right between you."

I don't really know how to respond to that, could everyone see that?

Pam surprises me further still. "It was another woman, wasn't it?"

I freeze mid mouthful of water, how does she know that? I swallow my drink. "At first it was, then it became more than one and…a lot more than one recently."

Pam shakes her head in disgust.

I go on. "I tried hard to forgive him but in the end, the love just went, he was a different person to me after that. I knew what I had to do, but he begged me to give things more time. Then I found out last night there had been more women so, he gave me the final excuse I needed."

Pam shakes her head. "Honey, he didn't deserve you. At least now you can find someone who does." She begins frantically looking around us. "…what about him over there?" She points towards a 40 something waiter.

I begin to laugh. "Pam!"

"Well, why not?" She continues. "You're still young, you're gorgeous, *you* could have any man you want! Don't leave it too long, someone as lovely as you doesn't deserve to be without love in their life, don't be afraid to love again. Just remember, life is short."

I smile solemnly. "Thanks for listening…"

"You seem to be really strong Luisa, I envy you…when I was your age I wish I was as comfortable in my own skin as you seem to be."

I wipe around my mouth with my napkin. "I got used to the idea of being single again quite a while ago. Even though we've still been together we haven't really been together…if that makes sense?"

She nods, patting my hand. "I'm just glad he hasn't made you doubt yourself with what he's put you through…"

"Well he did…when it first happened, I struggled for quite a while and then when I came to terms with what happened and we started to try again, I felt trapped. My Mom doesn't believe in divorce either…"

Pam shifts forward in her seat. "I can think of nothing worse than staying married to someone who treats you in that way. It takes real strength to pick yourself back up like you have."

Why does it seem like she's talking from experience?

"I feel like I had to get to know myself again…I had plenty of time to do that when he was 'working' every night and my writing helps…"

"Well you just keep on going…I think you're remarkable."

I watch Pam, replaying her words in my head that I'm surprised to find have made me feel quite emotional as Pete returns to the table.

"Right, another walk ladies?"

"I think I might just call my friend actually, if you don't mind?" I check, hoping they won't be offended if I go off on my own.

"Of course not, thanks for joining us for lunch." Pam rubs my arm affectionately.

I take out 40 euro's from my purse and place it on the table. "Lunch is on me."

"Oh no, you're not doing that!" Pam disagrees, giving me back the money.

Pete gets to his feet. "Ladies, lunch is on me…I've already paid."

Pam smiles at us both, I know there will be no backing him down.

"That's so kind, thank you." I've genuinely been really grateful of their company.

"See you back at the coach." Pam winks at me.

I head back towards the main square and back to our starting point of the gate, cross the road and sit on the wall overlooking the water with the breath taking fjords in front of me. I sit and stare at the view around me for a few minutes.

Relaxing back onto my elbows, feeling the sun on my face and feeling lighter and lighter as the time goes by. There's very much a fresh feeling in the air, I wonder if it's because of the mountains that surround me. I glance to my right to see a couple also sitting on the wall but they're completely lost in each other rather than the view with their arms wrapped firmly around one another and only pausing in between kisses to giggle. I can see why being here would make you feel more in love, with the natural beauty in every direction.

Chapter 9

It's 5:00.p.m back home now, perfect time to call Jodie on her way home from work. The phone barely rings before she answers.

"Hi Lu, how're things?"

"Good, I think. Jodie…..I've done it."

I tell Jodie the whole tale of Mark feigning illness, disappearing from the room, the website discovery with the various messages, the confrontation, the struggle and finally, him accepting the end and catching the flight home this morning. The only thing I leave out is Luka.

"Oh wow, Luisa, I don't know what to say…*more* women? What was going through his head?"

"I wish I knew, or maybe I don't…" I think better of it.

Jodie sighs heavily. "You're free now, how do you feel?"

"Relieved, I feel like I can get my life back. Mark can do the same, it's definitely for the best all-round."

"You can say that again. Are you staying out there? Will you be okay on your own? Of course you will…silly question."

I finally manage to get a word in. "Yes I'm staying. There's some really lovely people here, so I'll be fine." An image of Luka springs into my head but I don't just mean him, there's Pam and Pete too. Pam in particular has been great today.

"Oh yeah, lovely people hey? Have a holiday romance…it's exactly what you need! The love and affection of a hunky man, perhaps the lifeguard around the pool, *definitely* what you need."

I can feel my face going red, it's a good thing she can't see me. "Jodie…I can't do that technically, I am still married."

"Yeah, but you're not together anymore, heck you haven't even had satisfying sex for….how long?"

I look around me wondering if anyone heard what she just said. "That's beside the point."

"So what, the point is, you've only been married 'on paper' for a long time now and it's not like Mark was worried about it when you were together." She tries to back up her case. "Think about it…you need to feel loved again."

I'm silent and lost in thought as I listen to my friend as she takes on a serious tone. "Joking aside though…you are okay aren't you?"

"I'll be fine." I assure her and I know then that I will be.

We talk about work for a few minutes until Jodie reaches her car at the station, so we say our goodbyes and agree to talk again in a couple of days.

After more appreciation of the view and the biggest strawberry ice cream I think I've ever had, it's time to head back to the coach. Once on-board we drive back a slightly different way, meaning we get the car ferry at Kamenari. The coach waits beside the queue of cars and as the last car drives onto to the ferry, we follow on behind it. By this point I'm convinced the coach will be hanging off the back, there's so little room. Once were safely on the ferry, a few of us get off the coach to take a last look at the view.

There's a pleasant gentle breeze as we stand on the side looking at those amazing mountains once more. I take another couple of photos, including one of Pam and Pete together and Pete takes one of me with Pam, which will always make me fondly remember the kind words she said to me at lunch. It's a very short ride on the ferry and after just a few minutes, we're being called back onto the coach to head back onto dry land.

Last night's lack of sleep is really catching up with me now and as I continue to gaze at the scenery that surrounds us through the window, it seems to be soothing me into yet another sleepy state. The next time I look out after waking up, I recognise the road we're on as one which leads to our hotel. After bidding Tony our guide for the day goodbye, the three of us walk through reception and towards the lift. I'm definitely having a *siesta*, it's rude not to considering I'm half Spanish, well that's my excuse anyway.

I just about manage to kick off my flip-flops but I climb onto the bed in my clothes thinking what a wonderful day I've had, regardless of the uneasy start. After exploring Montenegro today, I'm determined to see more of Dubrovnik tonight and make plans in my mind to jump on the bus into town after dinner. I definitely feel like I have a new lease of life, well I will do after my *siesta*.

***

It's almost 7:30 p.m. and I literally have to drag myself out of bed. I have a long, lazy shower whilst I mentally decide what to wear. I go for my denim skirt and black off the shoulder top and wear my hair in a messy bun to the side. Some subtle make up around my eyes and a hint of bronzer later and I'm on my way to dinner. I begin to wonder how long I'll have to wait before I can tell Luka what happened last night. Jodie's words about a holiday romance begin to circle in my mind, if only…but I just couldn't see myself doing that. Could I?

The anti-climax I feel when I see Luka obviously isn't working tonight is borderline torture. I don't want him to think after everything I told him last night I've stayed with Mark. I'll have to pin all my hopes on him being at breakfast in the morning. Why this is such a big deal to me, I'm not sure.

There's plenty of free tables so rather than sitting down first I go straight to the buffet, taking a generous portion of beef stroganoff with rice. I hear the familiar sound of Pete's voice as he appears next to me.

"Now it's just an offer, there's a spare seat at our table." He gestures to the table where Pam's waving to me, all dressed up in a chic white shirt dress with gold jewellery, bold eye make-up and an inviting smile.

I wander across the restaurant and sit next to her. "Pam you always look so glamorous."

"Ohhhh…" She bats the way the compliment but I definitely see her sitting a little taller afterward.

She clasps my arm. "I don't know about you but I really enjoyed today. It was our third visit to Montenegro and I never tire of it."

"It's beautiful you're right. I went into such a deep sleep when I got back, I really needed it." I take my first mouthful of beef stroganoff, it's absolutely delicious and the meat so very tender is melting in my mouth.

"Your white wine madam." Franjo places a large glass in front of me as I look up in surprise, just as Pete reappears at the table with his plate piled high with different foods.

He gestures to my glass. "I took the liberty of ordering you a drink."

"Oh, thank you. Cheers." I propose a toast and the three of us touch glasses in the middle of the table. "What are the two of you up to tonight?"

Pam exhales, clearly worn out from the days sightseeing. "I think we'll just stay in the hotel bar, you're welcome to join us there, but you shouldn't be stuck with us, you get out there…" She winks.

I can't help but chuckle to myself at the wink she felt the need to add to the end of that sentence.

"I'm going for my first look around the old town tonight, time to start living…I want to see as much as I possibly can this holiday."

Just saying it out loud makes me feel alive and excited about the future, even though I know this is just the beginning of the end with Mark. Who knows what will happen when we start the inevitable divorce.

Pete starts nervously. "I hope you don't mind, but Pam told me about your separation…"

"Of course I don't mind, we're friends now. To be honest, it's good to have people to talk to about things." And I really mean that.

After a yummy chocolate torte dessert, which I know I'll regret later judging by how full I feel now, I wish Pam and Pete a good night and make my way outside to the bus stop.

Chapter 10

Leaving the hotel through the back exit, I get to admire the pool lit in all its glory again, the atmosphere is so intimate. Those teeny tiny lantern's get me every time. I see people sitting at the hotel taverna outside eating their meals, laughing, talking and enjoying their holidays. The waiters, all very smartly dressed in white shirts, black trousers and bottle green waistcoats rush around with that familiar sound of clattering plates as they clear the tables.

I walk through the gates leading out to the promenade and it's just a few minutes' walk around the corner to the stop for the number four bus and as I approach the stop I can see a few familiar faces from around the hotel waiting too, so at least I know I'm in the right place. Opposite the bus stop, I notice some fairly new looking apartments but I wouldn't say they look like holiday lets, and again, my mind takes me back to the conversation I had with Luka when he told me he lived in this direction. I shake my head to myself.

Once the bus arrives, I pay my fare to the driver and take a seat. I've been told it's only around a 10 minute journey into town, but with the speed the driver's doing I'm guessing it'll take half of that. As we move along the main road, I find myself reading the signs in my head. Names of apartments, names of shops, posters advertising music festivals and shoe shops, all in Croatian. It's not like I understand any of them, but I just want to take it all in.

The bus arrives at the last stop of the old town and everyone piles off the bus. The first thing that hits me is how busy it seems to be and how much hotter it feels. There's people here obviously on organised tours following their guide as I see clipboards being held in the air, so they stand out from the crowd for people to see.

Coaches are pulling up at the bus stop dropping off herds more people, other coaches picking up groups of tourists who fan themselves with leaflets and anything else they can get their hands on for some fresh air. I can hear so many different languages being spoken around me - French, German and I even recognise some Spanish.

Feeling the need to get away from the coach area as quickly as possible as it's just too crowded I squeeze myself through the mass of people which doesn't feel particularly easy. People are pushing and there's a distinct feel of sweating bodies around me as I get a sudden whiff of odour.

I head towards Dubrovnik city gates. To my left-hand side in the distance up the hill, I think I can just about make out the cable car gliding along. There and then I decide that tomorrow I will definitely come into town and get the cable car in the daytime to see those much anticipated views of the old town and maybe I'll even do the walk around the walls if I'm feeling energetic.

It seems slightly quieter as I walk through the gates before becoming just as chaotic again once I'm in the heart of the old town. Directly in front of me people are having their photo taken with a parrot on their shoulder as the bird perches proudly with his vibrant red feathers, giving way to hints of blues and greens on his wings. He repeats words as people talk around him and it seems he knows a few words in English as well as Croatian, as I hear him insulting a man next to him and I can't help but gasp. It's so funny to hear an animal talking like that.

There are dozens of signs for *sladoled* (ice cream) and a few buskers. I stop for a second to enjoy the music coming from a guitar and bongo drum played by two guys both wearing traditional hats. One of them has his eyes closed completely lost in the rhythm that they play together.

The town is full of pavement cafés, restaurants and beautiful little gift shops all adding to the overall ambience that can't be denied, the town has such a wonderful feeling. I walk on towards the bell tower and now it's almost dark, the lighting around me from the landmarks and the restaurants entice me to start taking photos. I follow the cobbled street around to the right and just at the corner near to the cathedral, a bar playing gentle jazz music gets my attention and I decide to stop for a much deserved glass of *vino*.

I take a seat making sure I choose one where I'll still be taking in the sights and the atmosphere, and place my order with the waiter. I can't help but reach for my phone yet again to take another picture, noticing how the beautiful cobbled streets make me feel as though I want to drop to my hands and knees and actually feel the stones on the floor. They look so smooth in this golden light which reflects from the buildings and yet they must be so old, holding so many memories. It's difficult to imagine how Dubrovnik was during the Yugoslav war, the town is just so impressive now.

Just two glasses of wine into the evening and I'm feeling really relaxed and almost carefree…and slightly tipsy - that is until Mark pops into my head. I think it's time to move on, so I pay the waiter and continue to follow another cobbled street which leads onto a different square, again so full of people and full of life.

This square seems to be louder with bars playing current music, almost making me want to stop and dance, I decide to walk on through and explore some more. There's definitely a younger crowd in this part of the town and as I walk through there's a strong smell of cigarettes.

I'm sure I can hear my name being hollered above the music and as I turn around the butterflies dart into my stomach as I see Luka walking towards me. He looks so good…yet again, wearing a black T-shirt which seems to enhance the darkness in his eyes, and a pair of dark blue jeans with white trainers.

"Luka." I can hardly contain the beaming smile that he always puts on my face, especially when I say his name.

"I thought it was you…" He looks around us. "You are erm…alone?" *At last*…I lean a little closer to him, his hand naturally resting on my arm as he leans to listen as I fear that the loud music and chatter around us might drown me out as I speak and I want to make sure he hears this.

"Yes, Mark went home this morning."

"*Dobro*…sorry…good." he smirks, making my pulse rate quicken. I'm sure he knows he has this effect on me.

He carries on. "I am here with friends, come and join us." he turns his head in the direction of two tables next to each other with a group of people in conversation, some of them singing along to the music and clearly having a great time.

"No, I can't interrupt…"

He then he takes my hand. "Wrong answer." He laughs, guiding me by the hand over to the tables full of people who are now watching us intently as they talk.

As I follow Luka, ripples of pleasure consume me and a warm tingly feeling appears to be travelling up the whole of my arm because of the feel of his skin against mine as he holds my hand. I recognise a few people as staff from the hotel restaurant, but having never spoken to them before, I'm thankful that my two glasses of wine have taken effect.

There seems to be one empty seat in the middle of the two tables and Luka leads me to that seat and introduces me to the two women and two men sitting either side of me as Vilko, Kristijan and Dea, who work at the hotel, and Melita who I definitely don't recognise. They're all immediately warm and friendly towards me and begin asking me about my holiday so far. Melita on the other hand, sitting to my right comes across as slightly cold and I can sense that she's wary of me. She's strikingly attractive with long, almost black wavy hair, olive skin and piercing green eyes and she wears the tiniest silver nose stud I've ever seen.

Luka reappears at the table, placing a hand on my shoulder and presents me with a large glass of white wine.

"Are you okay?" I can just about hear him ask above the music.

"Fine, thanks for the drink." I smile, taking a gulp.

He leans into Melita and I hear them exchange words in Croatian, before he disappears to the other side of the table to sit with some of the others. Melita begins to make conversation with me and I discover she's a couple of years younger than me and works as a hair and beauty therapist in another five-star hotel just a little further around the coast.

Now we're talking, I feel a lot more comfortable and relaxed, but I can't help but wish that Luka was sitting closer. We've caught each other's eye a few times but he remains deep in conversation and laughter with the others. Kristijan declares we need more drinks and catches the attention of the waiter. I meanwhile am desperate for the loo if only to have a breather and so I ask Melita where I can find them.

She rises from her seat and picks up her bag from the floor. "I will show you."

As I enter the toilet I wonder, is it me or is the cubicle spinning around slightly? After using the loo I check my hair in the mirror above the sink, and I'm joined by Melita who adds more lip gloss. I see her looking at me through the mirror.

She raises her hand to my hair. "Your hair it is so nice, is that your natural colour?"

"*My* hair? I've been admiring yours all night." I laugh.

She smiles gratefully. "Thank you, I have been growing it for a long time for our wedding."

"Oh, you're getting married? Congratulations...when's the big day?"

Melita puts her lip gloss away. "One week from Saturday." She pulls a nervous face and chuckles.

"You'll be fine...every bride gets nervous." I reassure her, having a flashback to mine and Mark's wedding day, which now seems so false.

Melita leads the way back out through the bar and outside to our table where we retake our seats.

She lifts her glass in my direction. "*Živjeli*…cheers."

I attempt to say cheers back to her in Croatian and realise I just sound really drunk. Everyone around the table joins in our *Živjeli*.

I start to wonder about Melita's fiancé. "So, what's your fiancé doing tonight?"

She sips her drink and turns to look at the others at their end of the table. "He is drinking I can see…" She laughs.

I look anxiously in the direction that she did *oh no, her fiancé, please don't let it be Luka*. Surely if it was, he would have introduced me to her as that, meaning I would have introduced myself to a bottle of wine instead of a glass shortly after.

I feel abruptly sober and deflated, but appreciate I still haven't replied to Melita and I notice she's looking at me worriedly.

"Luisa, is something wrong?"

"I erm…sorry, I'm fine. I-I just feel hot suddenly."

"It is always hotter in the old town, the buildings and with so many people." She shifts her chair back. "…let me get you some water."

Before I can argue with her she disappears into the bar and comes rushing back moments later with a bottle of water for me, which I gladly take from her.

"Thanks, sorry about that. I don't know what came over me."

I drink some water from the bottle and see Luka's watching me. He gets up and walks around the table in our direction to say good night to Kristijan who has decided to call it a night as he's working breakfast tomorrow. I listen intently to Luka and Kristijan, and wonder what they're saying to each other, I wish I could speak Croatian.

Kristijan says good night to Melita by enveloping her in a hug and kissing her on each cheek before taking me by surprise and doing the same to me. Kristijan looks around late 30s, wispy blond hair and seems to be well over six-feet tall, which makes me feel tiny by comparison.

"Nice to meet you Luisa, see you in the morning at breakfast."

"I'll be there, well, if I can get out of bed after all these drinks." I laugh before retaking my seat.

I wonder how I'm going to find out if it's Luka who's Melita's fiancé. Luka crouches down next to Melita and plants a kiss on her cheek. *I think I'm going to cry, I feel so foolish.* Time to get going I think, so I reach for my bag and stand to make my excuses to leave.

Luka stands abruptly. "Where are you going?"

"It's getting late, I'll get back to the hotel." On this I notice Melita look up at Luka expectantly.

I lean to make eye contact with Luka's other friends. "It was great to meet you all…"

Melita stands up. "You cannot go yet, I have not even introduced you to Patrik properly…" She beckons over one of the men from the other table, and puts her arm proudly around his waist when he reaches her side.

"This is my fiancé, Patrik."

Relief washes over me. "Hi Patrik, nice to meet you." *Oh, thank you, thank you!*

Patrick has long brown hair, just down to his shoulders, he's a good-looking man. He and Melita both look like models, such a good-looking couple. They look at each other before looking back to me.

Melita places a hand on my shoulder. "You will be here on the 7th July?"

I think for a second. "I'm here until the 9th."

"You must come to our wedding."

That's so nice of her. "Oh, I don't know, I haven't really got anything with me I could wear to a wedding."

"Don't be silly, you have to come. It is a Croatian tradition for the bride and groom to invite guests face to face, how can you say no?" She stops talking and gives me a pleading smile. "...you can come with my brother." She nudges Luka.

"Luka you never said Melita was your sister."

"I know, sorry." Luka and his sister exchange a look and I wonder if I've missed something.

Luka puts his arm around my waist. "I'll get you back to your hotel." I go to tell him there's no need but realise I haven't had any time alone with him all night, so I don't argue.

We leave the square, and walk along a side street as Luka drops his arm from around my waist. It's almost midnight now but bars and restaurants are still full, some people only just eating their evening meal it would seem, although it's becoming quieter on the side streets.

"Your sister is so nice, Luka."

"Thank you, I have always felt I have to look after my little sister."

"So, how old is Melita's big brother?" That actually sounded quite flirty…

"I am 33, I am guessing you are around the same age as her?"

"A little older, I'm 27."

"How old were you when you got married?"

The tainted memories reappear in my mind. "I was 24."

He seems to take a deep breath. "This morning, I thought you and your husband were…staying together."

"I was worried that was how it sounded."

A silence follows as we smile at each other, the chemistry feels stronger and I realise I've just admitted to him out loud that I didn't want him to think I was still with Mark.

I remember the waiter warning him at breakfast that his boss was on the way over.

"Is your boss always such a dragon?"

Luka frowns. "Not always, but he can be…when he is under pressure."

"Do you enjoy your job at the hotel?"

"Most of the time, yes. Sometimes it can be dull…but then one day something can change, you see someone who gives you reason to look forward to going to work just to see their face." He touches my hand lightly, his fingers lacing through my own as he brings me to a standstill. I can feel my breathing speeding up.

"Are you hungry?" He points to a pizza shop next to us, which has on display the biggest pizza's I think I've ever seen.

"I could definitely eat a slice of pizza." My stomach starts to growl at the aromas of melted cheese, tomato and oregano.

We break hands as we order two slices of pizza through the hatch and Luka goes to pay but this time I insist I'm paying, much to his annoyance. We each eat our slice of pizza as we continue walking along and we soon reach the old town gate.

"Do you normally get the bus home?" I ask, wiping around my mouth with a serviette.

We cross the road over to the bus stop and taxi rank.

"Usually, but the last bus is gone. We get a taxi?"

Luka signals to the taxi driver parked at the front of the taxi rank and the driver gives us the thumbs up. He opens the door for me and I climb onto the back seat as he sits in beside me as I start to hope I don't have any pizza topping around my mouth. Luka tells the driver where we're heading and off we go.

"I wish I could speak some Croatian, I do know a few words from my lesson yesterday…" I laugh to myself.

"You had a lesson? Okay, what did you learn?"

Oh why did I have to say that? I have to make an attempt now. "Okay…kako ste?".

Luka smiles. "Ja sam dobar. I am good." he exhales loudly and rubs his head. "želim da te poljubim!"

I see the driver watching us from his rear view mirror and think for a moment.

"No, not a clue, what does that mean?"

Luka goes to speak but the driver announces we've reached my hotel, so Luka pays the driver 50 Kuna and we climb out of the taxi. I jostle around in my bag and force 25 Kuna into his hand to pay my half of the fare.

"No!" He forces my money back into my hand and I shake my head in annoyance.

As the taxi has dropped us at the back entrance, Luka insists on walking me through the grounds as far as possible without anyone seeing him, so we begin the short stroll through at a steady pace.

I continue on our conversation from the taxi. "So what does that mean, what you said in the taxi?"

Luka looks up to the sky and shakes his head. "It does not matter. Did you enjoy Montenegro today?"

"I did the fjords were fantastic, it makes me want to get out and see more now. They've forecast rain tomorrow so if they're right, I think I'll walk the city walls whilst it's a bit cooler."

"Good idea." Luka comes to a standstill and glances around us and I assume as this is as far as he can walk me to be on the safe side.

"I take it you're not working breakfast tomorrow?"

He sniggers. "Thankfully not. I will see you tomorrow night?"

My heartbeat begins to pound louder in my head. "Laku noć." *Yippee, I remembered good night in Croatian.*

He tilts his head toward me and his lips discover my cheek, planting a kiss before very slowly moving away again. As he kisses my cheek his scent consumes me, then we study each other just for a split second, while I imagine what it would be like to kiss him on the lips.

He gently touches my hand again. "Good night, Luisa."

A giant grin spreads from my mouth, reaching up to my eyes. "Wow." I say under my breath, before realising I look like I'm talking to myself and do the two minute walk up to my room.

Chapter 11

My lips are stuck together, my tongue feels furry and as I try to lift my head from the pillow to check the time, I get the sensation someone has driven over my head. *Ouch!*

My mobile on the bedside table is flashing to tell me I have three missed calls from my brother, and a voicemail. His calls aren't the only things I've missed, I've slept in and missed breakfast. The one metre walk to the fridge for a bottle of water feels like a marathon but as I remove the lid from the bottle and drink as much as I can in one go, I start to feel more hydrated.

I open the curtains to see the forecast was right, it's raining. The outlook appears so different without the sun beaming down and with the dark clouds positioned above, but it still doesn't take away the natural beauty of the area.

I don't want to waste any more of the day so I take a quick shower and decide to dress in my leggings, green vest top and black pumps and take some shorts and sun lotion, just in case it brightens up later. I put my mobile into my bag, I'll call Ben once I've got some food inside me. I leave the hotel through the back entrance, strolling through the pool area. It seems strange it being empty during the day, there's a completely different atmosphere.

There's a couple of people lingering around the pool wondering what to do with themselves and as I look up at the hotel, I see people are sitting on their balconies hoping that the rain will pass and the sun will soon return.

When I reach the gates, I have a welcome flashback of Luka and I arriving back from the old town last night, which brings on a very satisfying daydream.

Out of the hotel grounds I turn left, walking rather fast because of the rain, in the direction of the bus stop and cut up some steps which I remember the rep telling us leads to a couple of shops including a bakery where I know I can get some breakfast. I order a coffee to wake me up, and two very appetising looking pastries. As I have a bit of a wait before the next bus to town is due, I decide to eat inside the bakery at one of the tables to shelter from the rain.

I take my first mouthful of pastry and feel glad I brought two as it's so tasty. The flaky pastry has just the right amount of sweetness and that, mixed with the apricot jam with a touch of icing sugar on the top is perfection.

As I'm eating I decide to listen to the voicemail from my brother. When the message starts I'm shocked at the angry tone of Ben's voice.

"Luisa, what the hell is going on? Call me as soon as you get this, I've just been to your house to move your post…call me now!"

I have a bad feeling about his. I allow myself to finish my first pastry before I call him back. I lick my fingers, not wanting to waste a single crumb of my breakfast.

Ben answers the phone straightaway. "Luisa…where are you?" He shouts so loud that I look around the bakery to check no one else can hear.

"What do you mean where am I? I'm in Dubrovnik, you know I am."

I keep my voice low, but detecting his angst I drink my coffee as fast as I can, wrap my pastry in serviettes to take with me and head outside, standing beneath the shop awning for shelter as I talk to him.

"Well Mark certainly isn't with you is he..."

"Well, no...he..."I try to speak, to explain but Ben talks over me.

"I came into move your post on my way to work like you asked me to and I could hear noises coming from upstairs. So I grabbed that vase you keep on the table by the door and slowly crept up the stairs, then I started to realise it was mattress squeaking and groaning coming from your bedroom. I thought it was you when I heard that, so, well, I don't want to be hearing that so I dashed back down the stairs to get out...." *Oh no, I feel the dread creeping in.* "...I thought maybe you'd come back early for some reason, but then I thought...why would you do that, especially without telling me? So I ran back up the stairs and burst into your bedroom..."

I have a horrible feeling about this, I know what's coming next. "Ben, it's okay...we're finished, that's why he's back at home and I'm still here. I told him to go, it's over for good this time and I want a divorce."

He lets out a long agitated breath. "I could've killed him Lu! No idea if it was that tart from his office again, or, well, whoever it was...."

I stare at the floor. "Oh well, maybe it was her, it could've been anyone." It wouldn't surprise me if his affair never really finished, although he swore to me it had.

My brother has quite a temper, so I know he would've hit him. "What happened?"

"I lunged at him, pulled him away from her, she was screaming..."

"Ben…" I cringe, putting my head in my hands.

"I knew when to stop…luckily for him, don't worry. I just punched him a couple of times before she pulled us apart."

The chaotic scene is playing out in my head as my brother begins to laugh unexpectedly and I actually laugh along with him.

"What's even funny?" I wonder.

"You should've seen him sis, the look on his face. Caught with his trousers down…well completely off."

I begin to wonder, is that the first time he's had another woman in our bed? This could have been going on throughout our marriage and I was completely oblivious. I feel tears start to sting at my eyes as I realise the amount of time and energy I've wasted on that man. I will not let him upset me, not anymore.

The rain is getting lighter and with my bus due in a couple of minutes, I walk out of the complex back down the steps and over to the stop. Still on the phone to Ben, I tell him about how I'd tried to split up with Mark a few weeks ago and how I discovered the website he'd joined, the whole truth.

"If I see him again…aggh, I'm so angry with him…how can he do this to you again?"

I see the bus approaching and so I end my call. I wanted to wait until I got home to tell Mom and Dad about Mark and I splitting for good this time, but I don't want them finding out by bumping into him in the street with another woman, or worse still, in a similar way to how my brother found out.

Ben agrees to break the news to Mom and Dad for me in the next couple of days. I think it will be better face-to-face rather than over the phone and I know Mom will be upset when she hears the word divorce, but I know she will be on my side 100% when she hears the full story. It might seem like I'm being a coward in asking someone else to tell them but I know how disappointed they'll be, my mother especially.

Once I'm on the bus and in my seat, I send Ben a quick text thanking him again for agreeing to speak to our parents for me and it's then I remember he still hasn't told me about him and Georgia setting the date of their wedding in Spain next year. Although he didn't really have much chance because of telling me all about his boxing match with Mark. I know Mom told me not to let on that I know, but now I've spoken to him, I'm desperate to tell him how pleased I am for them and so I decide to admit that I know about the good news over text too.

***

The drizzle is still falling when I arrive in the old town. It's noticeably cooler with the rain, but that doesn't stop many people from coming into town, myself included. Tourists are still piling on and off the coaches, laden down with maps with the addition of umbrellas and waterproofs today.

I slip into a small café on the corner near the bus stop to stock up on water for my walk and proceed towards the city gates to the ticket office. There isn't much of a queue yet, so I pay my entrance fee and begin to walk up the steps into the first section of the ancient city walls. The view from this height is incredible, looking down on the main square with people bustling in and out of shops. I can see the bell tower in the distance, hundreds of buildings with terracotta roofs that really stand out from the grey/white brickwork of the building structures, giving a real mediterranean feel.

Walking further on I move over to the right-hand side of the walls and the sea stretches out as far as the eye can see. The rain has now stopped and the clouds are slowly breaking apart with the sun trying its hardest to interrupt. Gentle shimmers of the sun are creeping through and reflecting on to the sea, making it begin to glisten.

I stop at one of the turrets to take more photos and visualise Luka, wondering what the quality of his photographs are like from his DSLR camera. I get a really good picture of the Fort of Saint Lawrence up on the rocks surrounded by greenery and of course, the Adriatic Sea.

I take a couple of minutes rest to admire the scenery and drink some water before continuing the walk. On the left-hand side there appears to be someone's garden, I'm surprised to see washing hanging on a clothes line just next to the city walls. Could you imagine living in one of those houses and having this superb view right at the end of your garden? Even having people walking past this close to your house, it would be more than worthwhile getting to see this view each day.

It's really starting to warm up again now and I actually feel quite foolish in my leggings, so at the first toilets I find, I'll certainly be changing into my shorts. I've now reached the harbour area of the old town. Boats line up, bobbing up and down amongst the different shades of turquoise and blue of the sea, with the walls and what appears to be another cathedral providing the backdrop. My stomach starts growling as I remember the second pastry I brought from the bakery still sitting uneaten in my bag, so I perch on a bench and devour the rest of my breakfast.

As I eat my mind begins to speculate about my future. In a week or so I'll be back at home, moving my belongings out of the marital home I shared with Mark and then it hits me, I'm homeless. Maybe I can stay at Mom and Dad's whilst I find somewhere to rent. At least I'm fairly certain I have a part-time job back at the travel agents with Jodie and co, which I'm really looking forward to and then, of course, I can write my book the rest of the time. Having said that, I can't help but question if the job's the right path to take at this moment in time. I have so many places I want to see, perhaps I should seriously look into travelling, seeing as I no longer have the concern of a mortgage or a husband. I can still write as I'm travelling and I know it will inspire me further as travelling always has.

I won't let anything hold me back any more. Look at me I'm in Dubrovnik on my own, exploring and discovering new things, and it's wonderful.

The steps in front of me leading back to the main square indicate the end of the city walls. I can't believe how fast that one and a half hours went, but I've got some great photos to show for it.

Next, I walk back out to the city gates, up the hill and around to the entrance for the cable car. For me, *the* image of Dubrovnik is that of the old town from an elevated perspective with the Fort of Saint John leading out into the sea and I'm really excited about seeing it from the cable car as I've always wanted to take that photo.

There's quite a queue forming at the cable car entrance, so I wait around 10 minutes in line for my ticket. Everyone seems to be sharing the same enthusiasm to get to the top. Couples, families, passengers from cruise ships and people alone like me, wait eagerly at the barrier for the next cable car to stop. The attendant's walkie-talkie bursts into life to tell him it's safe for us to board the next car.

Each car holds up to 30 passengers so it's rather cosy once we're all inside and the doors are closed. I manage to secure a spot against the window and poise at the ready to take a picture as we glide up the hillside with that magnificent view stretching out before us. In less than four minutes we have apparently climbed 778 metres and I feel like I've taken around the same amount of photos.

We disembark the car and I walk around to the first viewing point overlooking *that* view. It's simply breath taking. I get snap happy again, taking more pics and spend some time watching the world go by in the town from up above. I can just about make out cars moving along the roads on the outside of the walls, but my eyes are mostly drawn to the boats sailing along in the distance, the open sea stretching out before them.

I step inside for a peek around the gift shop and manage to resist the temptation of buying some of the impressive costume jewellery on offer which makes me think of Pam, and I wonder if she manages to restrain herself when she visits here.

I follow the staircase up to the next level and step back outside onto the further elevated platform. This is a much bigger area with wastelands to the left that lead around to the war museum and goats tucking into their lunch on the grass about 20 metres out in front of me. To my right there's a restaurant positioned with ample seating areas to take in the view as you eat, but before that is the fantastic vantage point that I intend to make the most of. I can't believe I'm really here, it's exquisite.

I lean against the railings to take it all in. It's quieter up here, but the chatter of people is never far away. I gaze upward at the huge white stone cross which I'm told by my guidebook was a new one erected at the end of the Croatian war of independence, due to the first one being destroyed during the war. Now seems like a good time to check out the museum.

The museum is housed in an old fort, which feels cold indoors away from the outdoor sun. The exhibition is really informative for someone like me, who knows very little about what happened.

There are rooms full of photographs, documents, maps and even old weaponry telling the heart-wrenching story of the conflict. I stumble across another room where a TV plays old news footage showing the war as it happened, and I do vaguely remember seeing news reports at home. I would have been around nine years old at the time. I sit watching the old bulletins and I can't believe that a lot of the area I walked through earlier today was destroyed. This included people's homes and livelihoods, not to mention the lives that were lost. It really makes you think and yet again my thoughts turn to Luka, he must've seen some awful things growing up.

On the next level in the fort is a disused area leading out to an even higher viewing platform with very few people around showing more of the town and I can't wait to come back here at sunset.

I've seen and learnt so much today, it really has opened my eyes, but my rumbling stomach once again tells me it needs food. I make the decision to get out of the crowds and back to the hotel for some much needed lunch, followed by the possibility of a cheeky afternoon snooze. All of those drinks last night have made me feel a little groggy all day.

On the bus journey back to the hotel I hear a text arrive, it's from Mark.

"Had a run-in with your brother this morning, I could do him for assault! Don't believe the lies he'll no doubt tell you Luisa, please. Remember, you're still my wife and I still love you xx"

I'm tempted to smash my phone across the floor of the bus, I'm so angry. Does he really think I'll believe his words over my brothers when all he's done for at least two years is lie to me over and over again?

I can't wait to get off the bus for some fresh air and when I do, I power walk as fast as I can to release my rage and almost knock Pam over in the process as I walk past her.

"Hey, slow down…"

"Sorry, I didn't see you there." I exhale, coming to a standstill.

Pam puts her arm through mine as she detects my irritated mood. "I think someone needs a drink."

"I probably do but I doubt it would help. Arrghh! I'm so angry, Pam…"

I'm almost having a hissy fit in the street by this point. She leads me around to the taverna just inside the grounds of the hotel where we sit at a table in the shade.

"Where's your better half?" I try to joke, failing miserably as a bucket load of tears erupt down my face. I put my head in my hands, almost afraid to look at Pam, or to look around me for fear of people staring.

"Sssh, it's okay." she rubs my back soothingly. "Has something happened with you know who?"

Composing myself with a deep breath and dabbing at my eyes with my serviette from the table I fill her in on the latest saga.

"I just don't understand. Even now, after everything…he still can't admit he's in the wrong…I just want to put it behind me and get on with my life."

"And you will do." She squeezes my hand. "Things will take time and I know it's difficult but the worst is behind you now, remember that. You've got your whole life ahead of you, so make sure you live it."

"Thanks, I really mean that. I just want to forget about him now, but how can I? It'll be a while before it's over properly, permanently."

"Yes it will be a while technically, but start living now, don't let him ruin another moment of your life or of your holiday even."

I smile my thanks to her as I consider her words carefully.

She leans closer towards me. "I am speaking from experience in case you hadn't already guessed?"

"I did wonder…"

A waiter appears at the table and I order coffee, Pam opting for a brandy.

She takes a deep breath. "It was a long time ago now, Pete had an affair when we were younger. The children were only three and five at the time."

I don't think I've ever heard her voice so dispirited, she's normally so enthusiastic, so happy.

"But you forgave him?"

Our drinks arrive and Pam takes a sip of hers, whilst I add sugar to my coffee.

"Eventually I did…it wasn't as simple as that. He had a baby with the other woman and I found it just too difficult to be involved in. I tried my best but months later, I was just so angry with him and I'm ashamed to say that I had a one night stand. Perhaps I felt the need to get back at him?"

I place my hand on hers as I listen, they're obviously very painful memories.

"Does Pete know that you…"

"I told him…a few days later. It was then that we decided to split, properly."

"Oh Pam…"

"About a year later, we got back together but it was never the same. We still loved each other and wanted to try again but it was mostly for the children and we both knew that."

"I'm really surprised to hear that, you both seem so happy together."

"Now we are, I say that honestly. It took a really long time and for so many years I wasn't happy, which is why I said what I said to you…that I envied you…how I wished I was as comfortable in my own skin at your age as you seem to be."

"Do you think you did the wrong thing? Back then?"

"I did make the wrong choice in us getting back together when we did but it was easier. But now I'm glad we did…who knows…if we hadn't got back together then, maybe we would still have done further down the line."

"Well you're happy now at least."

She squeezes my hand. "I am, maybe it's age on our side…it certainly makes you think. Anyway, things are good now and they will be again for you someday very soon."

"Well, I'm buying you lunch. Will Pete be joining us?"

"Put it this way, the last time I saw Pete he was blotto and just about managed to get inside our room before he passed out into a deep sleep."

"That'll be a no then…"

Pam begins to read the menu. "We saw you getting out of a taxi last night, he was very nice."

I feel embarrassed, just at the flashback that pops into my mind about last night and at the look on her face.

"Don't look so worried, you enjoy yourself and remember what I said yesterday about not wasting time."

***

Dressing for dinner that evening I feel excited at the prospect of seeing Luka. It takes me ages to decide what to wear for the fear of looking too overdressed or too casual. At long last, I slip on my Aztec print halter neck top and denim shorts and pull my hair into a high ponytail with the usual make up.

Yet again I'm quite late arriving at the restaurant, Franjo is actually now helping to clear the tables rather than escorting people to them, and so, I take a seat and order a glass of wine as I keep a lookout for Luka. I'm just helping myself to some pasta when I see him returning to the buffet area clutching a tea towel and wiping his brow. After my body momentarily calms itself down after noticing him, we exchange smiles. Who knew anyone could look so good in chef whites?

He reaches my side. "Did you have a headache this morning?"

I try to suppress my smile, but I can't. "Just a little. How are you?"

"I am good, how was your day?"

"Great, thanks."

"I am glad. I have to help my sister with some wedding preparations tonight, but I have the day off work tomorrow. We could meet?" He scans around the room, keeping watch for his boss.

"I… I have an excursion to the Elaphiti islands tomorrow." *Although I really wish I hadn't now.*

He shrugs his shoulders in a casual manner. Pam's words of wisdom from lunch about not wasting time echo in my mind as I have an idea.

"…if you're not busy, and you want to…you could come? I still have…another ticket." I'm almost having palpitations waiting for him to reply. Do I sound ridiculous? He lives here, he's probably been to the islands hundreds of times before.

"That would be good, shall I meet you outside? What time?"

I'm flabbergasted at his quick and certain response. "I erm…the coach arrives at 9:30…"

He motions to my plate with a huge grin. "I will see you in the morning, enjoy your dinner."

After picking at my food as I'm now too excited to eat with the prospect of spending the whole day with Luka tomorrow, I go for a walk in the fresh air along the pebble beach. I take in the distant music murmuring in the background coming from the various bars and for the first time in a long time, ideas for my book start to flow into my head. With my notepad back at the hotel, and the urge to write my ideas down strong, I make a quick stop at the supermarket for water for tomorrow's trip and dash back to the hotel.

From the comfort of my room I jot my thoughts down whilst sitting on the balcony with a good old cup of tea, courtesy of room service. I check my emails to see another from Asha, my publisher reassuring me there's no rush in sending my first draft as she has complete confidence in me considering how quickly I wrote my first novel.

I think back to the three chapters I've already written and smile contentedly at the fact my creativity has started to flow again like the old days and I start to feel really positive about my book that night as I gradually drift off to sleep.

Chapter 12

Next morning I'm up and dressed quite early, looking forward to the day ahead. I manage to read a little about the Elaphiti islands in my guidebook over breakfast in preparation for the day, before those friendly butterflies make their presence known in my stomach, as I go outside to meet Luka.

I sit on the wall outside of the hotel and retrieve my book from my bag again to give me something to do as I wait. I'll be so embarrassed if he doesn't show up. Thankfully, just a few minutes later, there he is walking towards me with his hands in his pockets looking really relaxed with a rucksack slung over one shoulder.

"I am not late am I?"

I put my bag on my shoulder. "No, you're right on time." I notice he keeps his back to the hotel, probably wise in case anyone recognises him socialising with me.

At first things feel almost awkward between us, but I know that's down to my nerves as Luka chats away confidently. Once we've made the 10 minute journey on the coach from the hotel to the Gruz Port, we're directed by the same guide from the Montenegrin trip - Tony, onto a two-storey boat. We climb the steps-cum-ladder onto the top deck and claim our seats to make the most of the view. The boat has a navy blue canopy shading us from the early morning sun, so I slip off my floppy hat - popping it into my bag.

There are so many boats surrounding us. Cruise ships, a couple of taxi boats and even some very expensive looking yachts. At the front of one of the yachts I can see a lady working out on an exercise bike as she enjoys the outlook across the sea, oh what a life she must lead. I can hear the sound of the sea lapping gently against the boat.

Luka nudges me. "You are miles away...what are you thinking?"

"Do you know how lucky you are to live here...in such a beautiful place?"

I sigh, not taking my eyes away from the sea. Luka doesn't respond and as I turn to look at him, his camera goes off, taking a photo of me.

I laugh with embarrassment. "That was sneaky..."

He leans in closer to me to show me the picture he's just taken on the screen. Our arms are touching and despite the heat I get goose bumps. I look down at my arm in close contact with his and I can't resist stealing a look up at him as he leans toward me, showing me his camera screen.

His voice sounds deeper somehow. "Look...now this is the view that I like." I push his arm away playfully and I can't help but smile.

It's getting hotter, yep, I'm definitely burning up. "I'm not sure how to answer that."

"I think you are uncomfortable to receive compliments?"

"I'm not uncomfortable as such, I just have a tough time believing them sometimes...considering the empty compliments Mark used to give me...they obviously had no meaning." I say it very matter of fact.

Luka considers my response. "I understand...but you do not need to think of him anymore...and just so you know - my compliments have meaning."

I smile. He's definitely upping his approach, and I like it.

We hear the hum of the boat engine starting up and our guide calling out for the last passengers to board. I look to my right to see a couple of people running towards the boat, their tickets are checked before the clattering sound of the gang plank being removed and pulled back onto the boat.

We enjoy a short ride taking in more of the marvellous sea views, to the first island of Kolocep where our guide gives us a brief history of the traffic free island before we're given some free time. Luka and I decide to walk along the beach to make the most of the sand, as there are no sandy beaches in Dubrovnik.

It's so good to feel the soft sand between my toes but three seconds later, the scorching heat from the sand feels like it's trying to remove the skin from my feet and I begin to dart from one foot to the other much to Luka's amusement. I think I'd rather keep my flip-flops on.

I really like a picture that I take standing at the beginning of a jetty with a little white fishing boat to one side with the green hills and trees in the background, the terracotta roofs of houses poking through intermittently.

Luka sees me eyeing my handiwork. "You have a good eye for a photo."

"Not as good as you I'd imagine, but thanks." I gesture for him to stand on the jetty as I take his photo and can't help but think how much better the picture looks with him in it.

He reaches my side again and I start to wonder about his hobby.

"Have you ever sold any of your photos?" I ask, retrieving my hat from my bag and placing it back on my head.

"Mmm, a few. I did an exhibition once and I sold some photos I took of Dubrovnik to a restaurant owner and a couple of local businesses."

"That's really good…I'd love to see some of your work."

"Anytime." he grins. "You never actually told me what you do…"

We walk up the steps from the beach and continue to follow the path alongside the sea.

"I'm about to go back to my old job when I get home. I was a travel agent, but I write too, I've had a book published."

"A book? That is great, what about?"

"Erm….. I guess you would call it a romance novel." I laugh awkwardly.

"Ahh, romance…" He looks at me intently. "You like romance?"

I turn towards him. "Books? Or actual romance?" I raise an eyebrow as he laughs.

"I mean the real romance…" He lightly touches my hand with his, those sparks return.

I say nothing for a second, tilting my head to one side. "Yeah… I think most women do."

He looks at me. "But you are not most women…you are you…"

Now it's my turn to laugh. "So…yes…I do."

"Did you enjoy working at the travel agent?"

I tell Luka about meeting Jodie, the laughs we used to have working together and of course the best part, the perks of the job - travelling.

"So why did you leave if you enjoyed this so much?"

Aggravation collects in my stomach, *I ask myself the same question all the time.*

"It was Mark's idea really, I don't think he thought being a travel agent sounded good enough...."

"...what? He did not want you to be happy?"

I shrug my shoulders. "In fairness, it made sense at the time. It meant I could do my writing full-time, but really I could have done both and still have been happy."

Our free time is almost over, so we make our way back to the boat. For the next leg of the journey we stay down stairs on the boat and sit on the side with our legs hanging over the edge. I go to lean against the railings but as they're scorching hot I recoil at first, amused as Luka does the same.

The sea spray flies up onto our legs and at one point as the journey becomes rather bumpy, lashings of water shoot up over the side missing me, but soaking Luka's shorts. I burst out laughing at the look on his face.

"You think that is funny?" He asks.

I nod in agreement, still giggling until he dips his hand into the newly formed puddle next to him and flicks the water sharply at me as I gasp in surprise.

"Okay, now we're even."

We arrive on the island of Sipan in the village of Sudurad, and walk through the harbour passing shops and small cafés with tables outside and that sound of the occasional jangling of cups and plates as people are served their morning coffees to the vista of the pretty harbour. Little wooden boats in bold blues and bright whites bob up and down on the water, their names painted on the sides. How lovely it must be to own a boat and to spend time trying to decide on its name.

Tony shows us the renaissance castle which has stunning grounds with beautiful plants and flowers, a real haven of calm. We have time for just a short stroll and then it's back onto the boat for the five minute sail around to a secluded cove to a restaurant for lunch.

Our lunch stop is literally in the middle of nowhere and you can only reach it via boat, which gives it a really isolated feel. We walk up the steps that lead to the restaurant to a delicious cooking aroma of smoked fish and right on cue my stomach begins to rumble.

Everyone from the boat takes a seat at one of the several long tables laid out ready and waiting for us. Luka and I sit opposite each other on the end of one of the tables and drink some much needed water, followed by some much desired white wine. Already it's a lovely relaxing setting and how can it not be with the outlook across the sea and the sound of birdsong coming from the trees. The birds are probably waiting for the food to be served so they can swoop down...let's hope they aren't as hungry as seagulls always seem to be in the UK.

Moments later, large plates of freshly smoked mackerel, salad and crusty bread are delivered to our table by the waitresses and I waste no time at all and dig straight in. The fish is the most delicious I've ever eaten, it's the smoky taste - it makes it so flavoursome.

When we've finished eating lunch the two of us amble down the few rocks leading down into the sea. We're only a few minutes' walk away from the restaurant where people are still eating, but as we sit down it's so peaceful. We can't hear a thing down here other than the gentle ripple of the water. I take a deep breath, close my eyes and begin to relax.

"Have you been to these islands before, Luka?"

"No. I have been to Lopud island and Lokrum, but today… I am a tourist with you."

We both sit down at the water's edge and he starts to gently throw pebbles into the sea, creating a calming splash with each throw as he raises the subject of Mark again.

"Did your family like Mark?"

"They did. Even after he cheated on me, my mother in particular wanted me to work things out. I'm not sure how she'll take it now though."

The image of my parents comes to mind and I wonder if they know yet. "…she's against divorce, she was brought up as a strict catholic in Spain."

Luka looks curious. "You are half Spanish? Ah, that explains the pronunciation of your name."

I laugh with him. "My Mom would be furious if she ever heard anyone mispronouncing my name when I was growing up. She'd say *it's Luisa-Maria.*" I do my best Spanish accent.

"So you think you will divorce?"

"Definitely, there's no question about it. As soon as I get home, I'll see a solicitor."

I find myself going on to tell him some more of what happened…about my discoveries of his further affairs just days ago and to say he's shocked is an understatement.

"Why do people do this? It is so wrong...the lies...it is terrible disrespect. Why did he get married?" He shakes his head and I sigh, wishing I knew the answer to that myself.

Luka leans back into the rocks. "I have been divorced for three years." I'm taken aback to hear this, I suppose I haven't really given much thought into Luka's past relationships.

"Really? What happened?"

He sits back up right, his arms on his knees. "Amra moved to Zagreb for her job, she is a dancer. It was not really meant to be anyway, things were...tense for a while before that. We argued a lot, I am not sure we were as compatible as we thought. "

At the mention of another woman's name, his ex-wife's name, I feel slightly green eyed. He talks about her in a rather casual manner which makes me think they're no longer in touch.

"It's weird how as you were getting divorced...I was marrying Mark."

Luka laughs. "If only you had known me...I do not think you would have married him."

I shake my head as I join him in laughter before he turns the conversation more serious, telling me more about his situation.

"Divorce is not easy, I found it very difficult...especially afterward. It made me wonder what I did wrong... why could I not make my marriage work? We loved each other of course, but a lot of the time we started to not even like each other very much."

I'm glad Luka feels like he can open up to me, it's clear he's finding it difficult as he stopped giving me eye contact...preferring just to look out at the vista before us.

I wait for a minute before asking anymore. "How do you feel about things now?"

"Hmmm... I know that we did the right thing, I blamed myself for a long time after the divorce was final but I know that we were both to blame. It really does hurt when you cannot make things work with someone that you love." He finally turns to look at me. "You will be fine Luisa, you are a strong woman." He nudges me and we smile at each other, a smile that tells us we realise we have a lot in common.

I feel like I need to make things more light-hearted and so I ask more about him.

"Three years is a long time, I take it you've not been short of...shall we say...female company?" I begin to laugh at how that sounded and luckily he joins in with me. I've actually surprised myself by asking this.

"Why do you say that?" He looks intrigued.

"Someone as good looking as you? Come on..."

He looks a little taken aback by this but he's still laughing along with me before clearing his throat to reply. "A few women, no one erm...serious though. Like I said because of what happened, maybe I have been weary of getting involved with anyone long term."

I can understand what he means. "I see..." Unsure really of what else to say.

He shuffles a little closer. "I also have not really met anyone that made me be able to picture being with them."

Silence follows as my mind conjures up pictures of Luka with his past girlfriends.

It seems he then wonders the same about me. "What about you…before Mark, I mean?"

"Well, from the age of 18 until two days before my 21st birthday I was with my boyfriend Rick. He went back to full-time university, but rather than staying local, he went to Glasgow so…"

He tries his best to do a Scottish accent. "Scotland?" I can't hold the laughter in.

"Yeah…so that ended with Rick. There were a few dates after him, but no one else really until I met…*him.*"

We sit in comfortable silence before Luka changes the subject. "Today is Croatia's last day outside of Europe…"

"I remember hearing about it on the news before I left home, so…it's tomorrow you join Europe?"

"I have a few friends coming to my apartment tonight for some drinks, some food, you should come…unless you already have plans?"

"I'd love to. I was going to get the cable car again tonight for sunset, but I can do that another night."

We see our fellow ship-mates returning to the boat, so Luka takes my hand to help me up the rocky coastline as we follow them. To my delight, he doesn't let go of my hand even when we're back on stable ground. It's an odd feeling, holding hands with another man after years of being with Mark, but because it's Luka…it can only be a good thing.

After another 30 or so minutes on the boat with our legs dangling overboard again and easy relaxed conversation, we reach our final stop for the day, Lopud. Again, Luka and I go straight to the beach and try to find a quiet spot.

I lay my towel down on the sand and throw my beach bag down on top before I see Luka has taken his T-shirt off. I desperately try to tear my eyes away before he sees me looking. As originally predicted, his shoulders are definitely very broad and although he doesn't have massive muscles, they're very clearly defined. It then dawns on me I'm about to strip down to my bikini and self-consciousness kicks in.

It's been a long time since I took my clothes off in front of another man, although it's no different to peeling off around the pool with my bikini on...it suddenly feels pretty nerve wracking because of my strong attraction to Luka.

He beckons towards the couple of shops we walked past. "Shall I get *sladoled*...ice cream?"

"Good idea." I decide, especially now whilst he's away, I can take off my clothes and already be lying on my towel when he returns, which to me will be less awkward.

I make myself comfortable on my towel and reapply my sun lotion before Luka returns with two ice creams, one strawberry and one coconut.

He sits down beside me. "Which would you prefer?"

"Mmmm I'm normally a strawberry ice cream girl, but, I've never tried coconut ice cream..."

"Well, you take the strawberry and you can try some of mine too." I see him casting a glance at me as he realises I'm now wearing just my bikini.

We each enjoy our ice cream quietly as we people watch. There seems to be a lot of families out today with it being Sunday. Luka holds his coconut ice cream out toward me so I can try some, and he holds the cone as I delicately take a mouthful. As I do so, Luka thinks it will be funny to force the cone nearer to me leaving ice cream on my nose.

"Luka!" I shriek as he laughs, while I flap about wiping it away.

Ice cream's finished, we both lie back to soak up the sun. The mere thought of Luka lying next to me without his top on makes me wonder how much longer I can wait to kiss him. I take a deep breath and encourage myself to just enjoy being in his company whilst I can.

I briefly drop off to sleep and wake up with a start, wondering where I am and hoping I haven't been snoring. Luka's now sitting up and staring out to sea, and I see the muscles in his back and shoulders straining around as he hugs his knees towards himself. I move forward, levelling alongside him.

My legs are still outstretched in front of me with my left hand resting on my towel when Luka takes my hand in his. Neither of us says anything, the attraction we feel for each other clearly hanging in the air, my heart thudding louder and louder with anticipation. Our shoulders are nearly touching we're sitting so close and just holding hands with this man feels so right. It's then that Luka turns to look at me and I wonder, is he going to kiss me? Finally?

With Pams' words echoing inside my head, I instantly know if he doesn't move to kiss me now - that I can't wait any longer and it'll be me kissing him.

Excitement begins to build as he slowly moves toward me placing his hand lightly on the side of my neck and places his lips on mine. Every molecule of my body feels awakened by his touch, I've never felt so alive. The kiss is tender at first, almost weary, before we both quicken the pace, his stubble grazing my mouth, only adding to the pleasure. The kiss is over in a matter of seconds, as I pull away. As much as it feels so right, in some way, it feels wrong, I feel in the wrong. Should I be doing this, what would people think? Mark only left two days ago.

"I'm sorry..." I gasp as Luka looks breathless. "...I'm...just...I can't, I thought I could but...it's only been two days, I'm sorry. What would people..." I raise my hands to my head as I go to explain but then I stop myself.

Luka puts his hand on mine once more to reassure me. "It is fine, I understand."

The rest of our time on the beach feels awkward. We both continue to sunbathe, but the change of atmosphere between us is clear. Luka tells me he's going for a walk, and I'm left sitting here kicking myself. *What am I doing?!* I really need to speak to Jodie.

Chapter 13

By the time we're back on the boat to Dubrovnik sitting on the side once more, the tension has eased slightly and we're back to casual chatting again, but it still doesn't feel the same. What have I done? I feel like crying, what a mess I've made of what was fast becoming a perfect day.

We stay together for the hour or so trip back to the mainland, other than when Luka takes his camera back out and walks around the front of the boat to take some pictures. I can't get it off my mind - that kiss, it was wonderful until I ruined it. I think it'll be best if I decline his invitation to his apartment tonight, I've clearly pissed him off so I'm not sure he'd want me there now anyway.

Back on the coach en-route to the hotel, regret really takes a hold of me. Ever the gentleman Luka walks me as close to reception as is safe, from the coach drop off point at the car park entrance.

He breaks the ice. "Thanks for today. I am sorry, I never even offered to pay for my ticket." Luka takes his wallet from his back pocket.

"It's okay, it's on me...you brought the ice creams." I get a flashback to us sitting on the beach, his lips on mine...

"Tonight..." Luka starts awkwardly.

"I erm... I think maybe I'll do the cable car...it's probably best." I feel sickened with sadness but I don't know how else to react now.

Luka looks almost hurt and I'm crushed. I wish I could erase what happened today, well not all of it, just the part where I stopped him kissing me, the rest of the day has been brilliant.

"Enjoy tonight." I touch his arm, maybe I'm trying to let him know that I regret pulling away like I did. I don't want him to stop trying to take a hold of my hand and being attentive with me...I know I'm giving off very mixed signals and it isn't fair.

"If you change your mind, Vilko will be working dinner tonight, you can come along with him. If not... I am working tomorrow, so..."

"Thanks...Bye." I wait awkwardly not knowing what to do, but quickly scurry away needing to be away from Luka, so he doesn't see the tears of frustration that now begin to sting my eyes.

Reaching my room I slam the door with a thud and let out a loud shriek of annoyance, before throwing myself onto the bed. I stare at the ceiling for a few minutes. I'm such a mess, why can't I just let myself enjoy a holiday romance?

I scroll through my mobile and call Jodie, I'm desperate to speak to someone that will talk some sense into me.

"Hello." It feels good to hear her voice.

"Hi, how's things?"

"Yeah, fine, thanks. How about you, how're you feeling out there?"
I fill Jodie in on Luka, how we got talking, bumping into him that night in the old town with his friends, our day together today and what happened on the beach.

"Oh, Luisa! I wish I was there to slap some sense into you..."

"You know what, so do I."

"I knew it, I could hear it in your voice the other day. As soon as I mentioned a holiday romance it was like you were bringing up every excuse you could think of as to why that would be a bad idea and frankly, I can't think of one reason why you shouldn't go for it."

Jodie seems so casual about this, I sometimes wonder why I can't be more like that, but the horrible fact still remains... I'm still Mark's wife and I can't wait for the day that isn't true anymore.

"You're doing it again, aren't you?" It's like Jodie can read my mind.

"Well..."

"Never mind well..." She interrupts. "Do you like him?"

I don't even have to think about this question. "Isn't it obvious?"

"Well then, this is just what you need to take your mind off Mark. What are you afraid of?"

"We only split up two days ago..."

She gives me an irate groan. "So what...in reality you split up over a year ago the way things were. You deserve some fun Luisa, listen to me...you know I'm right. I know you were together for years but look at the time you've wasted on him, forget him now he doesn't deserve another second of your thoughts."

My brain is full of confusion, but my heart has no doubts at all. When Luka kissed me today, it was amazing. It was my head telling me it was wrong, telling me I had to stop. I don't owe Mark anything... especially not loyalty, not any more.

"I could still take Luka up on his invitation, I could find Vilko in the restaurant like he said..." I'm up on my feet, the spring in my step has returned.

"That's the spirit, babe...just go for it. Don't worry about what anyone else thinks, do what your heart tells you."

I feel more like myself again after talking to Jodie and feel an overwhelming urge to look at the photos I've taken today. Just two in particular with Luka in them, one on the jetty and one on the boat, he's so genuine and I'm so attracted to him.

I send a couple of the pictures over to Jodie and she responds straight away with her opinion of how he's 'absolutely gorgeous' and she's certainly right there.

I begin to get ready for the night, still unsure of what to do exactly when there's a knock at the door. Wearing my towel fresh from the shower, I open the door to see a member of the reception staff standing holding a bouquet of flowers. My first thought is of Luka and I can hardly wipe the smile from my face.

I thank the receptionist and close the door, putting the flowers on the tiny bit of room left on the dressing table before opening the envelope to see they're from Mark. My heart sinks.

"Enjoy the holiday, I think this short time apart will be good for us. See you when you get   *home.*
All my love, Mark XX"

I should have known they wouldn't be from Luka. I can't even look at the flowers, I need them out of my sight.

Without thinking, I rush out of the room (completely forgetting I'm only wearing my towel) and straight to the other end of the corridor with no idea whatsoever what I'm actually looking for. It's then that I see a bin in the corner of the corridor so I push the bouquet as hard as I can, through the gap, leaving the stems visibly sticking out. I blow a satisfied sigh and storm back along the corridor, passing two elderly ladies on their way to dinner as I go. Who knows what they must think.

I reach my door just in time to see it slam shut. I try the handle in the desperate hope I can get in but no, it's well and truly locked.

"Great." I mutter to myself, just as a couple walk past me giving me a pitiful look.

I then have to make the humiliating walk down the stairs to the front desk whilst wearing only a towel, to admit I've locked myself out of my room.

Thankfully there are just a handful of people around as most people are in the dining room. So after pleading for another room key and getting a mixture of reactions from fellow holidaymakers ranging from disapproving looks and complimentary glances, five minutes later I'm back in the sanctuary of my room.

This is the kick I needed. Tonight, I'm going to Luka's.

***

I slowly consider the foods on offer at the buffet with one eye on the food and one eye scanning the room for Vilko in the hope my invite still stands. Back at the table, I start to eat my chicken and rice, I can still see that look in Luka's eyes when we got off the coach and I told him I wouldn't be going tonight after all.

The waiter takes my empty plate and with still no sign of Vilko, and with no other way of finding Luka - I admit defeat, drink the last of my wine and head outside to the bus stop.

Lapad seems busier tonight, local people that pass me as I stand at the bus stop seem in good spirits, excited for their country to be joining Europe. A group of teenagers walk by, one of them wearing a Croatian flag around his shoulders, another carrying cans of beer. I wonder if there are even more people out tonight…out to celebrate.

Arriving in the old town I register the humidity in the air in comparison to Lapad again, I can fully understand why people use those hand-held fans. It takes me a while to get out of the throngs of people who all appear to be standing around having just got off, or waiting for a bus. Eventually I do the walk up the hill to the cable car station and buy my ticket and join the queue for the next car to arrive.

I need to get to the top quickly so I can watch the town begin to light up from the view point. Five minutes later I'm blessed with that wonderful sight across the town. The sun is setting with a beautiful warm orange, flooding the whole of the sky, dancing down on the water and oozing out in every direction. The warmth of the sun slowly fades bringing a colder feel, the blue of the sea now stands out before hundreds of tiny lights begin to switch on all around the city walls and in between the terracotta roofs before finally, darkness descends. The air seems still and quieter now, although there are still plenty of people around.

I stand for what feels like hours, marvelling at the outlook and clearing my mind.

"Did you make it for sunset?" I'm suddenly brought back into the moment. I can't believe it, it's Luka just leaning on the railings next to me.

"How long have you been there?" My stomach begins its enthusiastic fluttering.

His eyes don't leave the view. "A few minutes, you looked deep in thought."

Neither of us speak, it's just quietness as we both gaze outward.

"I thought you were having people over, don't tell me the host got bored?" I joke, turning towards him to see him now facing my direction.

"The person I wanted there the most, she did not come." I'm once again mildly stunned into silence as he carries on. "…what are you afraid of?" Luka walks closer towards me, waiting for a reply.

I look down at my feet. "I'm not, I'm…"

"You are, you are afraid."

It takes me a few seconds to speak. "Mayyybe…but I…" I stutter "…about what happened today, I'm really sorry. I wanted it to happen…"

"…I know you did… so why did you stop?"

"I don't know!" I'm almost shouting by this point. The group of people next to us look in our direction before moving further on towards the restaurant, they must think we're a couple having a lovers tiff.

Luka walks closer and closer to me. "Želim da te poljubim." He's almost whispering as he looks deep into my eyes.

That phrase sounds familiar. "That's what you said, in the taxi that night, what *is* that? I'm sorry, I don't speak much Croatian, but if you don't tell me what it means, then what's the point in saying it at all? Or is that the whole idea?" I'm really starting to ramble on now.

Luka says nothing just watches me, which makes me aggravated as I throw my arms up in the air in disbelief.

"It means I want to kiss you..." I'm so glad to hear that. My legs turn to jelly as I know what's coming next and I can't wait another second.

I move closer towards him, glancing at his lips and then back into his deep brown eyes. I go to speak, but at this moment in time, words aren't enough so I move closer still and touch my lips to his.

Luka takes me in his arms and kisses me tenderly and it feels even better than I remembered when I was replaying it in my head after the beach. His warm hands cup my face before sliding down my back. The feel of his body against mine, I can feel how much he wants me and the feeling is definitely mutual. This time I certainly won't be pulling away.

I can't believe it, I really thought I'd ruined everything and now here I am, back in his embrace. As we part slightly I can hardly wipe the smile off my face.

Luka's first to speak. "That is why I had to come and find you, I was not letting you go without a fight." He kisses me again on the lips and smooth's my hair away from my face.

"I'm so glad you did. I think we can safely say I didn't put up much resistance." I giggle. "I looked for Vilko at dinner, I wanted to come, but..."

Luka gives a satisfied smirk. "Well, you can now. I can be your own personal escort."

We walk hand in hand to join the line of people waiting for the next lift back down the hill in the cable car. When we reach the bottom, we flag down a taxi for quickness and jump in the back. Things feel so easy between us now, the confusion and hesitation has gone, I know I've made the right choice.

Luka rests his hand on my leg for the duration of the drive back to Lapad. Even just a small act like that has such an effect on me, and I'm suddenly desperate to feel his lips on mine again.

Luka's apartment building looks to be a fairly new build from the outside, and is literally just around the corner from the hotel. We walk up the two flights of stairs to his apartment and as we approach, the party seems to be in full flow as I hear laughter, singing and music from the hallway. I have an impulsive urge to smooth down my black skirt to check I'm not showing more than I should be as we come close to the door. As we walk in the first person I see is Melita, and I'm glad to see a familiar face. She rushes over to greet us, looking stunning once again in her denim skirt and cropped vest top.

"I am so glad you came…" She kisses me on each cheek. "I knew he would find you." She elbows her brother.

I giggle happily. "I'm glad he did." I get a fleeting sense of things becoming very comfortable very quickly between Luka and I.

Luka squeezes my hand and carries on through to the kitchen where I see him pouring two glasses of wine. The small but cosy apartment seems relatively full of people chatting away cheerfully. I see Vilko and Kristijan on one sofa and they wave at me in acknowledgement in between their conversation.

The mood's very upbeat with the sounds of laughing and singing and the smell of buffet food lingering in the air. I notice the music becoming louder as a couple of people stand in enthusiasm and begin to dance, the others in good spirits as they watch.

Melita beckons me over to sit with her and Patrik and we get talking about their forthcoming wedding, which is now less than a week away. I really must think about what clothes I brought with me that would be suitable for the wedding, oh forget it, I might as well go shopping for a new dress.

Luka delivers my glass of wine, and perches on the arm of the sofa next to me and gently caresses my arm lazily with his one hand, meaning I'm now barely listening to his sister as the sensations this is creating are really distracting me. The next person to arrive is Luka's brother Aleksander and I can certainly detect the family resemblance seeing them next to each other. His brother is younger, with the same dark eyes, but is slightly shorter than Luka's five-feet-nine and without the goatee.

Luka introduces me throughout the night to a few of his school friends who waste no time in telling me stories about him growing up, much to his humiliation. Before long, I'm guffawing away at their jokes and I feel as though I've known these people for years, everyone has made me feel so welcome.

Just a holiday romance? Do you normally meet extended family members and old friends of the person you have a holiday romance with?

We are never far away from each other all night and when we're separated, the longing looks we give to each other only serve to remind me of the chemistry between us.

Midnight approaches and the sound of fireworks takes us all outside onto the street to fully appreciate the climax of the evening. Everyone I've met so far here in Croatia is really patriotic and genuinely pleased about their country joining the European Union. Most of the street are crowding outside to see the celebratory fireworks. We all stare upwards and watch as the beautiful reds, yellows, greens and purples fill the skies above us, the atmosphere is electric and I'm proud to be a part of it.

Luka stands behind me with an arm draped around my shoulders and his head resting on mine, it's magical. We make the most of the opportunity and enjoy another kiss as his friends are distracted.

After the fireworks, the atmosphere back indoors becomes more laid-back as the music is switched off and people seem to be winding down for the night. By this point a couple of people have made their way home and I'm wondering how the night will end for me and Luka. Tiredness has already crept up on me, so I tell him I'm calling it a night. He seems disappointed but understands and after I've said my goodbyes to all of the lovely people I've met tonight, he walks me back to the hotel.

"I've had such a good night, thank you so much." I almost feel emotional - nothing to do with the drink, of course.

Luka drapes his arm around my waist and pulls me in close. "Me too, I am glad you were there to share the festivities."

By now, things have quietened down outside around Lapad, there's just the odd straggler making his way home.

I stop at the rear gate of the hotel to say good night to Luka. "Right, well…"

Anticipation starts building inside of me as he puts both arms around me. "Let me at least walk you through to reception." he grins, releasing his hold around me and squeezing my hand.

It's the '*at least*' from that sentence that gets my mind racing and my legs trembling. To be honest, right now, nothing would make me happier than to invite Luka into my room to spend the night. Ever since I first laid eyes on him, I won't pretend that the thought hasn't crossed my mind on multiple occasions of what it would be like to be with Luka in every sense of the word. But it just wouldn't feel right, considering my room was originally mine and Mark's room. I suppose it's a way of keeping that part of my life with Mark separate to Luka.

He knows he can't risk walking me inside anyway. "You cannot blame me for trying, you know there is nothing shy about me." he continues, that lewd smile of his spread across his lips.

I nod my head, laughing. "I'm starting to realise that, yes."

We stand in each other's arms canoodling some more until the intensity picks up and I stop kissing him, placing my hand on his chest as we stare into each other's eyes.

"If it wasn't too risky for you to be in the hotel with me…"

He tries to catch his breath. "I am starting to think it would be worth the risk."

For fear of throwing caution to the wind and dragging him upstairs, I breathlessly break away.

Luka clearly understands as he picks up the conversation. "I-I am…working both shifts tomorrow but I want to take you to lunch."

"Okay, where are we going?"

"Just be ready at 12:00 p.m. Come prepared, we might swim too."

"Is this just a ploy to see me in my bikini again?"

He laughs naughtily. "Maybe, you will see. I will see you at breakfast first anyway, not in the way I want to, but…"

I can't help but kiss him again before I manage to somehow drag myself away and up to bed, alone.

Chapter 14

The next morning, as soon as I've eaten breakfast and very much enjoyed the sight of Luka cooking in his whites, I stroll back up to my room to prepare myself for the day. I dress in my red bikini and decide on my short cream dress with the little gold leaf imprints and smooth my hair into a bun. I still have a couple of hours until my lunch with Luka, so I've got plenty of time to enjoy some sun around the pool.

I relax down on my lounger and again, make some more notes for my book. I'm just about to enjoy some music through my earphones when I spy Pam and Pete entering the pool area. I wave in their direction and they come straight over to say hello.

Pam's carrying a small white sun umbrella I notice, which matches beautifully with her long white and blue print sundress, blue eyeshadow and just the one chunky blue bracelet. Pete's sporting a Panama hat today with the usual shorts and T-shirt. His nose appears to be a little sunburnt and I wonder if that's why he's wearing a hat.

Pam takes a seat on the lounger next to me. "Where've you been hiding?" She takes down her sun umbrella now she's comfortably in the shade.

I see Pete removing his hat and sunglasses and I try my best not to react as the extent of Pete's sunburn becomes clear. The whole of his face is bright red apart from the shape of his sunglasses around his eyes which still appears to be untouched by the sun.

"We erm…w-we did the Elaphiti islands yesterday, it was wonderful." That smile takes over my face again as I explain how picturesque the islands were.

Pete drops into the conversation looking confused. "I'm sorry, *we* went?"

I try not to stare at his extremely sore looking skin.

Pam's enthusiasm is apparent straight away. "Pete, why don't you go and get us a drink? Luisa?" She's obviously desperate to shoo him away.

"I've got my water thanks, I'm fine."

Pam watches him walk away. "Well…*we?!*"

I look at Pam open mouthed. "Sorry… I've got to ask whilst he's away…"

She bursts out laughing knowing exactly what I'm about to say. "Can you believe it?" She has to dry her eyes she's laughing so much. "…he fell asleep yesterday afternoon without his hat and in full sun… I couldn't believe it when I got back from doing a bit of souvenir shopping and I woke him up…"

She tells me how she spent most of last night putting natural yoghurt on his sunburnt face. We both have to pull ourselves together, Pam now having to use her hand held fan to cool herself down.

She glances behind her to check Pete's still at the bar. "Anyway…you were saying, you went on the trip yesterday…"

I say nothing and do my best poker face, but it's too hard to pretend. "The man you saw me with the other night - the chef, Luka he came with me…it was great."

"He's the chef? I bet it's not just your food he's heating up!"

"Pam…" I burst out laughing.

"Well he's absolutely gorgeous I don't know how you keep your hands off him."

Neither do I. "We're just having fun, it's definitely what I need."

"I can see that from the look on your face, I'm so pleased. You seem much more carefree. Have you spoken to your parents about you and Mark yet? Sorry to bring him up."

I shake my head. "Not yet, but Ben will let me know when he's spoken to them."

I chat with Pam and Pete for a while before they leave for their excursion to Mostar in Bosnia and Herzegovina.

Just before I'm due to meet Luka, I head to the ladies to tidy up my hair and when I step back outside into the sunshine I see him waiting, leaning against the wall opposite the hotel - picnic basket in tow. I remove my sunglasses to fully take in the view as I walk to meet him.

"A picnic?"

"What can I say, I know how to do romance." He flirts, stooping to kiss me hello and smelling absolutely divine.

We head out onto the promenade where we follow the coastal path as I slip my sunglasses back on.

"So where are we going?"

He puts his arm around me. "Just wait and you will see."

We continue to follow the path, past the '*Skriven*' bar which must be the best located bar in Lapad, with each table facing the unrestricted view of the sea. A few minutes further on, we come to another set of steps which lead down the rocks and down towards the sea. Luka stops to chat to a man situated at the top of the steps who's selling private boat trips, he seems to be offering boat hire by the hour, as well as full days' private sailing instruction. I assume that's what we're doing but then, the boat trip seller pulls his table to one side for easy access to the next level of steps down and Luka reaches for my hand to lead me carefully down the steps.

When we reach the bottom, we're standing on a secluded platform above the sea, with no one else around. If I walk to the very edge of the platform and look up to the top of the steps I can only just see the main coastal path.

Luka's busy laying out what looks like a padded beach mat, before laying a beach towel over the top at one side.

He points at my bag. "Do you have a towel?"

I open my bag to retrieve my towel, and place it next to Luka's on the mat. We then move them backwards a little so we're partially in the shade as we eat.

"What, no picnic blanket?" I giggle.

"How much do you think can fit in this basket?"

I peer inside to see various pots and tubs loaded with food and even a bottle of wine with glasses.

He gestures towards the very comfortable looking set up. "Take a seat."

I slip off my sandals and make myself comfortable beside him. At the same time, Luka starts unloading the basket of goodies in between us. I'm really impressed at the trouble he's clearly gone to as he relays a list of the items whilst removing the lids from each pot.

"*Lepinje* which are flatbread filled with pancetta and cheese from the island of Pag, salad with more local cheese, I hope you like cheese?" He laughs, and I nod in agreement. "Pasta with a cinnamon flavoured meat sauce, which is a local speciality and then *knedle* which are Croatian plum dumplings for dessert. "

"Mmm, you did all this?"

He opens the bottle of wine and pours two glasses. "Of course, I am a chef you know." Luka hands a glass to me. "*Živjeli*, cheers."

"Cheers." I sip my wine, it's delicious - sparkling and very light. "Where did you work before the hotel?" I take a bite of the flatbread and it's absolutely mouth-watering.

Luka swallows his food. "I worked in another hotel for a couple of years before this one, a three star hotel in town, but I did not have to do much cooking really, it was mostly preparing the food and chopping vegetables. When Kristijan told me there was a job at *The Sun Elegance* - five-star, I knew there would be more opportunities."

Next I try the pasta. At first taste, I'm not really sure on the spices but once the cinnamon hits my taste buds it's really good and I find myself piling more onto my picnic plate.

"It is tasty?" He asks, noticing the uncertainty on my face to begin with.

"Very…I wasn't sure at first, but…" I chew.

Luka pulls a satisfied face as he puts the lid back onto the now empty tub.

I've certainly eaten too much once I've tried some of the salad and delicious plum dumplings and so, I lie back to unwind in the sun. Luka finishes packing the empties away before removing his white T-shirt in one swift movement. *Uh-oh…control yourself, Luisa.*

Still wearing my dress over my bikini I sit forward and remove my dress before gently lowering myself back to relax. I without a doubt feel more confident in stripping to my bikini around him than I did yesterday, that's for sure.

He lies on his front with the sun on his back, his head turned to face me. "I bet you have been to some great places with your job, the travel agent?"

I mirror his positioning and turn to face him. "Yeah, it was brilliant." I close my eyes for a moment, there's a comfortable silence. "…before I met Mark I wanted to go travelling." I open my eyes to find Luka. "There are so many more places I want to see. I remember when I was younger, every year I used to love to watch the Eurovision Song Contest. All the different languages, all the different countries represented and I used to learn the songs, even though I had no idea what I was singing, I just loved the different languages and seeing the people from all over."

"Nothing to stop you travelling now is there?" Luka encourages.

I contemplate his words. "I was thinking that a few days ago. I could go home, pack everything up and just go."

"You do not seem so sure though." He rolls onto his side, resting his head on his elbow. "…I said to you yesterday, you are scared of doing what you want. I see that you hold yourself back and you should not."

"I think it's from having to consider someone else for so long…" Luka seems to know what he wants and he just goes for it. I really admire that about him and I tell him so.

He sighs. "When you have been around things like I was growing up, you realise what is important." I immediately know he's talking about the war.

"It must have been awful…I went to the war museum a couple of days ago. Can you remember much about it?"

"Not really, I think I must have blocked a lot of this out of my head, it is difficult to talk about."

I take a hold of his hand. Listening to Luka is heart-wrenching and it's not long before he changes the subject, clearly wanting to keep the mood upbeat.

"Anyway, let's make the most of the water. I actually did mean it when I said we would be swimming, it wasn't just an excuse to see you wearing very little, although…" He raises a mischievous eyebrow and kisses me firmly on the lips.

We tip toe to the water's edge where Luka confidently steps over the rocks and into the sea, plunging himself straight under the water to swim a couple of metres out, before swimming back toward me.

I stand with my hands on hips, giggling as he shows off before gently lowering myself into the water beside him.

The sea feels wonderfully warm from the sun and it's almost as though we're on our own private island, it's so peaceful. I gaze out across the sea, looking at the boats and letting my mind wander, imagining what life would be like if I did decide to go travelling. Luka flicks water in my face, bringing me back to the here and now.

I let out a squeal, laughing as I make an attempt to wipe the water from my eyes before Luka uses his thumb to smooth the water away from my eye as I steady myself holding his shoulder. He oozes sex appeal, his skin and hair wet from the sea. I ache to kiss him, to feel his lips against my skin and almost as though he can read my mind, he takes me in his arms and kisses me. My body feels on fire under his touch as my legs seem to find themselves around his waist and he continues to hold me close. Very close.

"Do you like it down here?"

That makes me grin as I look downwards. "Well...I don't really know yet do I..." I laugh. "But I have a feeling...a *good* feeling."

He throws his head back with laughter. "Oh *that*...you will love."

I prod him playfully as he gestures to the surroundings which is what he was actually talking about.

"I do like it, I would never have known it existed. You know all of the right people don't you, your friend holding your spot for you."

We enjoy an afternoon of swimming and make the most of the sun before walking back to the hotel, making plans to meet after Luka finishes his shift later. I enter my room with a distinct spring in my step and I feel so full of life that I change into a vest top and shorts, grab my earphones and head to the hotel gym.

I've always enjoyed exercising, but I don't tend to do it as much as I'd like to. I start off with 20 minutes on the exercise bike, 15 minutes on the treadmill and that, combined with the afternoon of swimming is more than enough for one day and so, its back upstairs for a shower and change before dinner.

I send a quick message to Jodie, thanking her again for her advice on the Luka situation last night, to which she responds pretty much straight away asking how things are. We send a couple of messages back and forth including a couple of pictures from today, before I promise to call her tomorrow to hear all about how her official role as manager's going.

Now, what to wear tonight? I'm slightly nervy about tonight, not in a bad way…it's more nervous excitement than anything else. I think my lemon yellow vest dress will emphasise my tan, so I choose this, along with a black belt at the waist and a black necklace. Peeking in the mirror, a calming confidence flows into me, something I'm feeling begin to build further, the more time I spend with Luka. I feel like I'm finally myself again for the first time in a long time.

Chapter 15

Later that night following dinner, I wait for Luka in a bar next door to the hotel whilst drinking the cocktail of the day and enjoying the soft jazz music flowing from the speakers. Luka makes his entrance wearing jeans and a blue T-shirt and looks so laid back, matching the mood of the surroundings perfectly. Luka's arm makes its way around my waist as he draws me to him for a long kiss on the lips, bringing my senses alive again. He then takes a hold of my hands and pulls me away from him at arm's length, looking at my dress.

"I was desperate to do that as soon as I saw you in the restaurant tonight, you look gorgeous in that dress."

I lean myself back closer to him, as that distance of about 20 inches between us was just far too much.

"Well thank you..." I rub his arm affectionately. "Are we staying here, or?"

He leads me towards the door. "We are going towards the sea."

I reach back towards the table taking a last sip of my cocktail, the taste now mostly of ice as he gently pulls me long with my other hand.

Luka takes me to a bar overlooking the sea, where all of the tables are littered with tea light candles, mirroring the lights of the next bay in the distance across the water. I notice in the far corner of the bar terrace, a band appears to be setting up ready to play as Luka orders our drinks.

He moves his seat slightly closer towards me. "After some typical Croatian food for lunch, I thought we could share *sladoled* tonight."

Luka gestures to the table next to us where a family of four are tucking in to the biggest ice cream I think I've ever seen, complete with sparklers and wafers.

My eyes almost pop out of my head when I see the waiter carrying our plate of *sladoled* a short while later, along with a bottle of beer and a white wine.

"Tell me that ice cream is for the whole of Lapad and not just for us?"

Luka laughs, rubbing my arm reassuringly. "Just wait until you taste it."

There's strawberry ice cream with noticeable chunks of the fruit itself mixed in, a white coconut ice cream with desiccated coconut sprinkled on the top. Next to that sits the creamiest looking vanilla I've ever seen with visible bits of vanilla extract, not to mention the crushed nuts, squirty cream and fresh pineapple that monopolise one corner of the plate. Oh, and not forgetting the wafers.

The pink of the strawberry stands out against the white and it's that I want to go to first. Luka however has other ideas.

He takes a spoon and fills it with as much of each flavour of ice cream as he can, including some cream, before feeding me the biggest spoon full. It tastes incredible but it's always the same, eating something like this makes you automatically assume that most of it's actually around your mouth rather than inside of it. The freezing cold temperature hits my teeth making me wince, my hand flies to my mouth in an effort to cover my expression.

To my horror, Luka starts laughing as some of the already melted ice cream finds its way onto my bare leg. He runs his fingers lightly along my thigh to remove the ice cream before licking it from his fingers, sending waves of pleasure along both of my legs. I suddenly feel really hot and as our eyes meet, the chemistry between us grows more and more by the second. I only hope he didn't taste any of my mosquito spray I covered my legs in earlier, and just as that thought crosses my mind I see him lick his lips, grimace and start to cough.

I reach for his beer encouraging him to take a drink before giving him a napkin to wipe his lips.

"Sorry I have insect repellent on my legs…" I grit my teeth.
He waves his hand to tell me not to worry as he continues to cough and wipes his mouth once again.

Coughing now subsided, the band begins to play and I drink some much needed wine, my throat suddenly feeling very dry from the intensity. Despite our hardest efforts, we don't manage to finish the ice cream. On my part it's due to the desire that I'm really struggling to keep hidden, I can't speak for Luka. I have my legs crossed towards him, and every so often as we move along with the music our legs touch, creating that spark between us once again.

My second glass of wine starts to relax me more so, as I sing along with some of the well-known songs the band are playing including a couple of Spanish songs I know from my mother, and from holidays growing up.

Luka sips his beer. "You speak Spanish very well."

"Thanks, I wish I could tell you I know what every word I'm singing actually means though."

The band begin to play a slow number, prompting several couples to take to the floor and to my surprise, Luka gets to his feet and holds out his hand to me.

"Come on, show me what you can do."

I laugh, wondering if he's actually being serious before Luka raises his eyebrows. "Do not make me drag you."

I give in and put my glass down on the table before taking his hand and following him to the edge of the dance floor. I've no idea what song they're playing I can't even concentrate on that, I'm just enjoying being with Luka.

We sway along to the music, our foreheads touching, the tension between us building as I feel the thud of Luka's heart against mine. He changes his hold on me, bringing us face to face, and I can take it no longer as I let my guard down and look deep into Luka's eyes once more.

"You never did show me any of your photography work…at your apartment."

An intense smile plays across Luka's mouth as he clears his throat. "I could show you tonight?"

"…Or now?" I lean in and kiss him.

He slowly leads me back to our table. Luka sits down looking around for the waiter to get the bill, and I perch on the edge of my seat to drink the last of my wine. A few minutes later, with still no waiters around Luka puts a handful of notes underneath the menu stand to pay our bill.

Part of me can hardly believe what I'm about to do, I'm about to sleep with a man who I've known for just under a week, but I can't help myself. The way I feel when I'm with Luka - he's intoxicating. We leave the bar and swiftly walk to Luka's apartment.

We walk for a couple of minutes, making conversation about the ice cream - neither of us really wanting to speak any more, not yet, not out here.

As we pass by the last restaurant on the promenade, Luka suddenly pulls me to one side for a passionate embrace, making me breathless with longing. We continue the short walk at a fast pace to Luka's apartment, barely saying a word to each other. Reaching his front door, he retrieves his keys from his pocket and manages to drop them on the floor. In the pitch dark we both crouch down hunting for the keys, feeling our way across the doormat as we bump heads. We laugh at the comedy of the situation as I clutch my forehead.

Luka takes out his phone and with the torch, finally we see them. He opens the door swiftly, ushering me inside first and closing the door behind us.

He puts his arms around me from behind me, and begins to plant kisses on my shoulders and around the back of my neck, grazing my neck with his goatee as he does so, making my knees weak.

I see three framed prints on the wall in the hallway that I didn't notice the night I was here for the party, I try to look at them properly to see if they're Luka's but as he's now pulling at the zip on my dress, my concentration on them is dwindling.

In one swift movement, he picks me up and carries me through to his bedroom, throwing the door shut behind us. I don't really take anything in about his bedroom at first other than the fact that I'm in there…with him…and that it smells of his aftershave. That scent alone is more than enough.

Our hunger for each other can wait no more as I remove Luka's T-shirt, revealing his torso and I take off my belt as he slips the straps of my dress off my shoulders, making my dress drop to the floor. We fall down onto the bed and I hardly recognise myself as I'm consumed with desire for him.

***

Luka turns to look at me and smiles, reaching for my hand. He looks gorgeous despite his hair now being in complete disarray, and I can't resist rolling onto my side to face him. He sweeps my now no doubt equally as messy hair away from my face, staring deeply into my eyes and traces my lips with his thumb, making me crave him once again. Moments later, we're savouring every part of each other all over again but this time the pace is tender - the urgency having been satisfied, for now.

Chapter 16

I wake up to see sunlight filtering in through the open curtains and feel briefly confused as I take in the surroundings. I have a moment of dread, where I think I'm back at home before I remember I've spent the night at Luka's. The other half of the bed is empty, but I can hear the water running in the bathroom and realise Luka must be getting ready for work. He strolls back into the bedroom with a towel wrapped around his waist and seems genuinely happy when he sees I'm awake.

"Morning." he smiles, climbing onto the bed to kiss me before continuing to dry himself off. "I was going to leave you to sleep whilst I went to work."

His towel is now completely off and my eyes go straight *there* and I'm wondering how much time he has before he has to leave for the hotel.

I sit up, pulling the sheet around me. "Oh thanks, that's sweet, but I'd better get back...." I climb out of bed and glance around the room for my clothes.

Luka gets dressed and styles his hair in the mirror catching my eye and grinning at me, sending butterflies soaring through me.

"You do not regret last night?" He asks almost awkwardly, I think it's the first time I've seen him unsure of himself.

I close the gap between us, reaching my arms up and around his neck, him now fully dressed and me in just my underwear. "Absolutely not!" I giggle before kissing him firmly on the lips.

After a quick coffee we leave the apartment, and walk around to the hotel. Luka lets me go in first and then, he heads through to the kitchens a few minutes later just in case anyone sees us arrive together.

The first thing I see when I open the door to my room is my mobile flashing on the bedside cabinet telling me I have six missed calls from my parents last night and two voicemails. Oh how I've been dreading this. I'm so glad I left my phone here last night, otherwise our perfect evening together would have been ruined.

It's not quite 7:00 a.m. so it's too early with the hour time difference to speak to my parents so, I listen to the first voicemail which is Ben warning me to expect a call, and then the second one is obviously my Mom, telling me to call her right away. It's way too early to deal with this, so I pass some time by having a shower and getting myself ready for the day ahead.

Showered and dressed and after spending some time on the balcony making yet more notes for my book and updating Asha once again, it's now or never as I pick up my mobile and call my parents. My mother answers after just one ring, her tone sounding very distressed.

"Luisa?"

Here we go. I roll my eyes to myself. "Yes, it's me, what's wrong?"

"Tell me it's not true?" She sounds in physical pain and I can hear my Dad in the background telling her to calm down.

"If you mean about me and Mark then yes, it's true."

"Are you sure you can't work things out *cariño?* Divorce...there's no going back - it's so final. Plus you are there on your holiday, alone."

Her panic stricken voice almost makes me feel guilty, like I've let her down as she carries on.

167

"…marriage isn't always easy, you need to work hard."

I sink onto the bed, staring up at the ceiling, does she really expect me to take him back again? Does she want me to be unhappy? I've had enough! I put my feet to the floor and stand up.

"I think I've worked hard enough considering he cheated on me and I took him back. Things haven't been the same since and now I find out there's been who knows how many other women since I took him back, I think, no, I *know* this is the end. I'm sorry if it upsets you, but we will be getting divorced."

There I've said it, well I've shouted it in fact. There's silence on the line. Then follows another 10 minutes of my Mom telling me she's trying to understand. I speak to my Dad, who is a lot more laid back than my Mom and he promises he'll speak to her.

I feel mentally exhausted as I lie back on the bed. Yet again, the thought of going back home fills me with dread. I really think there could be no better time for me to go travelling than now. Thoughts of Luka flood back into my head, maybe I could stay here with him. *Don't be stupid, Luisa, it's just a holiday romance, get a grip.* I push those thoughts immediately out of my mind.

I shake myself back to the here and now and go for breakfast. As I walk into the restaurant my eyes immediately reach the buffet station where Luka's based. I see him deep in conversation with Kristina. I leave my bag at an empty table and help myself to tea. On my way past, I look over at Luka to catch his attention but he's still talking. Sitting back at the table, I see Kristina work her way around the buffet and I see her watching him,

I'm sure she's flirting with him. She's giggling away, fiddling with her hair, she is - she's flirting.

Should I even be bothered? Whether I should be or not, the truth of the matter is that I am bothered. As she walks away, Luka replaces a tray of bacon on the buffet and as he does so, he notices me. He grins in my direction and looks around before beckoning me over.

I take a plate and pretend to be waiting for him to cook me an omelette so we can talk.

He looks up at me and back down at the omelette as he talks so it isn't so obvious how familiar we are with each other. "What are you doing today?"

"I'm not sure, maybe just the pool unless I get a better offer..."

"I do not know if I can compete with the pool but, lunch? I could cook for you, or we could go into town?" Luka flips my omelette before popping it onto my plate.

"Let's go into town, you made food for me yesterday, and now."

We spend the next couple of days together around Luka's shifts at the hotel and they're a blissful couple of days. He shows me around some more of Lapad, we have lunch at his favourite restaurant and we even go drinking and dancing with some more of his friends at a nightclub in the old town. I feel like we're really getting to know each other and the more I find out about Luka, the more I'm falling for him. It feels so nice to feel appreciated and to be heard.

I've spent the last couple of nights at his apartment which have been amazing. I feel like I can do anything when he's around, and he makes me feel so attractive, both in and out of the bedroom. The only downside is when we're together, I'm struggling to get out of my head that in just five days' time, I'll be leaving him behind and going home.

I'm hiding these thoughts, keeping them to myself as we both know this is just a holiday fling. I don't want to scare Luka away by mentioning the subject of me leaving too often, but the truth is when I imagine leaving him, I feel like my heart is being ripped apart.

After another wonderful night together, we walk hand in hand back to the hotel. I run into the supermarket across the road first to buy more sun lotion (I never seem to bring enough with me on holiday), as Luka carries on ahead of me through the car park.

Fully stocked up on factor 20, I'm approaching the entrance of the hotel and as I glance to the right I see Luka talking to Kristina as she leaves her car. Watching them talking, I get the sense that they know each other really well, and they seem so relaxed in each other's company. It would be hard not to find Luka attractive, and the same can be said for Kristina, she's simply beautiful. It's as though she's hanging on his every word, as they have what looks to be some friendly banter between them as much as I can tell, considering my lack of understanding of Croatian.

Kristina heads to the reception desk whilst Luka makes for the staff entrance to the restaurant. I continue upstairs, unable to shake off the empty feeling that's suddenly taken a hold over me. Watching someone flirt with Luka is the wake-up call I needed to make me fully realise just how much of myself I'm giving to him. I knew I didn't have it in me to just be a holiday fling, my feelings for him are much too strong for that.

I know I'm in danger of getting hurt and right now, the only thing I can think of to minimise the hurt is to not spend so much time with him. The idea of not seeing him makes me ache, we've grown so close in such a short space of time. Maybe it's been too much too quickly?

In my room, I shower and change my clothes and rather than eat breakfast at the hotel, I head to the bakery around the corner. I'm so angry with myself, how could I let this happen? I jumped in with both feet, got too comfortable too quickly and now I'm going to pay the price. I need a distraction, something to stop me thinking about him. When I've finished breakfast, I use the small internet café area back at the hotel to plan my travelling. Obviously, I'll ask Jodie to book the flights and accommodation for me, but first things first, where shall I start from?

I've spent a lot of time in Andalucia, but I never did get to visit Seville, so that seems as good a place as any to start from. Things may seem a little rushed researching my travelling now rather than waiting until I'm back at home, but I know once I get home, I'll end up talking myself out of it with everything going on with Mark. Putting as much distance as possible between me and Mark feels like the best thing in the world for me.

Right on cue, Jodie calls me and to say she's more than a little shocked when I ask her to book my first couple of flights for me now, is an understatement. I think she was expecting me to wait a couple of months until the dust had settled with Mark, but what is there to wait for, really?

"As long as you're sure you're ready babe?" Jodie sounds worried.

"I'm sure, trust me. I'll just need a week when I get home to speak to a solicitor and move what I can out of the house and then I'll be ready."

What I don't tell her is that I also need something to occupy my mind when I get home because the thought of being without Luka even for a day makes me feel so sad. In fact, I think I feel more upset about that than I did when I realised months ago that my marriage was over.

I hear her tapping away on her keyboard before she gives me some options of flights for the week after next.

I hear excited giggling down the line. "I've just had the best idea…I'm owed some holiday, why don't I do your first stop with you, I could come to Seville for a couple of days before leaving you to it?"

This is why she's my best friend, she's full of the best ideas. "That would be brilliant, let's do it."

"I need to obviously check dates with Darren first and hopefully the dog walker can come in for an extra walk a day…" I can literally hear the cogs moving in her head as she tries to mentally make arrangements for her beautiful fur babies.

Chapter 17

I end my call to Jodie feeling very different to when I started it. This holiday has made me realise I'm a lot stronger than I was six months ago. Meeting Luka has played a big part in making me understand my dreams and most importantly, he's made me realise my dreams aren't out of reach. If Mark and I had ended our marriage before we came to Dubrovnik, I think I would've cancelled the holiday rather than coming here alone, meaning I would never have met Luka, who has helped me more than he'll ever realise on my journey. I'm more convinced than ever that everything happens for a reason.

My positive attitude takes me to the pool, where I spend the afternoon soaking up the sun. Luka's never far from my mind and it feels a lot longer ago than this morning since I saw him last. My head is trying desperately to rule my heart. How can I forget about him? I'm supposed to be going to his sister's wedding with him in two days.

***

That night, I stick with my plan to see less of Luka and treat myself to dinner at the *Plaža Lounge* overlooking the beach. I walk up the wooden steps that lead to the restaurant to the sound of chilled house music playing from the speakers. I take a seat out on the terrace which I'm told by the waitress is normally completely open sided, but because the temperature seems to have dropped a little this evening and the wind has picked up, the canopies' have been rolled down.

The lounge and terrace are furnished with wooden tables and chairs with cushions in bright blues and pinks and has subtle lighting fixed onto the beams in between the canopies. The canopies still don't restrict the view of the beautiful hills and forest of Velika Mala Petka to the left, giving way to the deep ocean which is almost as dark as the night. I find the view soothing as I leisurely drink my wine, yet that emptiness I felt this morning about my life at home is beginning to find its way back in.

It's an effort to eat my food when it arrives. I went for the mixed pizza, which is all different types of meat with really flavoursome local cheeses and it tastes delicious, but my appetite seems to have disappeared. The waitress kindly puts my leftovers in a takeaway box and its back to the hotel I go.

Reception is busy as I walk through, with a queue of people with suitcases of all manner of sizes waiting to check in to start their holiday. It's the first time I've heard the grand piano being played in the reception and the soft cheery melody is actually very uplifting.

Hotel porters are busy labelling holidaymakers luggage with their room numbers, ready to whisk the cases away so they're in their rooms even before their owners - all part of the five star service of the *Sun Elegance Hotel.* I can hear the sound of laughter coming from the bar area and that unmistakable scent of lavender lightly drifting out from the bar and into reception.

My laziness and sombre mood leads me into the lift where I delve into my bag to find my key card before reaching the second floor. As I enter the corridor from the lift, I'm shocked to see Luka sitting on the floor outside my room.

"Luka." I clutch my hand to my chest "You made me jump…"

He gets to his feet with a serious expression. "I was worried something had happened. You were not at breakfast or dinner, I tried to call your room…."

I only then appreciate how it might seem from Luka's point of view and the guilt takes over.

"I'm really sorry, I didn't think." I open the door and usher him inside, not wanting him to get into trouble. I know the risk he's taken tonight coming up here to my room. *Is it me or does he look more handsome than ever tonight?*

It feels strange seeing Luka in my room like this. The guilt I thought I'd be feeling of having him here I now realise I don't feel it, it's all in my head.

"Have you been waiting long out there?"

Everything my head was telling me earlier - to spend less time with him and to forget about him, as I stand here now looking into his eyes…I know I can't do any of that. There's just something about him that draws me in.

He takes a step towards me. "About half an hour, I would wait all night if that is what it took." He gently cups my face in his hands, looking at me tenderly…mesmerising me. "What is wrong?"

I raise my hands to meet his as they hold my face and Luka gently brushes his lips against mine, making me almost gasp for breath and leaving me hungry for more. I pull myself together and take his hands from my face, not letting them go.

"It's just...sorry." How can I tell him that after only six days of being with him, the thought of returning home and never seeing him again is too much to bear? Luka squeezes my hands in comfort before I sit down on the edge of the bed.

"Sorry, I suppose everything that's happened is finally catching up with me. I guess I just wanted some time alone. Maybe we should exchange numbers?" I unlock my phone and hold it out towards him. "...I don't want you risking your job again just to find me."

He types his number into my phone and calls his number so he also has mine, before throwing my phone onto the bed and crouching down next to me, placing his hands on my legs. "Would you prefer me to leave? It is okay to need space."

Leaving is the last thing I want him to do, and judging by the fact his hand is slowly working its way up my leg, I think he knows that.

"Definitely not..."

I tug him closer to me, not wanting to waste another second of our time together. I should continue enjoying spending time with him now and just live for the moment. I'd rather do that than avoid him for the rest of the week and regret it for the rest of my life. Realising this, I kiss him more fervently than ever before.

I agree to stay at Luka's apartment again that night, not wanting to be away from him for another second longer than I have to.

A couple of hours later, I'm wearing one of Luka's T-shirt's as we sit together peering over the small Juliet balcony eating my leftover pizza and drinking a bottle of beer. There isn't much of a view from here, but it's still really pleasant all the same, just staring out at the world. I bring Luka up-to-date with my travelling plans and tell him with excitement how my first flight's now booked and is just a week or so away. He's really pleased for me.

Then he has some news for me. "I have something for you, for us. On Sunday, we have a day pass for the five star hotel, *The Grand Lapad Plaža*. We can spend the day together enjoying the private beach, we can eat and then..." He grins playfully, making me burst into fits of giggles.

"Mmm...that sounds perfect."

Luka and I stay up until the early hours, just talking. Things seem so easy between us, so comfortable. It's almost as though I've known him my whole life. When we finally get to bed at around 3:00 a.m. I fall asleep wrapped in his arms.

The next day, the day before Melita and Patrik's wedding, we do the usual walk back to the hotel. After I've eaten breakfast, I follow Luka's directions to Lapad's shopping centre in the hope I can find a dress suitable for the wedding. I do have a contingency plan of my black and white flowery sun dress but I feel like it's not dressy enough.

I think back to my wardrobe at home, if only I'd brought with me my new plum coloured off the shoulder dress that would have been perfect for the wedding. Oh well never mind, new dress here I come!

After two hours on my feet trying on nine different dresses, I finally settle for a strapless coral pink chiffon dress with just a teeny bit of diamante detail around the top. Along with this, I buy a pair of silver strappy sandals and thankfully, I already have plenty of jewellery with me and a silver bag, so I'm now fully prepared for what is set to be a wonderful day.

I'm almost back at the hotel when I pass by a shop I don't remember noticing before. They sell all of the usual beach goods, illuminous coloured li-lo's, hats, sunglasses and souvenirs, including some white lavender bags in the shape of angels. These are what catch my eye and I notice each one has a different word sewn across the front. Love, faith, believe and harmony, the words all stare out at me from the stitching. I feel like my subconscious self is compelling me to choose. I decide on 'believe' because I know that's what I need to do, to believe that everything will work out as it should.

For the rest of the day, I brush up on my Croatian in readiness for the wedding, at least if I can speak a few words of Croatian to Luka's relatives, I'll feel more polite.

I spend a few hours basking in the sun and catch up with Pam and Pete, who kindly invite me to eat with them that night. I'm so looking forward to the wedding that I make it an early night, but unfortunately without Luka. It feels quite strange not seeing him, but that feeling of excitement returns as I picture spending the day with him tomorrow.

Chapter 18

Feeling slightly overdressed for the bus in my wedding outfit, I opt for a taxi into town which takes me as close to the old town gate as possible. I pay the driver and step out into the hustle and bustle of the town and begin to walk as carefully as I can (stiletto heels and cobbled streets aren't the best mix) through the gate and towards Saint Blaise Church in the heart of Dubrovnik. I send a quick text to Luka to let him know I'm on my way down from the taxi.

Fellow tourists give me looks of surprise as I totter as best I can through the crowds, it must be obvious from what I'm wearing I'm on my way to wedding and a thought occurs to me, I wonder if they think I'm a local? Such an irrelevant thought I know, but one that makes me attempt to stride more confidently which can't be a bad thing.

As I turn the corner I feel the nerves begin, as I see the church ahead of me and what clearly seems to be the family of the bride and groom beginning to arrive outside. My eyes frantically begin to scan the group of people assembling themselves outside for Luka's familiar face and just as I start to wonder where to wait by myself until I see him, he emerges at my side.

My mouth immediately breaks into a smile when I see his face. He slides his arm around my waist and gently brushes my lips with his.

"You look stunning…" He tells me and my face beams all the more at his compliment.

Luka's wearing a perfectly cut navy blue suit, white shirt and navy blue tie, which only serve to make him look even more attractive. I'm struggling to keep my hands off him until I remind myself Luka's family are here and I don't want to give them the wrong first impression of me.

He maintains his hold of my hand as we walk towards the guests gathering at the church, it's now I begin to wonder what Luka's family will think of me being here.

Luka squeezes my hand. "There is nothing to be nervous about, they will love you…" He reassures me, obviously sensing my nerves.

Despite that and the fact that I'm fast falling for this man, faster than I thought could be possible, meeting the family already, it's like a whirlwind. Again, the thought strikes me that this is way too much for what is supposed to be a holiday fling. But if I stop thinking about what it's supposed to be and just enjoy the way things are going between us, it feels right.

The sea of people standing before me are dressed in wonderfully bright colours, all chattering excitedly between themselves as Luka leads the way through the throng of people and to another familiar face, his brother Aleksander.

Alek greets me warmly before we hear the sound of cheering and shouting as Patrik – the groom, his best man and two ushers arrive, following a flag bearer which I'm told is called a *barjaktar*. Luka briefly explains to me how important the Croatian flag is on a wedding day in Croatia. The photographer takes shots from various different angles as the *barjaktar* - with his obviously very loud personality, leads Patrik towards the church before the ushers announce we are to go inside for the bride's arrival.

I see guests taking endless photos of the scene around us. "Didn't you bring your camera?" I wonder aloud.

We climb the steps leading up to the door of the church where Luka gestures for me to enter first.

"I took photos this morning, Melita doesn't want me to take any more until tonight, she wants me to enjoy their day."

The church is as beautiful inside as it is outside and the altar is home to a huge statue of Saint Blaise. We take a seat near the front on the left-hand side, as I see various relatives and friends acknowledging Luka and looking at me in wonderment as he glances around us. A few minutes later, an elegant looking lady takes her seat in front of us as she waves various greetings in Croatian to the guests.

Luka leans in close to me. "That is my mother, I will introduce you later."

His mother appears to be in her mid-60s, has grey hair expertly styled into a French twist and as far as I can see is wearing a very flattering knee length champagne coloured scoop neck dress. She turns around in our direction, seemingly looking for her sons and smiling at them proudly before moving her eyes to me and lifting her hand to gesture a small wave in my direction, instantly dispelling my nerves with her friendliness.

Just a few moments pass before Melita on her father's arm enters the church. Melita looks absolutely radiant wearing an ivory dress with sweetheart neckline, mermaid cut around her hips leading to a fuller skirt of organza and lace with beautiful crystal beading. She wears her hair in a soft braided up do at the nape of her neck, with an eye-catching crystal hair slide visible on one side, giving her a very sophisticated modern day look.

Melita is followed by three bridesmaids, the first of which I'm told, is Patrik's six year old niece who looks so pretty in an ivory and burgundy dress. There then follows Melita's two closest friends, both wearing rich burgundy red dresses with a V-neck neckline with lovely tiny crystals dotted along the hem of the dress, which sits at knee length.

There's barely a dry eye left in the church (including myself) as they exchange vows. Even though I have no idea what's being said, the atmosphere is so charged with emotion that I can't help but shed a small tear. Much to my annoyance it also makes me think of Mark and of our wedding day, and as I take a sideways glance at Luka who's listening closely, I wonder to myself - is he thinking back to his wedding day too?

As though he can detect my gaze upon him, Luka reaches for my hand as it rests in my lap and squeezes it gently before letting it go again. A couple of hymns are sang where I do my best to pronounce the words from the hymn sheet to myself in my head, resulting in a slight snigger from Luka, as he witnesses the concentration on my face. Once Patrik and Melita are pronounced husband and wife, we retreat from the church and to my amazement, are greeted with the jubilant sound of an accordion and guitar being played outside as sightseers sit back and watch.

The bride and groom look blissfully happy as they stand at the bottom of the steps and are met with masses of colourful confetti being flung their way. The music starts up again charging the atmosphere further as people begin clapping, cheering and whooping in delight. The music is infectious as people sing the old folk songs at the top of their lungs.

Dancers in traditional costumes begin to *Kolo* dance, whereby they form a circle with their arms around each other and move round and round and in and out. I stand and watch, clapping along as Luka takes my hand for us to join in with some of the other guests. I'm genuinely having so much fun experiencing a Croatian wedding first-hand and feel giddy with the joy of such a warm atmosphere.

Family and friends in succession go over to congratulate Patrik and Melita, and when it's Luka's turn, he takes me along with him. I tell the happy couple how amazing they look as I kiss them both fondly on the cheek. Melita keeps a hold of one of my hands and squeezes it tightly.

"I am so glad you could come. We saw you doing *Kolo*, we will make you Croatian yet!"

People are still enjoying the music and chatting as I spy Luka's parents coming towards us. The pang of apprehension returns as Luka embraces them both one at a time as they talk, in what seems like definitely happiness (a good sign) in Croatian. Luka introduces his mother as Karmen, she once again greets me with a warm smile and kisses me on each cheek.

"It is lovely to meet you, Luisa. This is my husband - Luka's father, Alen."

Alen then takes my hand kindly as he also meets me with the standard two kisses. Alen appears slightly older than Karmen and is fairly stocky in his build with greying hair, I can definitely make out Luka's face in his.

Luka's parents chat with us for a few minutes before they are bombarded by more relatives, congratulating them on their daughter's marriage.

The wedding crowd then begin the procession of the walk through the town and around to *The Sands Hotel* for the reception, the folk music continues to play as the musicians follow us. Lookers-on join with the clapping and whistling and general merriment as we make the 10 minute walk to the hotel. Turning the corner a short while later, I see the welcome sight of the sea and the impressive structure that is *The Sands Hotel.*

The building is gleaming in the late afternoon sunshine with a glass fronted inviting foyer, complete with red carpet leading out to the footpath, especially for the bride and groom. As the wedding party stroll through the foyer, waiters and waitresses wearing white shirts, black trousers and blue waistcoats are on hand to offer every guest a glass of *rakija*, which is known as a drink of celebration.

I sip my *rakija* and am startled at how strong it is as it hits the back of my throat, causing me to cough out loud. Luka throws his glass straight back, drinking the whole thing in one before rubbing my back as I cough.

"It is strong for you?"

I take a deep breath. "Just a little."

Ladies on the left-hand side of the room give each guest a rosemary buttonhole wrapped in red, white and blue ribbon as we follow the rest of the wedding party through the hotel. We walk through a door at the back of the hotel and down a few steps, the dramatic sight before me makes me gasp in joy.

The outside terrace area of the hotel where the reception is being held houses round tables of 12, decorated with fresh white tablecloths with vases of iris croatica and red and white roses. Tea light candles sit waiting to be lit. Just over the wall is the magnificent view of the sea with some of the buildings of the old town also visible.

Luka tells me Melita and Patrik don't have a seating plan, other than for the top table with the bride and groom and immediate family, meaning Luka and I can sit together. We take a seat at one of the tables and are joined by a couple of Melita's friends along with Kristijan, Alek and some of Luka's cousins.

Everyone is so animated with the pleasure of the day, most people on our table speak good English, so I manage to join in the conversations. The wedding breakfast is served in buffet style and consists of different meats, vegetables and a variety of local sauces, salads and yummy cakes. After the meal, we are each offered a drink of schnapps - it would be rude to refuse and thankfully it's certainly weaker than the earlier *rakija*.

Darkness slowly fades in as the tea light candles on the tables now burn beautifully bright, bringing an air of cosiness and intimacy and Luka asks me to take a walk with him. I'm feeling rather merry after the endless drinks and as I stand to walk, my head feels nicely woozy with contentment.

We continue to walk alongside the wall overlooking the sea, through the hotel grounds before stopping to marvel further at the view. Luka puts his arms around me from behind, I can feel the lovely warmth of his breath on the side of my face. I look down at his arms around me, his jacket from the ceremony long gone and the sleeves on his white shirt rolled up, I feel happier than I've felt in a really, long time. The whole mess of things with Mark seeming like a lifetime ago.

Luka sighs contentedly. "I wish we were staying here tonight, no one would notice if we disappeared upstairs for 10 minutes." I can hear that cheeky smile of his in his voice.

"10 minutes..." I nod my head. "... or half an hour..." I giggle, suddenly aching to feel his skin against mine. I turn around to face him and give him a long kiss on the lips.

He runs a hand slowly down my arm. "Are you enjoying the wedding?"

"I am and your family are really nice. Your parents didn't mind me coming?"

I wonder what he's told them (if anything) about me. I can just see it now *'Mom, Dad, a woman staying the hotel where I work, who I am sleeping with is coming to the wedding'*. Luka laughs heartily before kissing me on the lips and leading me back to the reception, leaving my question hanging in the humid evening air.

The music is now increasingly louder and already, people are on their feet and dancing the night away. Luka and I are almost back at our table when a couple of Melita's friends who sat with us during the wedding breakfast appear at my side and attempt to drag me on to the dance floor with them. I can tell by the look on their faces and from the amount of alcohol we've now all consumed that it'll be far easier to give in and join them, so I resist the urge to turn them down and begin to enjoy the party as it reaches full swing.

As I glance around the terrace, I can see Luka laughing and joking with his friends and family and taking the occasional natural photo of the guests. Things are so different to how they were just a week ago. At this moment in time, on the dance floor with my newfound friends, I feel so unrestricted and that feeling that I can do anything that has gradually taken a hold over me since I met Luka, is becoming stronger.

Luka looks so relaxed, the whiteness of his shirt emphasising his light sun-kissed skin, the top button of his shirt undone and his sleeves rolled up. His stance now against the bar as he leans back on both elbows, drink in hand, makes me feel weak at the knees. However will I be able to leave him behind and forget about him? *I need another drink!*

The music changes to a slow number and I see Luka's watching me. He swiftly knocks back the last dregs of his drink, his eyes not leaving mine, before he strides purposely in my direction and takes me in his strong arms to dance. I get lost in the music, lost in this moment of perfectness under the stars, surrounded by these wonderful, warm and friendly people, with the heat from the day still holding out.

He smiles mischievously. "Do you remember the last time we danced together?"

Luka brings out a matching smile in me. "Mmm, hard to believe that was only days ago."

We lock eyes as he grins happily. Suddenly his gaze has such intensity which makes my pulse begin to quicken before he glances away, almost distractedly. He loosens his hold around me and lightly brushes my arms with his hands before steering me over to the bar.

Chapter 19

A feeling that my tongue is glued to the roof of my mouth and that I'm so thirsty I could quite easily drink the sea dry is what meets me as I wake the next morning. As I open my eyes, I see Luka walking towards me wearing just his crisp white boxers and thankfully carrying a large glass of water in my direction. I slowly drag myself into a sitting position as I take the glass from him before drinking the water down in one go.

I take in Luka's appearance. "How do you look so fresh?"

He smiles before taking the glass from me, and putting it down on the bedside table.

"I take it you are not feeling so fresh?" He laughs, kissing me on my forehead.

I close my eyes for a split second as I feel his lips meet my skin, which starts the immediate feeling of sparks flying throughout my body.

Considering when we got back to Luka's apartment at a little before 3:00 a.m. this morning he could barely stand - I'm not denying I wasn't struggling a little myself, there seems to be no signs of a hangover whatsoever for him. It was the first time we've spent the night together and literally just slept and nothing else.

"I know a good cure for headaches." Luka flirts, as a smirk forces its way onto my face.

Reaching forwards he tugs me onto his lap, my legs wrap around his waist as we kiss passionately, before he lifts me and places me down gently on the bed before taking my mind off my headache for the next half an hour.

***

Later that morning, we arrive at the five-star *Grand Lapad Plaza Hotel* to use our day passes. The reception area is wonderfully light and airy, decorated minimally in soft greens. The receptionist directs us through to the pool area, which is even more decadent than the *Sun Elegance Hotel*, which has been my home for almost two weeks, well, when I haven't been at Luka's.

We stroll through the pool area which has king-size day beds dotted around covered in extremely comfortable looking cushions. I see a couple of hammocks cleverly hung in a secluded area surrounded by palm trees. We walk out onto the private pebble beach, where a four poster day bed, complete with white canopies has been reserved for us. I feel like a child as I jump up to test out the comfort level.

Luka peels off his red T-shirt. "I cannot take all of the credit for this I am afraid. This is the hotel where Melita works, so she pulled some strings."

Luka slides onto the day bed next to me, his delicious masculine scent filling the air around us.

"She really likes you." He continues. "That is why I did not tell you, that night in town when you met her. I did not tell you she was my sister at first."

"Really? I'm confused."

"I wanted her to meet you, the real you. So, if I had told you who she was...you maybe would have acted nervously. Or maybe even thought it was too much meeting someone in my family..."

I laugh to myself, remembering that night vividly where I actually thought for a short time that Luka was Melita's fiancé. Just then, the waiter appears next to us to offer us a drink, and I think we surprise both him and each other when we order water, still feeling the after-effects from last night.

"You obviously value your sister's opinion then?"

I'm not sure what I'm hoping to achieve by asking this. What do I want him to say? *'Yes, I do, and she really likes you, which makes me like you even more... please stay here and live with me...'*

"She did not get on well with Amra, never did. My last girlfriend a while ago, Kristina, she was not sure about her and it did not last, so..." He shrugs his shoulders. "Our parents always joked that Melita was trying to be my mother."

I sit up, resting myself on my elbows. *Kristina? As in, Kristina, the rep?* I need to muster a response, I need to act casual so that he doesn't notice that I'm bothered if it is the same person.

"Melita's trying to protect her big brother, I guess."

The waiter arrives with our bottled water and pours us each a glass filled with ice and after just one sip, I can feel the water cooling me down instantly but it does nothing to dispel the knot of jealousy that I can feel in my stomach, since I realised that Luka and Kristina do have history. It's no good, I know I've got to ask. I take another sip of water.

"So is that the same Kristina from the hotel?" I shuffle awkwardly, hoping that I just seem as though I'm being nosy more than anything else.

Luka puts his drink aside and stretches out beside me. "Yes, but it only lasted a couple of months, we have stayed friends."

He closes his eyes and pulls his sunglasses down from his head. Why does this bother me? I'm wondering if it's because when I saw them talking a couple of days ago, she seemed to be openly flirting with him. It's none of my business. In two days, I'll be boarding my flight home, we both knew this would only be a fling so I've got no right to be jealous, especially when there isn't really anything to be jealous of.

After some time relaxing and enjoying the beautiful sea view and endless bowls of crisps that seem to keep appearing each time we order a drink, Luka manages to persuade me to hire a jet ski.

I feel pretty nervous at the thought of going on. "I've always wanted to try one, but I never have."

Luka jumps up from the lounger, and takes my hand. "Well then, what are we waiting for?"

I'm excited and terrified at the same time, but the promise that Luka will rescue me if I fall in makes it seem very much worthwhile. We walk to the shore and are given life jackets to wear, which suddenly makes it feel even more real.

Luka climbs on first and tries to steady the jet ski as I tentatively climb aboard and clasp my arms around his waist in readiness. He places his hand on my bare leg comfortingly before he reaches for the handle bars and starts up the engine as we feel the jet ski start to vibrate with the force of the engine. We begin with a steady pace, calmly flowing across the water before our speed builds up and we begin gently bouncing up and down, the wind in our faces and the cooling sea spray splashing intermittently upon us. The whole time I'm squeezing Luka, as I enjoy the seemingly endless view of the sea stretching out before us.

We arrive back to shore and I feel exhilarated as I swap places with Luka for my turn to drive…and his turn to be scared. As we head off bounding back out to sea with him holding me, his one hand around my waist and the other resting on my thigh, I can feel the heat flowing from his hands and I instantly know he's feeling at this point, as full of life as I am.

After another exchange of seats, we again reach the shore line where we're told our time is up. I can feel my legs shaking as we retreat back to our sunbed and we both leap playfully beside each other and lie down to catch our breaths. Luka pulls me over to him as he lies back and I support myself on one elbow, with my other hand resting on his smooth broad chest.

He traces the outline of my jaw with his thumb. "You cannot say you did not enjoy that."

"It was amazing, thank you for making me do it."

He lifts his head to meet his lips with mine and I can feel the urgency building between us. I pull away, trying to steady my breath and glance from side to side as we both laugh mischievously.

For lunch we decide to eat at the 'More Tavern' which is set alongside the beach with seats underneath a beautiful pergola with soft white sunshade's secured on the top, offering welcome cover from the sun as people enjoy their freshly prepared food. A chalkboard tells us today's special is slow cooked lamb with garlic and rosemary and if the aroma of the cooking is anything to go by it will be absolutely delicious, but it feels a bit heavy for me at lunchtime today after last night. I decide on a tunny salad as it's known here, whilst Luka opts for the spaghetti bolognese.

I stare out to sea watching people as they enjoy the different types of boats on hire. Along with the jet skis there are pedalos and water skiing also available at the next bay, along with paddle boarding.

I nod my head in the direction of the signage advertising the other water sports. "After lunch, why don't we hire a pedalo?"

Luka looks like he needs to think about it before responding. "Okay, but I want you to know that you will be doing most of the peddling!"

He signals a waiter over to our table and to my surprise, he asks him to take a photo of us together. The waiter enthusiastically agrees, although he looks terrified when he takes a hold of Luka's camera.

Luka gets up from his seat and walks around to my side of the table before crouching down next to me, our eyes level with each other's as he puts his arm around me and we mould together, closer to each other. The waiter snaps away, before almost dropping the camera, but managing to take another photograph as he thankfully catches the camera before it drops to the floor, much to our relief. The waiter mutters his profuse apologies and hands the camera back to Luka.

After lunch, we gently stroll along the shore line of the private beach taking in the views. The beach is only sparsely full of holidaymakers, meaning that all we can hear is the soothing sound of the waves and the gentle crunch of the pebbles moving beneath our flip-flops.

I look skyward, feeling the heat from the sun intensifying on my face as I take a deep breath before releasing it slowly.

Luka tugs lightly at my hand. "Are you okay?"

I turn my head towards him, my smile growing as I do so. "I'm fine." ...*and it's all thanks to you,* I continue in my head.

I feel that wrench in my heart once more as he smiles at me. I'm feeling so much more optimistic with my travel plans ready and waiting and I've made a great start on my second book, but I know that the contentment I have when I'm with Luka will soon disappear, a thought which makes me feel as though I'm leaving a big piece of my heart behind.

We scramble onto the ready and waiting yellow pedalo and let the sea begin to carry us outwards.

I note Luka slouches back in his seat which makes me have to pedal harder.

"You really weren't joking when you said I'd be doing most of the hard work then?"

He laughs and shrugs his shoulders before giving in and helping. "If my legs are hurting later, I may need a massage."

"I'll have to see what I can do."

Luka leans to his right, skimming the water with his hand. "You are looking forward to your travels?"

I'm suddenly aware that the pedalo seems to be rocking more to the right, making me attempt to lean more to the left. "Yeah, definitely."

The sound of the waves rings louder in my ears as I try to push out of my mind the heavy heartedness of leaving Luka behind. "Have you ever wanted to travel?"

He sits back up right. "There are places I want to see, photographs I want to take… I have always been satisfied that one day I will go, but not really thought about when."

"You should really get your photos out there more, they're brilliant…maybe you should go to local restaurants again?"

He thinks momentarily. "Mmm, I would like to…perhaps I should."

"You definitely should, the pictures you take are too good to be hidden away from people."

He smiles, looking rather coy for the first time.

We enjoy a couple of minutes rest from peddling, our pedalo keeping us afloat in the calming waters. I realise I don't even know if he's ever been to the UK and so I ask him.

"No…I have never been…maybe I can visit you some time…one day?"

My heart lurches at the thought. "I'd like that."

Without warning, Luka yanks off his T-shirt and jumps into the water, making the pedalo sway sharply from side to side. His head appears from under the water as he laughs, whilst I lean embarrassingly across the other side, desperate to keep the balance.

He swims around to my side of the pedalo. "Stop panicking…you will not fall in." His strong shoulders and arms are moving him closer in my direction as he beckons me into the water to join him.

"No way…we can't both get out, this thing might capsize."

"Says who?" He watches me, his eyes penetrating almost through me. "Come on, I know it is deeper out here but I will look after you."

How can I resist? Without thinking about it, I peel away my dress leave it on my seat, and attempt to slide down the slide at the back of the boat and into the sea. Straightaway, Luka swims up close to me and takes me into the safety of his arms. I wrap my arms around his neck as he frees his arms from around my waist and pulls my legs up around him.

"Just hold on until you get your confidence and then you can swim alone."

It springs to mind how that's what we are, me and Luka. Since we met he's built my confidence more so and my self-esteem, made me realise I can do things I only ever dreamt of doing and now, *'I have to swim alone'*, only I don't want to swim alone…not without Luka.

Eventually I brave it and begin to swim around our pedalo and even enjoy just floating, looking up at the cloudless sky. Time seems to slow down as I try my hardest to empty my mind of any negative thoughts about going home.

Luka climbs back on board and helps me to join him as gracefully as I can before we head back to shore. Jumping off the boat, he shakes his legs around one at a time.

"I will definitely need a massage." He jokes. "Come on, I need to run to loosen my muscles."

On that, he grabs at my hand and begins to jog, with me following behind. I pick up the pace, let go of his hand and begin to overtake him.

With our sun lounger in sight I hear Luka gaining on me and finally, he wins and makes it back first.

I slow down to a walk as he stands next to our lounger teasingly looking at his watch. I'm nearing him when he jogs back to meet me and to my surprise, he scoops me up into his arms, quite literally sweeping me off my feet before resting me down on the sun lounger and falling down laughing beside me out of breath. I playfully punch him on the arm.

He looks amused. "You are a sore loser?"

I lean back as I wait for my breath to return to normal as I hear my mobile spring to life from my beach bag. We look at each other as I yank my bag towards me by the strap and shuffle around inside it before locating my phone to see a message from Mark.

"Hope you're okay, I'm missing you but will see you very soon XX"

Irritation fills my body rapidly and I sharply exhale.

Luka watches me. "It is him?"

I hand my phone to Luka, with the message still on screen as my mood drops.

"Ovaj čovjek!" He snarls. "Sorry…" He rubs my leg before re-reading the message and handing my phone back. "You should change your number when you get home…"

I switch my phone off and purposely bury it at the bottom of my bag in the hope that the further away it is, the less Mark can get to me. Luka edges his way to the top of the lounger to be next to me and enfolds me in his arms, holding me close with my head resting on his chest, I can hear his heart beat quickening as he holds me.

Chapter 20

As our day comes to an end, I head back to my hotel to get showered and changed. I look in the mirror and my lightly bronzed skin is a refreshing sight.

I step out of the shower and wrap myself in one of the hotel's gloriously soft towels, enjoying the scent of jasmine from the fabric softener. I take a bottle of water from the mini fridge and I sit out on the balcony, resting my legs on the second chair and watching the people below enjoying the last few hours of the sun. I'll really miss Dubrovnik when I go home.

Glancing inside I spy my beach bag in the corner of the room where I left it and the memory of me earlier burying my phone at the bottom of it returns to me. I contemplate calling my parents.

I heave a heavy sigh to myself and return back indoors to grab my phone. My Dad answers and hearing his voice, I realise how nice it is to have some familiarity from back home.

I can hear the concern in his voice. "You sound well sweetheart, but how are you?"

I head back indoors, sliding the balcony door closed and make myself comfortable sitting cross-legged on the bed. "I am well Dad in fact, I feel better than I have for a really long time." It feels so wholesome hearing myself say this aloud.

"That's good to hear. Are you looking forward to coming home…sorry, that's probably a stupid question…."

I interrupt him as I recognise how awkward he feels from his tone of voice. "That's okay. If I'm honest, no I'm not looking forward to it but…"

Now it's his turn to interrupt. "Well, it won't be for long, your mother said you've been keeping in touch with a few text messages. You know you're welcome to stay with us for as long as you need to and I mean before you go travelling and when you come back."

I smile to myself, grateful that I haven't disappointed them too much and that they're on my side.

"Thanks, I'm really grateful for that. Ben hasn't done anything stupid has he, not seen Mark I mean?"

My Dad falls silent.

"… Dad, tell me he hasn't?"

"Luisa, we're your family, and we're not going to stand by and watch that man make a fool of you again. Ben and I have been around to the house, yes."

I get to my feet, and begin an aggravated pace around the room. "He's not worth it, Dad. I wish you'd have just left it!"

My Dad continues to tell me they didn't just go to confront Mark, they filled two suitcases with as many of my belongings as they could. Tears spring to my eyes as he continues to talk, I actually feel quite moved they thought of doing this for me. At least now I don't really have a reason to have to go back to the house, other than to get the last few bits and pieces, a far cry from the picture I imagined of fighting with Mark as I packed my things to leave him.

I stifle a sniff. "Thank you."

"Anything for my girl. If you need us to pick you up from the airport when you get back, let us know."

I get dressed in my cream short-sleeved skater style dress with the different coloured butterflies, a dress I'd been saving for one of the last nights of our holiday in the hope I'd look more tanned. I leave my long hair down and emphasise my eyes with eyeliner and mascara, before adding a hint of bronzer on my cheek bones.

As Luka isn't working tonight at the restaurant, we made plans for me to meet him at his apartment before going out to eat. Although I don't leave until Tuesday night, as Luka will be working for the next two nights…this will be our last full night together.

As Luka opens the front door when I arrive, he greets me with a much needed kiss on the lips.

"You look gorgeous, as always."

I squeeze his bicep beneath his grey shirt. "Mmm, so do you."

Making my way over to the small breakfast bar area at the kitchen-cum-lounge he follows me and produces a red rose.

"Now, I am not normally this…how would you say…soppy, but…for you."

This makes me blush as I take the rose from him. "It's beautiful, thank you."

He leans down to meet his lips to mine.

To finish off our wonderful day together, we choose an intimate restaurant in a picturesque spot along the coastal path. As we sit down opposite each other, the sun is slowly beginning to set over the sea next to us, filling the air with the warmest glow I think I've ever seen. It's truly amazing.

I can't believe it as I take it all in. "Wow…"

Luka follows my gaze and our legs meet underneath the table, forcing goosebumps to appear as we make eye contact. Our first course of a tuna pâté arrives and although we're still chatting with ease, I've noticed a definite shift of something in the air between us. Luka barely touches his main course and seems distant somehow. When the waiter asks if we want to see the dessert menu he answers no for both of us and requests the bill.

I wait until the waiter's out of earshot. "Is something wrong?"

He leans to take my hand across the table, flashing one of his side grins. "No, sorry, I just…cannot wait for us to be alone."

His words do something to my insides, making my temperature begin to rise. I start to wonder how Luka feels about me leaving, is it hurting him as much as it's hurting me, the thought of us being apart and most likely never seeing each other again? I'm sure it isn't, but I know that our fling…our time together has meant something to him at least.

As soon as we pay the bill, we walk back through the humid darkness of the night and back to his apartment.

The air around us seems still and somewhat calming on the walk back. We walk slowly, with no great rush, pausing every now and again at the railings along the coast to look out into the distance. Each pit stop we make, although the angle is slightly different, the view doesn't change. Each one is equally as beautiful as the last with the moonlight dancing on the sea as the boats anchored in for the night join in, bobbing up and down. Feeling Luka next to me as I contemplate the vista is equally satisfying.

"I can't believe I'll be leaving all this behind." I rest my elbow onto the rail and lean forward supporting my chin with my hand.

Luka leans forward alongside me. "At least you have happy memories of Dubrovnik." He nudges me playfully with his arm before looking at me, and at this moment, I don't want to be anywhere else in the world.

I lean my head onto his shoulder and continue gazing out, before he brings me back to reality with a kiss on my hand and pulls me in the direction of his home.

Closing the front door on our day, we head straight for his bedroom and immediately begin to undress one another, slowly taking in every inch of each other before collapsing down onto the bed as we kiss tenderly and curl up in each other's arms before drifting off to sleep. Although kissing is all we've done tonight, it feels right somehow. For me this is about more than just the physical, I'm falling in love with him and there isn't anything I can do to stop it, even leaving the country in 48 hours won't stop my feelings for him.

***

Opening the door to my hotel room the next morning after leaving Luka's, I feel sad that our familiar routine of walking back to the hotel together each morning is almost at an end. I do my usual shower and change and dress for breakfast, today in my black shorts and red vest top.

Retrieving my phone from the safe, I walk across the room, waiting for my phone to switch on and settle down into the armchair in the corner. A message from Jodie comes through, telling me to enjoy my last full day in Dubrovnik with, as she calls him, *'your gorgeous Croatian man.'* I snigger to myself before typing a short reply telling her that I fully intend to.

Unwelcome tears begin to appear in my eyes…I've got to pull myself together. As it's still early, I lay down on the bed in an attempt to relax myself and calm my mind before drifting off to a light sleep.

I jolt awake at the sound of persistent knocking on my door. The confusion of having been woken up suddenly makes my heart almost beat out of my chest. I remember now I didn't put the do not disturb sign outside, maybe it's housekeeping.

I smooth my hair down and as I open the door, I can't believe it. Surely, I'm still asleep, surely this isn't real. I feel like my whole world has just come crashing down around me, as standing on the other side of the door, is Mark.

Chapter 21

His face lights up like a Christmas tree when he sees me and in contrast, I feel my expression darken as extreme exasperation fills my body. For a split second, I think he's going to try and kiss me hello, before he senses my anger and casually takes a step backward.

"Aren't you going to invite me in? After all, it is our room."

There are no words, what more can I say to this man?

"What the hell are you doing here?" Realising the door's open and the neighbours can probably hear me loud and clear, I turn down the volume before speaking again. "Why have you come back here, Mark?"

He looks disappointed but what did he expect me to say?

"Luisa, I'm sorry, it's time we talked properly face-to-face. Now, are you going to let me in, or do you want everyone to know what's going on between us?"

I open the door wider for him to walk in, his small trolley case dragging behind him.

"Nothing *is* going on between us Mark, now tell me what are you doing here?!"

He makes himself at home on the corner of the bed, slipping off his pumps and doing his best to make eye contact with me but I'm otherwise engaged, pacing the room with my hands to my head in pure irritation.

"You look well…really well in fact."

His compliments only help to increase my frustration, forcing me to snap. "Maybe it has something to do with being away from you!"

He sighs before shaking his head in that mocking manner that he uses so often, igniting my anger as I vent some more.

"Stop it, I can't keep going through this over and over again. I've had enough of your bull shit! What the hell is wrong with you? What do you want?"

He gets to his feet. In the light, I can see he looks like he hasn't slept in days. "I've come to take you home, back to our home."

"Did the fact that Ben and my Dad came to fetch most of my belongings not tell you anything?"

He looks at the floor as I continue. "...I'm not coming home, not back to you, we are finished for good, forever, do you understand?!"

He gestures towards my left hand. "You took your wedding ring off?"

I reach for my jewellery roll and see my wedding and engagement rings sparkling back at me from where I left them a little over a week ago. It seems like such a long time ago since I wore these every day, I was a different person then, a person who was trapped and desperate to live their life without knowing how to. I grab for Mark's hand and force the rings into his grip, his eyes staring at me as I do so.

"I don't want them back you should be wearing them, I want my wife back." He holds them out to me and I push his hand away forcefully. "...I know a lot has happened, but you can't leave me..." He looks like a broken man.

If I was watching this moment in a film I'd almost feel sorry for him, that is until I remembered what brought us to this situation in the first place - his affair followed by, who knows how many other affairs.

I feel like I'm talking to a brick wall as no matter what I say, he just isn't listening, I'm exhausted. I sit in the armchair with my head in my hands as he kneels down beside me, prompting me to move away, I can't bear to be this close to him.

He spins around and begins to follow me across the room. "Tell me what I can do, I'll do anything to make it right, what will it take?"

"What will it take?" I yell. "…try turning the clock back to the first affair you had. Actually, no, don't! I don't care anymore, Mark, I really don't care. I just want to get on with the rest of my life."

Luka's face comes into my mind and I remember our plan to meet outside when he finishes work, 10 minutes ago.

Mark catches me checking the time. "What? Am I keeping you from sunbathing? This is our marriage we're talking about here and you're checking your watch. You didn't even want to let me into the room did you, into *our* room?"

He opens his suitcase and much to my disgust, starts to hang up the few items he has with him.

I can't take any more. "Our room? I've hardly slept in our room, since you went home!"

Mark stops unpacking, looking at me with concern. "You mean…you're having trouble sleeping?"

"I've met someone Mark, someone who makes me feel good about myself, someone who has helped me realise I can follow my dreams…"

He sits down, I don't think he was expecting that. "Okay…. so, you've had your fun, maybe it will help you understand what I did and help us to move on together." He holds out his hand. It's like he thinks he has the answer for everything.

"No! You're not listening to me…I haven't done this to get back at you, it just happened and he's the best thing that ever happened to me…"

I take the door card from the light slot and without thinking I head down stairs, through reception and out onto the car park. I dread turning around for the fear that Mark has followed me, but when I do, thankfully he's not there.

Luka's leaning against the wall when I reach his side. "Luisa, I thought you had gone back to bed." He laughs, before seeing my hassled expression. "What is it, has something happened?"

"It's Mark, he's here - he's come back…" I rub my head despairingly with a rising sense of panic filling my body.

Luka looks back towards the hotel. "Does he know about me?"

"I told him. I'm sorry…he was going on and on about me going home to him and it just came out. I thought maybe it would make him realise." Luka glances over my shoulder and takes my hand as I see Mark pacing towards us.

"Look, do not panic. Pack your things…everything and I will be here waiting for you."

Mark stands next to me, glaring at us. "You do realise he's probably sleeping with every other lonely woman, every tourist he can get his hands on? You've chosen the wrong one this time mate, she's married so go on, crawl back home and mind your own business. If I wasn't sure she was only doing this to get back at me, you'd be on the floor by now."

Dread washes well and truly over me as Luka storms in his direction and I use all my strength to pull him back. "No, Luka I don't want this, it's ridiculous...he has to realise."

Luka stares at him, I've never seen anything bother him before... until now.

"I know she is married, but you do not deserve her! As for sleeping with other women, maybe that is what you do but I do not." He shrugs his shoulders as he speaks.

Something about the way he says those words, very brief but they ring true. They're more powerful than anything Mark could say.

Mark laughs to himself. "You expect me to believe that? I suppose she does..."

Luka looks at me questioningly. I know by the look on his face he's respectfully biting his tongue as he knows I don't want a scene.

"I will be here for you." He mutters.

I look back at Mark before answering Luka. "It's fine you can go, I'll see you back there..."

Mark begins to laugh again, self-righteously before walking back towards the hotel.

Luka shakes his head. "I will wait. Promise me you will call security if you need to. Actually I will come with you..." He begins to walk towards the hotel until I pull him back toward me.

"No Luka, he'll make a scene, I know him. You wait here, I'll be fine."

Back in my hotel room, I tug my case from underneath the bed and frantically begin to pack my things. Mark opens the mini fridge, and begins to pour whiskey into a small tumbler, as he laughs to himself. "You really do look pathetic Luisa, you're making a fool of yourself."

If he does that one more time, I think I'll scream.

"Do you know something Mark? It's clear to me that you don't want a wife… I don't think you ever did. But the problem is you don't want anyone else to have me either!"

Everything gets thrown into my case, no folding, and no carefulness. I just have to get away from him as I continue to bombard him. "…when I get home, I'll be filing for divorce." I snap, not even looking at Mark as I speak.

He drinks his whiskey back in one sharp gulp. "I can't get divorced, how will that look at work?" He slams the glass down in fury.

I fling my toiletries into my case before starting on my shoes. It's amazing how quickly you can pack when you need to. "That's all it boils down to for you, work, work, work. Well, guess what, you *will* be getting divorced. Considering your colleagues knew about that first trollop I doubt it will be a great surprise anyway."

Next I open the safe, throwing my passport, ticket home, mobile and remaining cash into my bag before one final check around as I notice my bikini on the balcony where it sat drying overnight and dash outside to retrieve it.

Mark stands hands on hips. "You know I love my job, just like you loved yours at that little travel agents." His patronising tone returns.

I zip up my suitcase and heave it onto the floor. "Yes, I did love my job there, much to your disappointment. I know it was never good enough for you, but I don't care anymore."

He throws his head back laughing. "And you have the nerve to criticise me for sleeping around when that's exactly what you've been doing since I went home? I bet you were so pleased when I left, went after the first available man did you?"

I shake my head in despair. "Now who's pathetic? I thought we were happily married, I loved you more than anything in the world and you ruined everything. I would never have dreamed of cheating on you, and that's the difference between us..." I pull the handle of my suitcase up. "...you and I have been over for a really long time, and you know that as much as I do, I've moved on now. You had no problem in moving on to other women when we were together, my brother even caught you in bed with that woman a few days after you left here...so don't you dare judge me!

I pick up the handle of my case and leave the room before Mark even has a chance to reply. As I reach the top of the stairs, I'm surprised to see Pam and Pete waiting for the lift with their cases packed, I forgot they were going home the day before me. Pete does a double take when he sees me with my case.

Pam turns around, her short hair freshly curled with tongs and her makeup expertly applied, but I can still see the look of concern on her face. "Luisa, I thought you weren't leaving until tomorrow?"

"Mark has comeback...I've got to get away."

Pam's mouth falls open in shock. "Ohhh no..."

The lift announces its arrival with the usual *ping!* and the three of us and our cases shuffle inside. As the doors of the lift close I breathe a sigh of relief.

Pam places a protective arm around my shoulders. "Where're you going?"

I smile at her and realise how much I'm going to miss her. "I'll be spending my last night at Luka's, but anyway, enough about me...have you both enjoyed your holiday?"

Pam tilts her head with an expression of empathy, clearly understanding my need to change the subject. "Luisa...our stay has been wonderful, it's just a shame it's come to an end."

Leaving the sanctity of the lift, I glance around hoping I won't see Mark. Pam and Pete join the queue of people waiting to check out and I wait with them for a moment, realising I'll have to say my goodbyes to two people who have been such good friends to me for the past couple of weeks.

Pete looks really sad for the first time since I met him, his savage sunburn now giving way to peeling, as Pam parks her case down and rummages in her handbag before producing a pen and an old receipt.

"You must keep in touch with us..." She begins to scribble down a telephone number and email address. "...and I really mean that Luisa, we can't become those people you meet on holiday and swear you'll keep in touch with but don't."

"You see this is why you need a mobile."

She holds out the scribbled details towards me and I take it from her, before throwing my arms around her in an embrace.

"I'll keep in touch…I promise." Pulling away, I notice Pam has tears in her eyes which in turn makes me feel emotional too.

Pam leans to whisper into my ear. "Just remember to always follow your heart, it's the only way you will always be happy. Tell him how you feel before it's too late…" She gives me a knowing look which stuns me for a moment, certainly giving me something to think about.

"Oh, Pam, I can't thank you enough for listening to me, for your advice…"

She rubs my arm in comfort. "Just *remember* that advice lovely Luisa."

I take the pen from her hand and grab at the first piece of paper I see in my bag that being the hotel spa menu, and I reciprocate my details as best as I can around the prices. I hug Pete goodbye before kissing them both on the cheek, grabbing a hold of my case and heading for the door.

"Keep us updated on your travels…" Pete shouts after me, to which I turn and wave.

Feeling that wonderful sun upon my skin as I walk outside feels revitalising after the morning I've had. I begin to think about what Pam said, but there's no way I can tell Luka that he means more to me than he realises, I can't risk getting hurt again.

I head through the car park to see Luka talking to Kristina next to her car again and the feeling of envy that crams into my chest is unreal. When I go home who knows what will happen between them, but I can't think about that now, today is our last day together.

I feel slightly awkward as I approach them, almost as though I'm intruding on their conversation. Kristina sees me first and throws me one of her sweet smiles. "Dobro Jutro…"

Luka turns around, a weary expression on his face. "Luisa, you are okay?" He takes my hand as I see her watching him whilst tucking her black hair behind her ear. "…I hope you do not mind, I told Kristina your situation."

I'm embarrassed, but try my best to hide it. "No, no, that's fine. Actually, I think its best tomorrow if I make my own way to the airport. I can't face getting the coach with him as well as the plane."

Kristina smiles sympathetically. "Of course, I understand. I will change my paperwork so we don't wait for you at the hotel."

She turns back to Luka finishing her conversation in Croatian, before returning her attention to me.

"I hope you enjoy your last day together, if you need anything…I am still here." And with that she walks inside the hotel.

Luka takes my suitcase. "Come on, we do not want him following us." We begin the walk to his apartment.

I don't feel like speaking, just being. Seeing Mark again, it's like he's brought me back to reality. I listen to the sound of the birds chirping with the rolling noise of the wheels on my suitcase in the background. Luka nudges my arm, almost as though he's frightened to touch me.

"You are quiet…he cannot ruin your last day."
I know he's right, at least I'm away from Mark again now.

Once we're inside Luka's apartment, I take a seat on his sofa and he brings me a glass of water. I take a sip and put the glass on the floor. Luka

214

crouches down in front of me, staring into my eyes and I feel my pulse start to accelerate. Before I know it I'm guffawing out loud, which then makes Luka laugh along with me.

"That is better…" He declares, his hand gently traces the inside of my leg. "What shall we do on your last day in Croatia?"

"I'd love to take the cable car again, if you don't mind?"

"I do not mind…shall we go now?"

Desire begins to creep in, I can't imagine never feeling his lips on mine again after tomorrow.

"Not just yet, there's something else I'd rather do first."

Understanding my figure of speech, he leans up onto his knees and immediately meets his lips to mine. His hands run through my hair before making their way down my body as he tenderly kisses behind my ear and down my neck. He unexpectedly stops and leans his forehead to mine, our eyes meeting and the connection between us making our breath ragged with hunger for one another. He picks me up, I wrap my legs around his waist and we continue kissing as he carries me through to his bedroom.

Sometime later, I wake up with Luka snuggled against my back and it feels so comfortable that I just lie there and enjoy it for a while. He begins to stir so I creep out of bed to make us coffee, pulling on Luka's T-shirt as I reach the kitchen. The kettle has hardly boiled when I hear his feet on the tiled floor and turn to see him leaning against the wall, wearing just his shorts.

"I will miss seeing you in my T-shirts…"

I pour two coffees and turn to take the milk from the fridge. "I'll miss wearing them." I smile fondly, passing him his cup.

I stare at my hot coffee before taking a cautious sip, feeling the warm liquid heating my throat when Luka wakes me from my thoughts.

"I would love to see you wearing that all day, but…get dressed and we will go. I have work at 6:30."

"What if Mark recognises you at dinner? That's assuming he'll eat at the restaurant. I don't want you to get into trouble, Luka…"

"Relax. Even if he is there, the chances are he will not even notice me anyway."

Chapter 22

I feel as though I couldn't eat another thing for the rest of the week after finishing my lunch in the *'Izgledi Restaurant'* at the highest point of the cable car station. This restaurant would be so intimate at night with the darkness, giving way to the splendid views of the old town twinkling with the lights and the surrounding islands. I could kick myself that we haven't eaten here sooner.

I've just eaten a delicious medium cooked steak with a huge Istrian salad and now Luka's trying to tempt me to dessert. I could sit here all day and stare at the horizon as it meets the cloudless blue sky and for the first time since I arrived here almost two weeks ago, as I look out there is not one boat in sight, just never ending clear blue ocean. I'm filled with calmness, like the calmness of the sea has just washed over me and in some way, renewed me. As I come to, Luka's watching me and when he sees he's caught my attention I giggle.

Luka begins to laugh along with me. "Whatever has just made you smile, it definitely suits you."

I play with my glass awkwardly on the table. "It's this place, the views. I know I've told you this before but you're so lucky living here..."

He nods in agreement.

"...seriously, where I live the views consist of a shopping centre and numerous multi-storey buildings surrounded by cloudy skies."

Luka pulls his chair out from under the table. "We should go back outside in that case and make the most of it."

As we meet the outside air, the heat of the sun is a very welcome feeling and it's like I've been inside for far too long. We both take more photos of each other with the view in the background and a couple more of us together.

Luka begins to put his camera away as he smirks to himself. "The last time we were up here…"

An image of that night appears in my mind, it feels like years ago. Luka puts his arm around my shoulders and pulls me in to his chest, where I rest my head as we both gaze out.

"I wish I didn't have to go…" There, I've said it out loud. I close my eyes and take a deep breath.

He doesn't respond, just simply rubs my shoulder as I stay in his embrace.

I wish I knew what he was thinking or how he's feeling. *Uuugghh!!* Maybe I could test the water, speak to him about us, but no, I know it's for the best. Between me and Luka, things are and have been nothing but perfect and I won't risk it being anything less than that.

Coming back down from the cable car, Luka leads the way back towards the old town gate, and I assume we're heading back to Lapad until I see him take his mobile from his pocket.

"We should go for a drink somewhere else, stay in town longer."

"Okay, where shall we go?"

He gently pulls me down one of the cobbled side streets. "I know just the place, this way."

The street we're walking down is a lot narrower than some of the others and is a lot cooler as it's more shaded. We walk past an elderly man staring into a shop window, retrieving a small comb from his pocket he begins to comb his hair, the window providing the perfect mirror for him.

We walk further on, rounding a corner where the street meets a small square, home to a couple of bars but no music playing, just the gentle sound of birds chirping in the bushy green trees in the centre of the square, and the subdued sound of occasional chatter.

Luka gestures to the left to a bar with chairs and tables underneath a large sunshade. "Here?"

I look at Luka and see a satisfied grin spreading across his face, and it's only then that I see Melita, Alek, Kristijan and Vilko at one of the tables, smiling and waving in our direction. I look back at Luka, who starts to laugh.

"Have you planned this?"

"I might have done…" He kisses me on my cheek before I follow him over to his brother, sister and his friends. I'm so touched they've planned this between them that I'm almost speechless.

Melita rises from her seat and hugs me. "We worried we had missed you, we have been here for a while." She looks over to Luka.

"Sorry, I had to drag Luisa away from the views…"

Melita looks radiantly happy and I notice she's wearing her work uniform of a white beautician tabard with the *Grand Lapad Plaza Hotel* logo.

I turn to Melita. "How's married life?"

"It is good. Patrik is working, he tried to change his shift, but…"

"Don't worry, I understand. I can't believe you arranged this, I didn't think I would get to see you all again."

She puts her hand on mine as it rests on the table. "Of course. Although it was my brother's idea but we all wanted to say goodbye to you properly."

At the mention of the trouble Luka's gone to, I feel a warm smile appearing on my face but at the same time, I feel like I could cry. "He's very sweet, although he tries to pretend he isn't."

Melita laughs with agreement. "Luka and Alek are both like that, they have a…a soft side too."

I then chat to Alek who is definitely shyer than Luka, just as I suspected at the wedding. Vilko has to leave after just one drink, so I don't really get much chance to talk more to him. We say goodbye as he leaves and it dawns on me that this is the next of a few goodbyes I'll have to make over the next 24 hours.

Sometime later, as everyone has to go back to work, despite the urge to have a couple of drinks in the sun everyone is fed up of water and coffee so we make a move. Alek has driven into town and so he offers us all a lift as far as Melita's hotel. It's a 10 minute walk to where he's parked and Melita and I talk non-stop all the way. I really think we could be great friends, the more we get to know each other…if things were different, but never mind.

When we arrive at the car park of the *Grand Lapad Plaza Hotel* a short while later, I climb out of the car and I feel the atmosphere for me change slightly as I feel my emotions begin to do their best to come out via my eyes. Melita and I hug and as her slight frame meets my own, a couple of stray tears make their way out. She pulls away and beckons me a little further away from the others.

She takes out her mobile from her bag. "Let me take your number Luisa, we have to keep in touch."

I tell her my number, hoping I've remembered it correctly. I purposely didn't bring my phone with me today in a bid to avoid Mark even more so I can't take hers, a decision which I'm now regretting. She immediately sends me a text so I'll have it the moment I get back to my phone later.

Melita looks around at the others before turning back to me and I notice Aleksander and Kristijan are talking between themselves whilst Luka looks miles away, lost in thought.

"I know you will come back one day." She smiles knowingly.

"I hope you're right."

She sees me watching Luka. "You and my brother, there is something there, more than you realise…"

I try to laugh her comment away as I begin to blush. "It's just…" I struggle to find the words. "… I go home tomorrow, it can't be anything more than what it has been."

I'm trying to tell myself that as much as Melita, but I don't think either of us believes any of it. We make our way back over to the lads and I kiss Aleksander goodbye as Melita continues into the hotel to work and Luka, Kristijan and I head back around the coast into Lapad.

They walk me back over to Luka's apartment and as Luka lets me inside, he places both hands on either side of my waist and slowly kisses me on the lips, filling the air between us with his aftershave - the scent of which reminds me of summer, of sea salt and coconut mixed with a woody fragrance.

"Be ready to go out when I get back, I have a surprise planned." His lips have barely touched mine and I can feel them tingling from the after-effects, my body needing more.

Kristijan waits patiently in the doorway and as Luka goes to leave, Kristijan gently takes my hand between both of his. "It has been a pleasure knowing you Luisa, take care of yourself." He enfolds me into a hug.

They continue on to the hotel to work, leaving me with a few hours to myself. I check my phone and receive Melita's text instantaneously.

"Keep in touch! xx"

I'll remember Melita fondly, she has always been so openhearted and friendly to me and I really hope to see her again someday. I reply to her message to wish her and Patrik a fantastic honeymoon in Venice before storing her number in my contacts, smiling at her profile picture of the two of them on their wedding day.

Next, I call Jodie to fill her in on Mark's unexpected arrival. She sounds just as shocked as I felt.

"I can't believe he's done that! What did you do?"

"What could I do? He refused to leave so I had to. I told him about Luka, maybe I wanted to get back at him in some way or maybe I was telling him to make him realise that things between us are over, that I'm getting on with my life without him." I make my way into the kitchen and pour myself a glass of water.

"I'm guessing he didn't take that well?"

"He thinks it's a 'tit for tat' thing." I swig some water.

"And is it…?"

I almost choke on my drink at this question "Absolutely not…"

"Just checking babe, no one could blame you if it was. I'm glad you've been having *fun* anyway, you'll have to fill me in on all the *fun* when you get home!" I can hear the cheekiness in Jodie's voice as she uses the word fun as a euphemism. "So where are you now, by the way?"

"I'm at Luka's he's just left for work, but he'll be back in a few hours."

I hear the sound of cutting scissors, assuming that she's doing her usual 'not working on a Monday as I worked on Saturday' routine of grooming the dogs. I go to ask her but her excited questioning continues.

"What are your plans for your last night together?"

"I've just been told to be ready as he has a surprise planned."

"Ohhh, that's so sweet…"

"He is, he's so…he planned a surprise drink this afternoon, so I could say goodbye to his brother, sister and a couple of his friends."

"Luisa, it sounds like you two have become really close. Is there more to it than you're letting on?"

I stutter. "No…don't be silly, of course there isn't…anyway…is that the sound of the doggy pampering parlour I hear?"

She laughs. "It certainly is…my babies are getting a quick tidy up before their class tonight."

As I end the call with Jodie a few minutes later, I know I could have been honest with her about my feelings for Luka, but there really is no point.

I hunt through the chaos that is my suitcase in an attempt to find something to wear. I end up emptying the whole thing out onto the bed and taking out what I need for tonight and tomorrow before repacking everything for the journey home. I have a shower and get dressed into my denim skirt and cream halter neck top, which has beautiful delicate black lace around the neckline and I leave my hair lose.

I still have some time before Luka will be back and I wonder aimlessly around his studio apartment. I pick up a couple of framed photos of him with his family when he was younger. On one of the photos he looks around 20 years old. Without his goatee he looks completely different, but he still looks like the man I've grown to love. I think about what could have happened between us if we'd met five years ago and were living in the same country, but this does nothing to defuse the sadness which has been constantly fighting to get out for the last couple of days.

When Luka returns a little later, I've fallen asleep after making myself a little too comfortable on his sofa. He must creep in through the door as I have no idea he's there until I wake to see him sitting on the edge of the sofa gently stroking my feet.

"You were tired?" He asks as I slowly awaken.

I sit myself up and swing my feet to the floor as he moves up alongside me. "Sorry, I blame the amount of food we ate at lunch time."

"Are you ready to go out? You look like you are."

"I'm ready if you are?"

224

Luka picks up a small rucksack from the kitchen worktop and I hear him open various cupboard doors as I quickly freshen myself up in the bathroom.

Daylight has given way to darkness when we leave the apartment. We slowly walk hand in hand down the promenade passing busy bars and restaurants, and we see the live band that we danced to, albeit for just a few minutes last week are playing again and I realise it's been a week since that night.

It's then almost like a switch going off in my head that I start to look around behind us, dreading bumping into Mark, dreading him ruining our final night together. Aware of my agitation, Luka stops walking and slips his arm around me.

"Don't worry, there is no way he will find us where I am taking you."

I take one last peak behind us and then remind myself to live for the moment and this moment is now and with a wonderful man beside me. The music and chatter from the bars fades into the distance as we follow the path around the coast, passing just one or two people every couple of minutes. We reach the steps where last week, we climbed down to the bathing platform and we come to a standstill. The boat trip seller's stand/hut is still there, but with the padlocked barrier across the steps entrance.

Luka retrieves his rucksack from his back and brings out a set of keys and I can't help but smile as he looks back at me.

"I thought we could go back to the place you enjoyed the most." he begins fumbling with the lock and after a couple of minutes, he opens the barrier to allow me through before locking it behind us.

The subtle lighting on the main pathway thankfully gives just enough light to get ourselves safely down the steps without me making a prat of myself by falling down. Reaching the bottom, all I can hear is the gentle lapping of the sea against the rocks and the distant music coming from the '*Skriven Bar*' a couple of minutes down the bay. The night sky is clear except for a handful of stars shimmering above us.

Who knows how long I've been staring, but finally when I turn around, Luka has been busily laying out the padded beach mat again, a bottle of chilled wine, glasses and crisps in front of the mat. There are even several tea light candles dotted around in front of him.

"I can't believe you've brought me back here, thank you. It's perfect."

"You are welcome. We should have a toast…" Luka holds out my wine glass towards me as I take my seat on the mat next to him. "To the future and to wherever your travels take you."

Our glasses meet and I can't take my eyes away from his as I take my first drink of the evening.

We relax back, and begin to talk about our past travels. Luka starts to tell me about the north of Croatia. "You would love Plitvice National Park, it is very… erm…picturesque?" He asks, checking he has the right word. "It is less than two hours from Zagreb, if you have chance when you get to Zagreb you should go."

I change positions, sitting upright and turn myself in his direction. "I remember reading about that place, I'll definitely try to go. What's your favourite place you've been to?"

Luka refills our wine glasses and opens the large bag of crisps before lowering himself back down.

"I would say, Venice."

"You've been? What made it your favourite?" I reach for a handful of crisps and I'm pleased to discover they're my favourite, cheese and onion.

"Even though I had an image of what it would be like, it was so much bigger and better than that." He shifts his weight almost uncomfortably, onto his side facing me. "It was our honeymoon, four nights in Venice." I give an understanding smile before he continues. "I recommended Venice to Melita, I know she will love it. How about you, where is your favourite place?"

I laugh a little as I contemplate my similarly ironic answer and swallow my mouth full of crisps. "It has to be Mexico, where we went for our honeymoon."

Luka raises his eyebrows and laughs along with me shaking his head. "It is a shame we were not with better people at the places we loved the most although, we thought we were with the best people in the world at the time."

He stops laughing, and watches me as I drink my wine before he continues. "With all of the places you want to see in the world, it seems that this holiday could just as easily have been in any of those other places. I am glad it was Dubrovnik you chose this time."

"I'm glad it was too."

We hold each other's gaze, both of us clearly deep in thought and then Luka pushes himself up and touches his hand gently to the side of my neck and my skin begins to tingle beneath his touch. I edge myself closer to him and the familiar feel of his lips sends a shiver down my spine.

In the distance I can hear music playing, it sounds like live music from one of the bars that we walked passed on our way here. It's a song that I've always loved, the recognisable guitar melody makes me pause and as the singer begins, I can't help but grin.

Luka smiles. "You like this song?"

I'm still poised in concentration as I listen to every word.

"I *love* it!"

Luka gets to his feet and pulls me to mine by my hands. Surrounded by candlelight, the sea, the stars and the arms of the most amazing man I've ever met, I'm dancing to one of my favourite songs, it's so romantic. My head is resting against Luka's, his arms are around my waist as I absorb each and every word of the song. The song which talks about unexpectedly falling in love…

How fitting that this song should play tonight, the words mirror my thoughts entirely. I will not cry, I can't be thankful enough for meeting Luka, for the fantastic time he's shown me and for everything he's made me realise. Tonight is the perfect end to our time together.

Once the song has finished, we lie back down on the mat, my head resting on his chest as he lightly runs his fingers through my hair. We lie there for ages, listening to the background music and the gentle swaying of the sea until we almost fall asleep and decide to call it a night. We walk hand in hand back to Luka's apartment, and I realise I'm starting to get hungry, especially as we pass the small stall on the promenade selling hotdogs and popcorn. I order a hot dog and as we wait for the lady to cook it, I realise as I look back down the promenade we've just walked up that this is the last time I'll see Lapad and Dubrovnik in the darkness and I desperately try to take it all in for one last time.

I take my phone from my bag, and walk slightly away from the stand, adjusting the settings to take the best photo I can of the promenade with its subtle lighting as it leads down to the sea. I re-join Luka and pay for my hotdog and as we go to walk away, the 'hotdog lady' - obviously not her official name, offers to take a photo of us together on the promenade.

She puts my food back on top of the grill to keep it warm, before following us with my phone. Luka puts his arm around me and I turn myself comfortably in towards him, as we smile.

By the time we reach Luka's and have playfully argued over the last bite of hotdog, I'm surprised to see it's almost 1:00 a.m. After a quick trip to the loo and check of my make up, I leave the bathroom and see Luka's leaning against the window sill waiting for me. I slowly walk towards him.

"Thank you for tonight, it's been perfect." I kiss him on the lips.

He smiles, he has the most gorgeous smile and wish I could see it every day.

"I am glad you liked it."

He holds out his hand in my direction, his head tilted down as he watches me and as I reach out my hand to meet his, I know this will probably be the last time we are 'together'. We begin to kiss and my hands automatically find their way underneath his shirt. His one hand is behind my neck, his thumb gently stroking my jaw line and the other working its way, teasingly up my thigh and underneath my skirt. We stop kissing and as I look into his dark eyes, I know I'm in love with him and I desperately want to tell him that, but I can't.

I lead the way into his bedroom where our kissing becomes more sensual as we begin to peel off each other's clothes. Each time we make eye contact, it's as though we understand each other completely and on every level, I have never felt so attracted and attractive in my life.

Chapter 23

Since I woke up this morning, things have felt so final. Yes, I'm going home today and I really don't want to but, when I think back to how different I felt two weeks ago, I feel more focused on what I want now and I know just how to get it. Well saying that, Luka is a different story. Maybe one day we'll see each other again but if we don't, I wouldn't change anything about our time together.

Luka left early for work and insisted I stay in bed which I did, but without sleeping. I have too much on my mind to sleep and I refuse to waste my last few hours in Dubrovnik. So after forcing myself to leave Luka's bed for the final time, I get dressed and decide that for my last day I'll enjoy breakfast at the bakery.

Two pastries, one coffee and an orange juice later, I sit and relax for a few minutes in the small outdoor complex that houses the bakery, a supermarket and a cinema and watch as holidaymakers head for the supermarket to stock up on bottled water and essentials and local people head to the cinema to catch an early morning film. I hear the slamming of doors and rattling of cans as the supermarket receives a delivery of breads, bottles and various tinned goods.

I could kick myself now for the day that I wasted last week that I didn't see Luka, instead deciding to avoid him to stop myself from getting hurt. I know I'll be hurting like crazy when I leave him. Right now, I honestly feel that I will never meet anyone like him but I won't regret any more. I'll just be glad of what we had and who knows, maybe we'll keep in touch and become friends and at least I'll still have him in my life, albeit thousands of miles away.

After breakfast I take a look around the local shops to buy some presents for my family. I buy my Mom, Jodie and Georgia a lavender angel the same as my own and choose some *bajadera* chocolate for my Dad and Ben. The urge to look over my shoulder suddenly returns, I know I'll see Mark at the airport later but I'm really hoping I don't have to see him before then.

I continue into the next shop which is adjoined to a restaurant that I don't remember noticing before. The shop sells T-shirts, bath salts, trinkets and paintings of the old town, but the thing that really sticks out to me is a framed photo of the sun rising over the old town.

The picture seems to speak to me and it's better than anything I could take myself. I'm so tempted to buy it but if I do, I'll feel terrible that I could have brought one of Luka's from him, so I put the picture down but as I do so, I notice the signature in the corner '*L. Domitrovik*'. I'm in shock, it's one of Luka's and I can't believe it. I go straight to the till to pay for it, a feeling of proudness filing my heart.

I get back to Luka's and whilst I wait for him to return from work I cautiously look at my phone and continue to pack my last few toiletries. Within seconds, I'm alerted to one voicemail and three texts, all from Mark. I clear these from my screen and type out a text to my Dad asking him if the offer for a lift from the airport's still there, before switching my phone on to silent again. I don't want to hear anything from Mark.

A knock at the door tells me Luka's back and I rush to open the door to let him in. The first thing I notice when I see him is how tired he looks.

"It is strange knocking the door to my own apartment and waiting to be let in." He laughs, shaking his head.

"Well thanks for leaving me with your keys today."

He's wearing a light blue fitted T-shirt which shows off his muscular arms and a pair of cream shorts. As he walks past me he grips the top of my arm with one hand and kisses me on the lips. I'm so excited about my purchase I can't wait another second to mention it.

"I went shopping whilst you were working…"

He rolls his eyes and smirks. "Of course…"

I rush into the bedroom to the frame. "Look what I've brought…"
I hold out the photo and as he registers what I'm holding, he looks really happy.

"You brought one of mine?" He smiles, gently clasping my hand. "I would have let you have one for free."

"That's the thing, I picked it up and wanted to buy it and I didn't even know it was yours and I thought I might offend you, if I brought someone else's work."

"…you could never offend me…" He puts his hand to the back of my head and looks deep into my eyes. "Thank you."

I gaze at his mouth before meeting his eyes again and trace my finger along the line of his goatee and his bottom lip. He kisses me softly and I feel like I'm glowing with joy.

"I spoke to Kristina, she has managed to re-book your seat on the plane, so you will not have to sit next to him."

I'm really relieved, although I get a flash of nerves through my body as I'm reminded I'm leaving... very soon. "Can you thank her for me? I won't see her if I'm getting a taxi to the airport."

"Of course I will." Luka pours himself some water before offering me some as I make myself comfortable on the sofa. He walks towards me with a glass.

"Me and Kristina - it wasn't for long, just a couple of months that is all..."

I'm silently stunned for a moment. "Where did that come from?"

Luka sits next to me on the sofa, his feet underneath himself. "I just wanted you to know."

The fact that he said that to me, what does that mean? Is he concerned that I'm thinking something will carry on between them when I'm gone? And if that *is* the case, does he feel something more for me, the way I do for him? I really wish he did.

For my last couple of hours in Dubrovnik, we take a walk along the pebble beach. Families are taking out pedalo's into the sea and I'm reminded of our jet ski and pedalo day.

Luka nudges me. "What are you laughing at?"

I slip my arm around his waist. "I was just remembering when you jumped into the water, leaving me fearing for my life and our pedalo."

He laughs along with me, his arm around my shoulders as we reach the end of the beach and follow the path around the coast again until we reach the 'Skriven Bar' where we stop for lunch. The only free table, luckily for us, is right on the edge with the amazing views of the coastline right under our noses.

We order coffees and food, deciding to share the huge club sandwich with fries.

Luka stirs his coffee. "When you go home, do you think you may continue to learn Croatian?"

I take a drink from my cappuccino and think about the answer. "Erm…" I laugh. "Maybe…"

"The few words you can speak, you speak them very well."

"Well, thank you. I'm not sure what my Mom would think of me learning a language other than Spanish though."

Luka looks at me inquisitively. "Do you look like her?"

"People say I do, although I have my Dad's colouring rather than hers."

"You are very close with them?" He adjusts his seating position, meaning his knee now touches mine underneath the table…my senses awaken.

"Not massively close no, but we get on well. Anyway, maybe if I had a good teacher, I might be tempted to learn Croatian. Three languages under my belt could be pretty good."

He laughs. "You will not find a teacher as good as me, I teach you all of the best phrases."

"I have to agree there…"

A silence follows, where I'm replaying in my mind moments when I've listened to Luka talking Croatian to his friends and family, thinking about how attractive and intelligent he sounded and how attractive and intelligent he *is*.

Over lunch, we talk about Melita and Patrik's wedding and his parents' reaction to his divorce as I ponder how smoothly mine will go.

Luka gives me some sound advice. "You just have to remember the reasons behind your divorce, although I am sure you will not forget. It will not be easy but if it is the right thing for you, you have to sit through it."

I smile, grateful for his honesty. "It will be worth it when it's all over, finally." I laugh uncomfortably.

"We had better make a move…your taxi, only an hour away."

I look at my watch in surprise at where the afternoon has gone, and get a sudden rush of sadness as I contemplate saying goodbye to Luka.

Back at his apartment, Luka flicks on the radio and lies down on the sofa and gestures for me to join him. I lie down on my side, with my head on his shoulder and my hand on his stomach as he holds me close, with his hand on mine. We lie there, simply listening to the music and intermittent chatter between songs, just being together for the last time. I can't help but keep looking at the clock on the wall, counting down my final minutes as I wonder how things will be as I leave. I'm planning on texting him my email address - he did promise to email me the pictures of the wedding once he's taken them from his camera.

Five minutes to go and I get up from his comfortable embrace and do the heart-wrenching thing of dragging my case to the front door. Luka's now also on his feet, leaning against the wall by the door and staring down at his bare feet. As the horn of the taxi sounds outside, it's complete silence between us, I don't think either of us knows quite what to say and

I have this horrible tightness in my chest, the kind of tightness that I know will give way to tears if I'm not careful.

Luka carries my suitcase down the stairs for me and lets out a sigh of relief as he reaches the pavement, my case landing down with a loud pounding noise that matches the heavy pounding of my heart.

He gives me an unsure smile. "Are you sure you do not want me to come to the airport?"

It was lovely of him to offer, but the thought of saying goodbye surrounded by hundreds of people would just be too much. At least this way it's just me, Luka and the taxi driver, who is making a conscious effort to look the other way.

"I'll be okay, but thanks for the offer."

Luka nods politely and the taxi driver opens the boot and heaves my case in before returning behind the wheel. I take a deep breath, walk closer to Luka and he throws his arms around me and I squeeze him tightly as he holds me near. I take another deep breath, breathing in his aftershave and letting it fill every molecule of my being, as I try to hold on to as much of him as possible.

We pull away from each other and as we look into each other's eyes, he flicks my hair from my shoulder out of the way. His hand slides its way to the back of my neck and his finger traces small circles there, giving me goose bumps.

"I am so glad we met." He smirks.

Another deep breath, *you can do this is Luisa*. "I'm glad we met too…more than you will ever know." Tears fill my eyes.

"I will not know what to do with all of my free time now." He laughs.

I try my best to laugh with him but I'm finding it really difficult. "Well with this free time on your hands…get your photos out there and let everyone see the world as you do."

Luka gives me a sexy grin, making me giggle - thankfully. We kiss and in some ways, it feels like our first kiss all over again. Our hands travel over each other's skin and I wish I could drag him back indoors, but I can't.

Luka holds onto my hand tightly. "I hope you have a fantastic time going to the places you always wanted to go. I will be thinking of you…"

"I'll be thinking of you too." I take a deep breath, for courage. "If you ever want to sample the delights of the UK, you know where I am…"

Luka laughs. "I do… *brinuti* Luisa…take care."

He squeezes both of my hands before planting one last lingering kiss on my lips. I open the taxi door and close it behind me and smile one last time at the man who made me feel so alive for the first time in a long time.

Chapter 24

Once the taxi's left Luka's street, I reach for my phone to distract myself from the tears hovering in my eyes. I text him my email address telling him he now has no excuse for not sending me those photos to which he replies with a laughing emoji. A message then comes through from my Dad. He's telling me he'll be there waiting for me at the airport when I get to Birmingham, which lifts my spirits fleetingly.

I stare out of the window at my last views of Dubrovnik and feeling cold for the first time in two weeks I wrap my arms around myself, too lazy to retrieve my jacket from my bag. I rest my head against the window and close my eyes as the realisation of never seeing Luka again sets in.

***

Arriving at the airport not long after, I pay the taxi driver and he once again heaves my suitcase from the boot. I make my way inside to meet the air conditioning that the departure terminal always gives and that feeling alone is like its telling me…the holiday's over, Luisa. Think I'm definitely going to need my jacket soon.

Hundreds of people are queuing to check-in for their flights, travel reps are assisting passengers with overflowing suitcases and children run riot around the airport in boredom, people are hovering around the screens wondering which direction to go in. I locate my check-in desk and am pleased to see I've made it here before the coach that Mark will be on.

Checking in takes just minutes and now free from my case, I head to the toilets to inspect my make up after the struggle with the tears situation. I use the loo before checking in the mirror to see that my make-up is still fully intact and return back out into the terminal, following the signs for departures.

As I reach the security area where my hand luggage will be checked, I stop to rest my bag on a nearby table as I drink the last of my bottled water, before throwing the empty bottle away. Passport and boarding pass in hand, I join the queue of people waiting to head through to departures. It always feels so very strict and regimented at this part of the journey.

As the queue slowly gets shorter and I get closer to my flight home, I can't resist looking behind me through the crowds of people. My imagination conjures up an image of Luka running towards me, moments before I disappear through the security, begging me to stay with him but the reality is of course very different.

"Excuse me, miss…" The lady behind me in the queue disturbs me from my thoughts as she ushers me forward as I'm now front of the queue. I show my passport and boarding pass and with one final glance over my shoulder, place my bag on the conveyor belt as it travels through the x-ray machine.

The departure area is really crowded, and all I want is some time on my own and some quiet. I walk to the far end of the area to a coffee shop and after ordering a drink, I sit down with my back to the world as I face the wall, desperate for some space and time with my thoughts.

I stare partially out of the window where I can see planes being pushed back ready for departure, people in fluorescent vests holding those coloured bats that look like they're signalling they're ready for a game of table tennis. I look back to the wall in front of me at the poster advertising the nightclub that I went to with Luka and his friends just last week, and it's all I can do not to burst into tears.

When my flight's called for boarding, I head towards the departure gate and my fellow passengers as they queue to board the plane. At first I can't see Mark, so I join the back of the queue in the hope I won't see him until I'm on the plane and then it will be virtually impossible to speak if we're sitting far apart. I search inside of my bag for my passport and boarding card and when I locate them at the very bottom of my bag, I look up and see Mark halfway along the queue.

As I see him - literally seconds later, he turns around in my direction and as we lock eyes. I get a heavy feeling in my stomach, I really hope he isn't going to make a scene. He continues to move along the queue before turning around to face me again. I half smile, unsure of the correct way to greet my estranged soon to be ex-husband. He simply nods my way and looks hesitant, beginning to step out of the queue before stepping back in and looking around at me before finally, slowly walking towards me.

As he nears closer, I see his grey T-shirt almost matches his skin tone. His normal olive complexion has given way to an ashen appearance and his eyes look heavy and withdrawn. When he reaches my side, he places his bag down at his feet next to me.

"I was worried about you…"

"There was no need to worry about me, you knew I was with Luka."

"That's the problem!" He shouts angrily, his voice seemingly echoing around the busy terminal meaning everyone in the queue and nearby turn around and look directly at us.

As he realises he's raised his voice, he softly smiles in apology as the people around us continue to talk amongst themselves. I turn around to see there are only a dozen or so people behind us in the queue, so I take Mark by the elbow and steer him to the very back of the queue so we can talk a little more privately.

"Mark, I don't want a scene, I don't want everyone knowing my business." I explain calmly, creeping forward again in the queue.

"You mean you don't want everyone to know that you've been sleeping with the cook at the hotel, whilst we've been on holiday?"

I actually want the ground to open up and swallow me, I'm mortified as everyone turns around to look at me.

"That's not the issue here Mark and you know it. The issue is what you've been up to behind my back for who knows how long." I manage to find the right level of anger with a hushed tone, although he deserves to have everyone know exactly what he's been up to.

Gradually we reach the gate in silence, show our passports and boarding passes before making our way through the tunnel and on to the plane. Mark steps in front of me and he's kindly told by a member of the cabin crew to take his seat in row 10 and as we reach his row, he's alarmed to see one empty seat by the window with an elderly couple taking the two remaining seats next to him.

"Sorry, I think you may be in my wife's seat." He politely explains to the lady.

I know I should stop and tell him that actually, they're in the right seat and that I'm no longer sitting with him, but I just can't bear to speak to him any longer and so, I continue along the aisle to the safety of row 24 and take my seat before he can come after me.

As I settle into my seat next to an elderly man and who I'm assuming his grandson, the cabin crew commence their announcements that all mobile phones should now be switched off ready for take-off. Scrambling around in my bag, I locate my phone…checking, hoping for a message from Luka, anything, just as long as I know he hasn't forgotten me already. The blank screen staring back at me makes me ache with sadness as I switch off the phone and lean my head back against my seat.

***

The pitch black view of Birmingham from the window greets me as I sleepily open my eyes and we come into land. Moments later we touch down and it hits me all over again, I'm now without Luka. I shake my head in annoyance with myself, I've got to forget about him, though how I'll do that I have absolutely no idea. I hear the chorus of unbuckling seat belts and wish I could stay on the plane and go straight back to where I came from. I purposely hang back, so I'm the last person to leave the plane, wanting to avoid Mark again for as long as possible.

Queueing up at passport control I'm almost hoping they refuse to let me into the country for some reason or another and send me back to Dubrovnik, but that doesn't happen.

When I reach the luggage carousel, I busy myself once again with checking my phone for messages as I switch it back on, but all I get is more disappointment. My case appears in front of me and as I reach out to pick it up, Mark's beside me and beats me to it.

"What do you think you're doing?"

He pulls my case onto the trolley with his. "A thank you would've been nice actually...come on I've already called a taxi, it shouldn't be long."

He continues on ahead with my case on his trolley and I desperately follow him, tugging at my case bringing it crashing down to the floor. Mark freezes, looking at me like I've completely lost it and then I do lose it. My temper reaches boiling point.

"I am NOT coming home with you, I've told you!"

I hurry on in front of him, hoping there are no customs officers around as I probably look like I'm smuggling something back into the country with the rush I'm in. As soon as I'm through customs and out into the open, I immediately spot my Dad standing by the door waiting for me.

As he sees me, he walks forward to meet me and envelopes me in his arms and I break down in uncontrollable tears. The emotion of seeing my Dad, everything that's happened with Mark and knowing what I've lost with Luka all comes to the surface and out through my eyes in heavy sobs.

My Dad squeezes me tightly. "It's okay sweetheart, you're home now." I'm desperate to tell him that being back home is part of the problem, but I dry my eyes and do my best to usher my Dad outside before Mark can see us but unfortunately it's too late, I can already hear him.

"Luisa... Luisa, where are you going?"

My Dad turns around sharply, I don't think I've ever seen him look so angry. "If he knows what's good for him, he'll leave you alone!" He puts a protective arm around me.

"Dad…please, let's just go."

My Dad's stern expression on his face is enough to keep Mark away for now, as he stands and watches us leave the airport.

For the journey back to my parents' house I sit in silent thought and my Dad is kind enough to let me be, noticing how exhausted I am. It's gone 11:00 p.m. when we pull up on their drive and it feels really strange walking into my parents' house and knowing that other than whilst I'm travelling, this will be my home for the foreseeable future. As soon as my Mom hears the noise of the front door, she rushes into the hallway and throws her arms around me. This time I'm strong, even though she must be able to tell I've been upset she doesn't comment.

Over a cup of tea and two slices of toast which my Mom insists I eat, I fill them in on my holiday (obviously omitting the Luka story), and the beautifulness that is Croatia, before dragging myself off to bed in one of the spare bedrooms.

Reaching the top of the stairs I pause, looking inside the room that will be mine for now. The room is in darkness, albeit a small lamp switched on sitting beside the bed. The room's filled with memories as a stash of teddy bears sits gathering dust in the far corner and various photographs hang from the wall in frames. Photos from past family Christmases and holidays with *Tito*, which my parents have displayed there over the years since I moved out.

As I go to close the door behind me, I hear my mobile burst into song. Straight away my heart lunges in my chest as I empty the contents of my bag on the floor, *'please make it be Luka'* I think to myself. Locating my phone, I'm gutted to see Mark's name on the screen and I promptly end the call before sinking onto the bed in a slump, leaving my phone on the floor amongst my bag contents.

How can it feel like such a long time since I saw Luka already? It's almost as though it didn't happen...like it was all a dream, a really lovely uplifting dream. I'm really not sure how but, I've got to push myself through this.

Glancing at the floor, I grab once again for my phone as it sits amongst my passport, old tickets and receipts from the grand emptying of my bag. Flicking through the photos, I'm instantly back in Croatia. Surely it has to have been a dream to have been so good? As I enjoy reliving the memories of the wonderful time spent with Luka I have the strongest urge to text him, but as I take my phone in my hand, something stops me. Let's face it, I wouldn't be doing myself any favours by getting in touch with him. As far as I'm aware we were just a fling to him, so I've got to leave it there. At least I still have the truly happy memories.

Chapter 25

The next morning there's a tapping on the door, followed by my Mom sneaking in with a tray loaded with tea and what smells suspiciously like a bacon sandwich.

"I thought you may be hungry." She has a self-satisfied smile on her face as she places the tray down next to me.

"Thanks." I pull myself up into a sitting position, taking a welcome sip of tea.

Mom sits down on the bed next to me. "Jodie called for you, she said she'd been trying your mobile all morning."

"It's on silent, Mark kept calling last night."

"Perhaps you should change your number, although you will need to speak to him sometime."

Mom had a point, maybe I should just change my number, but there's no way I'm doing that at the moment, I need to hang onto the tiny bit of hope that Luka might get in touch.

Ever persistent, my Mom won't give up. "What are your plans today? It's almost 2:00 p.m., I take it you slept well?"

The truth is I hardly slept at all and I'm shocked to hear it's well past lunch time. It took me ages to drop off to sleep and when I finally did, I seemed to wake up every hour, wishing I was in bed beside Luka, back in his apartment.

"Cariño?"

I realise I haven't replied. "Sorry, no, I didn't get much sleep…..too much on my mind."

"You need to think of the future now, perhaps you should make an appointment with a solicitor to get the ball rolling before you leave for Seville, I can come with you if you need me there?" She squeezes my hand, and I'm grateful for her support.

"That's a good idea. Thanks, but I think I'd rather go alone."

She kisses me on my forehead before leaving me to eat my delicious bacon sandwich as I scroll through the seven missed calls on my phone. Three are from Jodie and the rest, of course are from Mark. Seeing his name once again on my screen, I feel so agitated. It's with that I climb out of bed, almost throwing half of my uneaten sandwich across the room with haste and make my way across the short landing and into the bathroom where I ferociously switch on the shower.

The wonderfully warm water feels sublime against my skin, refreshing me from top to toe. I feel a sudden longing for Luka and the ache I get in my heart is enough to bring tears to my eyes. I miss him so much despite the fact it hasn't even been 24 hours since I was in his arms. I rub the shampoo into my hair even more firmly hoping to distract myself from my heartache, but this just proves pointless. I have to focus on myself, getting the ball rolling for the divorce and preparing for going travelling.

Stepping out of the shower cocooned in my towel, I hear a message arrive on my mobile. With relief, I see it's Jodie and not another message from Mark. Seeing Jodie's name brings a smile to my face as I know seeing my best friend will start to make me feel better. I apologise for not managing to speak to her earlier and she suggests us getting together tonight over a bottle of wine and a takeaway at her house to catch up, which makes me feel more upbeat.

I blow dry my hair and apply some bronzer to my face to enhance my sun kissed skin, followed by my trusty mascara. It's then I remember as I look down at my case on the floor, Ben telling me how he and my Dad collected all of my belongings from the house.

I look over at the double wardrobe in the corner of the room and as I open it, the sight of all of my clothes hanging there seems rather strange. The last time I saw these clothes they were hanging in my bedroom, or our bedroom at what *was* mine and Mark's house. I'm so thankful I don't have to go back there to get my belongings now, the thought of seeing that man makes the feeling of agitation begin to build up yet again.

I pull on a pair of jeans and a cream vest top and after a quick glance out of the window, I put my umbrella into my bag and don my black blazer jacket.

Deciding to walk for 20 minutes to the local shopping centre rather than catching the bus is something I started to regret after walking for 10 minutes in heels for the first time in two weeks, other than the heels I wore to Melita's wedding. To be honest I felt like I needed some fresh air - even though it's a little too fresh for my liking after the heat of Croatia.

After walking into a couple of solicitors offices and being told there are no appointments available today, I realise I should have called ahead. But I'm not giving up, there's plenty more where they came from.

Entering the offices of Wilson Weaver and Co, I'm met with the smell of leather furniture and strong polish. The offices aren't very modern but what they lack in décor, they will hopefully make up for in service. The reception area is quite dull with dark wooden furniture, bottle green carpet and black filing cabinets. There's a tall potted yukka plant in the corner of the room which at least does bring a little colour into the place and a worn, yet comfortable looking burgundy leather sofa. The receptionist, seems friendly enough.

"Our family law solicitor has a cancellation if you'd like to wait 10 minutes?"

I'm so glad to hear that. "Yes, please. Thank you."

"Can I get you a tea or a coffee?"

I'd much prefer to take off my heels and soak my now sore feet in hot water, but resist the urge to tell her this, and I kindly accept the offer of coffee.

Mr Weaver introduces himself at reception a short time later and escorts me through to his office. His office is fairly large, with numerous framed certificates proudly displayed on the walls. Filing cabinets run alongside one full length of the room and bookcases sit behind his desk, full of various legal titles. His office appears a little brighter than the reception area, with two huge windows allowing the light to flood the room with the blinds pulled to one side.

Mr Weaver is well over six-feet tall and with his rather stocky build, I feel like a mouse next to him. He beckons for me to sit down in the armchair opposite his desk and insists I call him Peter.

"So Mrs Powell, I understand you would like to start divorce proceedings against your husband?"

I clear my throat…it all seems so formal. "That's correct."

Peter opens his notepad and with one click of his pen, he's poised and waiting for me to begin.

Chapter 26

As I step into Jodie's hallway later that evening, shaking the rain off my hooded jacket, I hand over the scrumptious smelling three lots of fish and chips I've picked up on my way to Darren, as Jodie and I exchange a hug.

"I've really missed you, Luisa."

Darren laughs from the kitchen. "I don't know how, you've spoken to each other almost every day…"

Jodie frowns at him. "You just concern yourself with plating up the food, we're starving here."

Right on cue Zack, Belle and little Molly come running towards me with their beautiful glossy coats as I bend down to pet them.

"Ohhh there you are…it's lovely to see you too." My voice takes on the high-pitched tone which is obviously mandatory when talking to dogs and cats. They soon head off to the kitchen once they smell the delights of the takeaway, on their best behaviour staring up at Darren for some titbits.

Jodie hangs my jacket over the banister of the stairs before reaching for her purse from her bag.

"Here you go, let me give you the money for the chips…"

I immediately push her hand away. "Oh no you don't. The deal was I supply the food and you supply the drink."

Moments later, we're relaxed in front of the TV, plates of grease balanced on our laps. The food smells so nice, and that tang of vinegar so inviting but after just a couple of mouthfuls, I'm really struggling to eat and find that I'm much more enjoying poking my food around the plate.

There's only so many bits of fish I can get away with giving to the dogs… although the way that Zack's clutching my leg I have a feeling he would happily eat the whole portion to himself.

I hear Darren clear his throat, obviously trying to get Jodie's attention by the guilty look on his face when I look over at him.

I see Jodie studying me. "Are you not hungry?"

"I thought I was, maybe not after all."

There's a suitable silence in the room as Darren and Jodie continue to eat before Darren brings up the subject of Mark.

"Have you spoken to Mark, since you got back?"

Jodie looks daggers at him. "Darren…"

I softly smile at her. "It's okay Jode. No I haven't, I'm ignoring him. It's easier that way."

Darren and Mark have always 'got on', but never as well as Jodie and I had hoped. The four of us have got together numerous times over the years and although it hasn't been awkward between them, it's always been abundantly clear they're quite different. After what's happened, I'd love to ask Darren's opinion on things, but I don't want to put him in an awkward situation.

Darren's mid mouthful of food as he stops and looks at me. "I think, as no doubt you do too, he's a prat and you shouldn't have taken him back the first time."

It seems I didn't have to worry about asking Darren's opinion after all. Jodie looks furious, her eyes are almost popping out of her head.

I laugh at her expression. "Calm down, I've told you it's okay."

After Jodie and Darren have finished eating, Darren makes himself scarce and leaves us to it.

Jodie pours me my first glass of wine of the evening. "How did it go at the solicitors?"

I relax back onto the sofa tucking my feet underneath me, Molly now lying on her back next to me insisting on a tummy rub.

"Not too bad I suppose. It was quite humiliating telling him the tale, but I guess he's heard worse." Jodie listens as I tell her the story of the solicitors office.

"Basically, I can divorce him on the grounds of adultery and unreasonable behaviour, I'm sure Mark will be thrilled when he receives his letter. I can claim half of the house but I don't want it, it was never mine to begin with and I certainly don't want it now."

Mark already lived in the house when we met, so I moved in with him there. Obviously I've been paying towards the mortgage and bills when I was working, but I don't want any of it, I just want to be away from him.

I take a drink of my wine and rest my head back on the sofa. "I just hope he doesn't start to contest things."

Jodie looks puzzled. "How do you mean?"

"Well, now he knows about Luka, what if he tries to make out he's the victim in all of this?"

Belle jumps up on to Jodie's lap. "He wouldn't dare! What he's been doing has been going on for a long time, you and Luka has been what just over a week?"

Luka, just hearing his name makes me ache and my mind recollects the times we spent together until Jodie brings me back into the room.

"So, come on tell me everything about him, I'm dying to know…" She has a beaming smile on her face, which is obviously contagious as a smile creeps upon mine too.

"Oh, Jodie, he's just…he's…" And before I know it, I've burst into uncontrollable sobs.

Jodie immediately gets up from the other sofa leaving Belle looking very put out as she sits next to me, offering her arm around me as I cry into her shoulder. She says nothing, just comforts me until I'm ready to speak again. When I finally come up for air, I dry my eyes and blow my nose and do my best to compose myself. I know Jodie's my best friend and I can tell her anything but, I'm trying not to let on (although I'm not doing a very good job at the moment) the true extent of my feelings for Luka.

She squeezes my hand. "Are you okay?"

I giggle nervously as I dry my eyes and shift back into the sofa. "Sorry, I'm not sure what came over me for a minute then."

"It's probably just an accumulation of everything….you needed to get the tears out."

Jodie looks at me as though she's trying to read my mind and part of me thinks she's actually succeeding, but she isn't letting on. I need to carry on telling her about Luka, otherwise she'll know something's wrong, so I fix a smile on my face.

"He's wonderful Jode, he really made me realise a few things I should have been conscious of a long time ago."

"That's good, I'm really pleased he *'showed you a good time.'*" She winks at me, giggling uncontrollably.

I feel myself begin to blush as I think of the nights, the afternoons and the mornings spent in Luka's arms, the way he made me feel about myself and the way I feel about him. Another fit of giggles follows as Jodie tops up my glass of wine.

"That's more like it!" She laughs, raising her glass towards mine. "You have to show me some more photos of this man…"

I do my best to smile, but I can't help but feel sad at what I've left behind. I'll get over him. Keeping busy over the next few months will certainly help.

"Do you think you'll hear from him, are you going to keep in touch?"

"We did exchange numbers, but… I think it was just a holiday fling." Even I don't believe those words as they come out of my mouth, I wonder if she does.

Jodie looks disappointed. "Ohh, that's a shame. Still, at least you had fun and he's certainly put some colour back in your cheeks with all of that se…"

"… Jodie!" We both burst out laughing.

We spend the rest of the night talking about Croatia and going through our plans for when we get to Seville. Jodie's staying two nights with me in Seville, before she leaves me to it. A good girly few days will do me the world of good I'm sure. I can't wait. Jodie fills me in on how she has arranged a night out with the girls on Saturday for my leaving do, which will be great.

Two glasses of wine later and I'm climbing into the passenger seat of Darren's car for my lift home. Only a couple of glasses and I actually feel really drunk. I was drinking more than this on holiday and not feeling quite this merry, it just shows what being on holiday and feeling that bit more relaxed can do.

I feel like I've stepped back in time as I open the door to my parents' house to hear the TV blaring away, wondering what their comments will be when they see I'm under the influence. They both turn their heads as I walk into the living room, my Mom eyes me suspiciously.

"Did you enjoy your night?"

I slip out of my jacket and take a seat on the sofa next to her. "Yeah we did, thanks."

I can tell she wants to ask more, but after filling her in when I came back from the solicitors earlier, I think she's trying to let me be. It can't be easy for them either having me back at home after all these years. I hear a beeping noise and a pang of excitement engulfs me, *could this be him?* I scramble across the room for my phone to where I left it on the dining room table, only to see my Dad picking up his phone. I'm flooded once more with disappointment, I make my excuses and head up to bed.

Lying in bed, I'm consumed with thoughts of Luka but I force myself to think positively. Only five more days before my travelling begins, I have to focus on that. Maybe, just before I get to Zagreb on my final stop in a few months' time, I could contact Luka to tell him I'm back in his country, maybe he might have time to meet up. But, by then could he have completely forgotten about me?

I awaken abruptly, scanning the room and wonder what's woken me. I see a hint of light reflecting onto the curtains and as I trace the light back with my eyes, I see the light disappear on my phone next to me. I drag myself across to the other side of the bed to pick up my phone and my heart almost skips a beat as I see a text from Luka. I bolt upright, fumbling for the switch on the lamp next to me, flooding the room with brightness. Flooding *myself* with brightness.

"Remember me? Hope things are okay for you back at home. Luka x"

I'm smiling from ear to ear. I type out a reply, hoping I don't sound like I've been desperately waiting to hear from him.

"I'm not sure I do remember you actually, remind me who you are again? Things aren't too bad, thanks. How's Croatia? I miss it already! x"

"Just Croatia, you don't miss me? :-("

I giggle as I read his response. I want to tell him exactly how much I miss him. He's flirting with me, being playful. Why oh why do we analyse these things so much when it comes to the opposite sex? I need to be quite casual in my response so I give it some thought before typing yet another reply.

"You? Well, maybe a little…x"

As I send the message, I realise maybe I should have asked him something to keep the conversation flowing. I feel like a schoolgirl again, playing mind games with boys, trying to play things cool but potentially putting my foot in it.

Ten minutes go by before he responds. It feels so good to have this playful banter with him again, I picture him relaxing on his sofa, a bottle of beer in hand.

We spend the best part of two hours texting each other, catching up on the last 24 hours since we were together. I tell him about my trip to the solicitors and what it's like living with my parents again and he fills me in on his morning shift at work followed by his night off, where he met up with Aleksander and Vilko for a drink.

As our texting marathon comes to an end, I'm buzzing with excitement but at the same time, I'm longing for him even more. At least now we're in contact he's still in my life and I'm really grateful of that.

***

The next day, I'm up early and after breakfast I set my laptop up in my room and set to work in adding into my book the notes I made on holiday. I've barely made a start when the doorbell rings. Rolling my eyes in annoyance at the disruption, I make my way downstairs and after opening the front door, I'm shocked to see Mark standing on the other side of the porch door. I stop in my tracks tempted to leave him there and close the door on him but I know he won't give up, so I open the door.

"Mark."

"I got your letter, or should I say, your solicitor's letter?" He holds up the envelope as proof.

"That was fast."

"Couriered to me at 8:00 a.m. this morning!" He snaps. "Sorry, Luisa. Look, can I come in?"

I open the door wider for him to walk in past me before closing the door behind us. I motion towards the living room and follow him inside where we sit at opposite ends of the room.

Here we go…. "Say what you came to say…" I'm finding it increasingly difficult to be polite to him.

"Adultery Luisa? I think we're both guilty of that now, don't you?"

I shake my head. "I must be psychic. How did I know you'd try and pull that one? What I did with Luka is hardly the same thing as what you did to me time and time again Mark! I've seen it with my own eyes, thankfully not in the flesh, that was Ben's bad luck, but I saw the proof on your laptop."

To my surprise, Mark doesn't try to deny anything in fact, he doesn't really say much at all after that he just looks at me as I continue.

"My solicitor has advised me to go for half of the house, but I've told him no. All I want is a fresh start away from our marriage."

Mark huffs and puffs at this. "Half of the house when it's my house?"

"Like I say - I just want to get out of this, I want our divorce to be as quick and smooth as possible."

Mark begins to laugh. "Oh, I see…you're fooling yourself, Luisa."

"What are you talking about?"

Mark stands up, slowly pacing the room. "You think by divorcing me as quickly as you can, you can get back to *the cook* who I suppose you think is pining for you in Dubrovnik? As soon as you were on that plane home, he was shagging somebody else!"

I'm annoyed at his comments. "For your information…Luka's a chef not a cook, why do you do that? Does it make you feel good trying to belittle peoples jobs…their passions?"

He shakes his head, smirking so I continue my tirade. "…and don't assume everyone is the same as you Mark, but even if he was shagging somebody else already, he has nothing to do with this. Don't try kidding yourself this is someone else's fault, it's yours and yours alone."

Mark knows exactly how to get to me after all these years. "Oh you want him to be waiting for you, don't you?"

"Just leave, you've said what you had to say, now go!"

Mark stands staring at me, shaking his head and chuckling to himself as he slowly walks out of the living room and out of the front door which I rightly slam behind him.

I'm infuriated that he can still upset me and as I do my best to hold my tears inside, I start to wonder how I would feel if what Mark said about Luka was true. I know it isn't true, and I have to remember that. I trusted Luka implicitly, something I never thought I would manage with a man again after Mark. Even if Luka did go looking for somebody else now, that's his business.

I think back to my various conversations with Luka last night. Do I dare think that maybe, just maybe he has real feelings for me? I didn't expect to hear from him, but he got in touch. Surely that has to mean something?

My steaming hot coffee and I settle back down in front of the computer, but I'm easily distracted. Thoughts of Mark and our impending battle for divorce, thoughts of my writing, and of course, Luka, all occupy my mind. I close my eyes and attempt to relax. Breathing in slowly and out slowly, it's no good. To take my mind away from the multitude of unanswered questions swirling around my brain, I open up my emails to check my flight itinerary for my upcoming travels. At least my travels are something stable in my life at the moment amongst all of this uncertainty.

I reach for my notebook and make a list of all of my flights, along with the dates and the accommodation in which I'm staying. On the next page, I make another list of things I need to buy in readiness and decide that after lunch, I'll head into town and pick up a few things.

I'm just about to call it a day on my laptop as let's face it, I won't be able to concentrate enough to do anything productive when the whistling noise plays out from my computer, signalling a new email. Clicking on the envelope icon I feel like electricity has just surged through my body when I see who the email is from - Luka Domitrovik.

I swear I'm almost shaking as I do my best to control the mouse and click on his name. Opening the mail, I notice various attachments which seem to be pictures.

Luisa,

Just a few photographs from the last couple of weeks. I could not help but laugh looking back at some of them, you have certainly given me some great memories.

The woman on the photographs is someone who deserves so much happiness and I hope I gave her some of that, even in just a short amount of time.

Luka xx

His words are enough to make a gigantic smile exude across my face. Clicking on each of the attached pictures in turn, I gasp in happiness and giggle as I see a photograph of me on the boat going to the Elaphiti islands. Luka had a way of making me feel at ease and I think that shows from the look on my face.

A couple of pictures follow from the party at his apartment with his friends - the night we celebrated Croatia joining the European Union. One of me and Luka together having just finished our lunch at the *Grand Lapad Plaza Hotel* and an action one of us lunging forward as the waiter dropped the camera (still managing to take a photograph at the same time), before catching the camera again. I remember that moment like it was yesterday, it must only be four or five days ago although, it feels a lot longer.

Then follows a picture of me, Melita and a couple of her friends on the dance floor at the wedding which makes me smile fondly, remembering how welcome they made me feel.

The last picture is still at the wedding, but is of me and Luka. It must have been taken when Alek was taking some shots with his camera. We're smiling from ear to ear as we look at each other in what seems to be an extremely natural photograph. I stare at this picture for a few moments, taking in the scene which transports me back to the day itself. It was such a magical day, one that I didn't want to end. I can't help but notice how happy I look in Luka's arms, and I begin to wonder if I'll ever truly be that happy again.

Without even thinking, I forward the email onto Jodie at work before closing down my computer and I send Luka a text, thanking him for the photos.

Chapter 27 – Luka, Dubrovnik

The day that Luisa went home, back to her life in the UK…back to the life that she knew before she met me, hit me harder than I thought was possible.

As I watched her taxi drive away I felt that I would never feel that way again. The way that we connected in such a short space of time, looking back now it does not seem possible for this to have happened, yet it did.

I knew that she wanted more from me, I knew what she wanted was for me to tell her how I feel but the truth is I was afraid, I am still afraid. Do I even know how I feel? I am not sure. To think that I accused her just last week of being scared of doing things that she wants and now here I am in the same situation.

After sending her an email with the photos from the wedding and of our day at the hotel together, she sent me a message, yet I could not reply. What could I say? There was so much that I wanted to say to her but I did not know where to begin.

She had been trapped in an unhappy marriage and now she was finally getting out…the two of us together, could it be real? She never made me feel that it was not but, how could I be sure?

Losing my job at the hotel the day that she went home, I had to protect her from that. If I told her I had lost my job because of Mark making a complaint about me, she would be distraught with guilt.

I am nothing like Mark. In some ways he held her back only pushing her forward into the limelight when it suited him and made him look better. If I told her how I have feelings for her I felt she may have stayed here with me so she *still* would not have followed her dream of travelling…I could not stop her doing that. I knew that I had to do my best to move on with my life, without her.

Chapter 28 - Luisa

Saturday rolls around and with the plan to meet the girls at 8:00 p.m. I start getting ready early giving myself plenty of time to decide what to wear. It's now been 48 hours since I text Luka and I'm still yet to receive a reply. I'm doing my best not to think about it too much.

Numerous times I've re-read the last message I sent to him just simply saying thanks for the photos and how great they are. This is the longest I've gone without speaking to Luka since we met and it's tearing me apart. Maybe this is it now, it's just something I have to get used to.

Dressed in my plum coloured off the shoulder dress, black peep toe heels and my hair pinned to one side and draping onto my shoulder, I leave the house and meet the girls in the waiting black cab outside. I can hear the laughter and cackling coming from the taxi as soon as I open the front door which instantaneously makes me smile. Yes, this is exactly what I need.

"Helllloooo…" I call. I can hear the excitement in my voice as I greet my friends as the taxi becomes a mess of flailing arms as we hug each other hello, whilst we make our way into town.

This is the first time I've seen Zoe and Ashlee for a couple of months and it's really good to see them. After the awkward but, thankfully short conversation about Mark, we get down to the important business of admiring each other's outfits.

We arrive at our first destination of the evening - a lively bar, which is usually one of our regular haunts called '*Golds*'. It plays contemporary house music and always gets busy, but has a good crowd. The darkness of the bar with its black and slate grey walls is lit with several expensive looking gold chandeliers which are hung along the length of the bar, giving a relaxed yet sophisticated vibe.

Jodie and Zoe head to the bar whilst Ashlee and I are so busy catching up that by the time we reach the girls at the bar, the drinks have already been ordered and Zoe is busy pouring four glasses of white wine from a bottle as shots sit on a silver tray next to her.

Since I saw her last, Ashlee has had her beautiful black hair cut into a stylish crop which emphasises her long neck and high cheekbones. As she fills me in on her latest boyfriend, she has me in fits of laughter. We always say that Ashlee should have been a comedian, she never fails to make us laugh.

The four of us sit ourselves at some newly available stools at the bar, as we do our best to talk above the music.

As soon as we've sat down, Ashlee eyes me suspiciously and I instinctively know what's coming.

"So, come on Luisa, Jodie tells us you've fallen in love with an Adonis..."

Zoe makes suitable *oooh* and *ahhh* noises as I feel myself begin to blush profusely. I turn to look at Jodie next to me, just in time to see her looking daggers at Ashlee who in turn, looks appropriately scorned as her cheeks flush to almost the same shade of red as her midi dress.

Jodie places her hand on my arm. "I never said that you were in love with him...I was just keeping the girls telling up to date about your holiday fling."

It's not that I mind the girls knowing about Luka, I want the world to know. I would happily shout it from the rooftops given half a chance, but the pretence of it having been nothing more than a fling is getting harder and harder.

I tell the girls about Luka, playing my feelings down as best I can, before Ashlee changes the subject onto Zoe's ex-boyfriend. Zoe has only recently turned 21, but she looks older than her years despite her almost waist length brown hair.

Jodie suddenly stops the conversation. "Ladies..." Gesturing with her eyes and as we turn to follow her line of vision, we see a group of four men next to us, clearly talking about us.

One of them, dressed in a tight white t-shirt has arms so muscular, I swear they're bigger than my thighs. He promptly winks in our direction giving Zoe a fit of the giggles as she flutters her eyelashes in his direction.

"Oh, look at him." Zoe begins. "...you can just picture him in the mirror at the gym, kissing his muscles."

The rest of us begin laughing so heartily, we're in danger of falling off our stools. Ashlee drags herself to her feet, knocking back the last dregs of her wine. "Come on, I think it's time we hit the dance floor next door."

We battle our way through the crowd towards the bar in '*Hot House Nightclub*', and promptly order two shots each followed by another glass of wine each. I already feel rather merry to say the least by this point and I know that drinking shots is the wrong move for me. Even with this thought in mind, I have a desperate need to forget things for tonight and to relax as I follow the girls and throw the drinks back.

Looking around the bustling nightclub, even though there are dozens groups of friends enjoying themselves, the only thing I really take in are the couples dancing closely with each other and the newly formed pairs smooching on the dance floor and in every available corner. The smell of the club suddenly hits me and starts to turn my stomach. The waft of stale beer and energy drinks lingers around us.

I gulp my wine back much to the surprise of the girls who stare at me as though they've never met me before in their lives.

I slam my glass down on to the bar as Jodie looks at me nervously. "Are you alright, Luisa?"

Jodie waits for a response as Zoe leads the way with Ashlee on to the dance floor. "...only you've been staring into space for the last five minutes and now you're drinking like there's no tomorrow."

I squeeze Jodie's arm in affection. "I'm fine..." Although that seems to come out of my mouth as 'I'm f-f-f-iiiiiiin-n-n-e' and I wonder for a second if that was actually me speaking because that person sounded really rather drunk.

I take her hand and guide her onto the dance floor, joining the others as they strut their stuff. It feels good to relax and forget for a while.

A few songs later, Zoe decides it's time for another drink and saunters off to the bar with the help of Ashlee. The drink is clearly wearing off as my concentration on dancing is definitely wavering, and so, I delve into my bag on the hunt for my phone and feel elated to see a message from Luka.

"I am glad you liked the photos. Are you ready for your trip? xx"

I stand in the middle of the dance floor, eagerly typing a response. Even being nudged by the flying limbs of the enthusiastic dancers behind me doesn't put me off. I tell Luka I'm out with the girls for my leaving party before continuing dancing with my phone in my hand. I can see Jodie looking at me from the corner of my eye.

She shouts to make herself heard above the music. "Is that Luka?"

I can barely contain my happiness as I nod at her with my beaming smile before another response comes through.

"I hope you have fun. Be careful of male attention xx"

I giggle to myself as I read his message before telling Jodie I'm going to the ladies, purely so I can think about my reply to Luka.

As I'm slightly under the influence of alcohol, I type a flirtatious text back to Luka…I really hope I don't regret this in the morning.

"A girl can never have too much male attention…"

I use the loo and apply some more lipstick in the mirror before my phone pipes up once again.

"I think you are trying to make me jealous? X"

I smile smugly to myself. Something inside is telling me not to reply until tomorrow when I have a clear head, but the tipsy Luisa knows better.

"…*Is it working?*"

There, response sent. But for some reason I have an uneasy feeling about this. I put my phone back into the safety of my bag as Ashlee joins me in the mirror to inspect her make up.

"Oh, you missed it, Luisa. Those blokes from next door are here, Mr Biceps is all over Zoe and she's loving it!"

I laugh to myself as I take hold of her arm and we march back outside to the heat of the club, me now feeling buoyed from Luka's flirtation. Ashlee wasn't exaggerating when she said he was all over Zoe, the two of them are busy playing tonsil tennis as the others including Mr Bicep's friends, continue to dance - apparently oblivious.

An image of Luka comes into my head and I wonder how on earth I fell this hard and so quickly for someone.

Chapter 29 – Luka, Dubrovnik

That night I met Aleksander and Vilko for drinks, we went to *'Baldo's'* - I had not been there since that first night I went out with Luisa.

We were talking about my work situation when my brother, Alek brought up the subject of Luisa.

"Why did you let her go? It was like the two of you had always been here…together."

I sipped my beer, the bottle dripping condensation onto my blue shorts which was a welcome distraction for me whilst I wondered what to say.

"There is much you do not know Alek, she was here for a holiday…"

"It does not mean you cannot keep seeing her, does it?"

I see Vilko cast a glance toward my brother before he also chips in. "He is right my friend, there was so much more there - there was more spark between the two of you than there ever was between you and Amra. You are going to throw that away?"

I clear my throat in awkward feeling as I tell them how I feel, about not holding her back and about us both getting on with our lives, with the thousands of miles in between us. They continue to tell me I am making a mistake.

I change the subject, telling them about the possible interview Melita may have got me and I need to focus my energies on that.

Later that night back at home, I cannot get Luisa off my mind. 48 hours ago I made the decision that email was to be the last contact with her but I am already struggling. I decide to get in touch and her reply is almost instant. She tells me she is out with her friends and immediately we have that easy flowing flirty conversation back between us. She is so uncomplicated, so easy to communicate with. I tell her to be careful of any male attention and I snigger to myself as I type the message. She tells me there is no such thing as too much of this so I ask, are you trying to make me jealous?

When she replies to ask if it is working, I stop. I have to. It will always keep leading back to the discussion of us. There can be no us.

Chapter 30 - Luisa

The next morning, after realising I drank far too much last night, Luka and the text he didn't reply to is the first thing on my mind. I have a moment of panic, where I can't quite remember what I sent to him. Locating my phone on the floor, I again read the message I sent asking if he was jealous...desperately willing him to reply. I wonder if he would've been bothered?

I keep thinking about speaking to him and being in his arms, this is ridiculous. I need to either tell him how I feel, if he doesn't already realise or, stop pining for him. The truth of the matter is, having Luka as a friend would be better than nothing at all, but being friends with him would never be enough.

I feel as though I'm covered in a thick fog of misery this morning - my hangover certainly doesn't help. How could anything so perfect be given a time limit of two weeks?

In two days' time I'm jetting off to make one of my dreams come true...going travelling and yet the feel that there is a definite missing piece just won't go away. I'm annoyed with myself at how I'm feeling, I've done such a good job at picking myself back up over the past year or so and I've let myself become soppy and way too involved in the Luka situation. This stops now.

I pull myself together and practically leap out of bed, but as soon as my feet touch the floor, the after effects of last night's drinking get worse. Spotting my glass of water on the side, I gulp the full glass down before resting my poor hungover self back down on the bed once more. *Right, that's it.*

I spy my trainers in the corner of the room and before I have time to talk myself out of it, I'm dressed in my grey joggers and white vest top, scraping my hair into a ponytail and forcing myself out for a jog.

***

Despite having stitch for most of the circuit and receiving some strange looks from passers-by in their cars as I attempted to get moving, I actually feel quite invigorated after my jog. It probably ended up being just more of a fast walk more than anything else but it was good to get out in the fresh air.

Now freshly showered and changed I join the rest of my family, including Ben and Georgia for Sunday lunch. Ben and Georgia fill us in on their wedding plans and I have to say I'm really excited.

Georgia tosses her shoulder length blonde hair over her shoulder and moves in closer to me as she attempts to explain the type of wedding dress she has in mind.

"Seriously, all I want is something classic and simple. I keep picturing a dress cut to just below the knee, something in chiffon to match the location – light and carefree."

I can see the image of her clearly in front of me, wearing a dress just as she described. "Ohh, you'd look so beautiful in something like that, it sounds very you..."

Wiping the soppy grin from my face that arrived as soon as my brother started to talk about the wedding, I tuck into the delicious roast lamb with carrots, cauliflower and several different types of potato. The lamb has been marinating overnight in garlic, rosemary, mustard and honey so now it has the succulent taste of sweetness against the garlic as it melts in my mouth.

I look momentarily around the room as I drink some water and realise something looks different on the wall next to the table.

It takes me a couple of seconds to realise what it is exactly, but I soon appreciate by the nail in the wall with nothing hanging from it and from the colour difference in the wallpaper clearly a picture frame has been taken down. It's a picture from my wedding day - I'd got so used to it being there I must have stopped noticing it at some point.

Mom meets my gaze and smiles solemnly. "I didn't think it right to keep the photo on the wall, Luisa."

"I'm glad I don't have to look at it…"

My dad tries to make light of the situation as he puts his cutlery down rather noisily on the table.

"We will get a different picture, to replace it."

We spend the rest of the afternoon talking with excitement about the wedding plans and my travelling and I fill them in on my planned route.

Just then I hear my Mom begin to sniffle, prompting my Dad to lean in close to her and squeeze her hand.

"I'm so proud of both of you…" She looks at me and then at Ben in turn.

"We are both proud of you." My Dad adds. "You getting on with your life and going travelling…" He looks at me before putting his attention on to Ben. "…and you getting married."

My brother gets up from his seat and pulls me in for a bear hug…I think he's worried I'm about to get upset. He squeezes me so tight I feel I'm about to pop.

"Have an amazing time sis, I'll miss you."

I kiss my brother on the cheek before squeezing him back. "I'll miss you too. Thanks again for your help with…you know."

He pulls away. "You don't have to thank me. At least now you're getting divorced I won't have to waste my energy on him.

Later that evening as my parents begins to doze off in front of the TV, I decide that now is as good a time as any to start packing. I look around the mess that has become my room over the past few days. My open suitcase still sits on the floor with the few bits I haven't bothered to unpack still sitting inside. I kneel down on the floor next to the case and begin to take out my guidebook of Croatia, various maps and receipts.

I reach for the paper bag in the corner of my case and discover my lavender angel with 'believe' embroidered across her chest. Staring at the words in front of me, I feel a tinge of sadness forcing me to glance fondly at the photo that I brought of Luka's of the old town as it sits on top of my chest of drawers.

I smile to myself, grateful now more than ever for what my holiday in Dubrovnik gave to me. I hook the ribbon that's attached to the angel around the handle on my drawer and realise once again, the positivity that seems to radiate from her.

I'm startled to hear my Mom clear her throat softly behind me. "You are miles away…well, you literally will be in a couple of days."

"I can hardly believe it's happening to be honest, it actually really is one of my dreams coming true."

My Mom walks further into the room, rubbing my shoulder affectionately before sitting on the end of the bed. "I know it is *cariño*, that's one of the reasons why your Dad and I are so proud of you."

I take a seat hesitantly next to her on the bed. "Really? Even though pretty soon I'll be divorced?"

She shakes her head furiously. "I know I reacted badly. I probably didn't support you as much as I should have done when Mark did what he did to you the first time." She clasps my hand in hers, looking me in the eye. "…I struggled to hear you speak of divorce, but it was wrong of me to make you feel that you could not speak to me about things. I wish I could turn back the clock."

"Mom, it's okay, I know what your beliefs are, and I don't expect you to change them, I wouldn't want you to…"

"No…" She interrupts. "They are my beliefs yes, but sometimes things happen. How could I ever have thought that man would change?"

I rest my head on her shoulder. "How could any of us think he would?" I sigh. "But we did what we thought was right at the time. It doesn't matter now *Mamá*." I lift my head and turn to face her.

She smiles fondly. "You haven't called me that in a long time…"

When we were younger we would always call her that, I think she always preferred it to the English version.

She stares momentarily into my eyes and smiles proudly. "That holiday, I don't know what happened but you have come back a different person. You know what you want and I believe that nothing will stop you now." If only she knew who had come into my life and turned things around.

As she stands to leave the room, she spookily notices Luka's photograph of the sunrise for the first time and goes closer to marvel at the vision, taking the frame in her hand.

"What an impressive photograph, Luisa." She turns her head towards me as I move closer to her, joining her in studying the image.

"I know, I just had to buy it when I saw it…" I imagine Luka, poised in readiness to take the shot that now sits framed before us.

She kisses me on my cheek, still clutching the frame. I feel as though she wants to ask a question, it's like she knows something about this picture is very dear to me. She puts the frame down and smiles, not shifting her eyes away from it for even a moment.

"Such an inspiring place, huh?" Mom moves her hands into the back pockets on her jeans and sighs, making eye contact again. "I know you will be happy again one day, Luisa-Maria."

I paint a smile on my face as she leaves the room, but inside I still have the agonising longing.

After attempting to decide what to pack for my three month trip, I still only have a few items actually packed in my huge hiking bag which I've decided to take rather than a case hoping it will be easier to carry around.

The next morning I feel so tired, having not got to sleep until gone 4:00 a.m. After breakfast, I haul my hiking bag onto the bed and retrieve my positive frame of mind and actually manage to pack everything I'll need for my trip. Feeling satisfied that not only am I actually packed and ready to go, I also resisted the urge to over pack which is what I normally tend to do. I had recurring pictures in my mind of me heaving a suitcase around with me, almost slipping a disc in the process. Apart from my first stop in Seville with Jodie, I'll mostly be relying on public transport for the duration so travelling light is a must.

With my packing completed I do my best to eat some lunch but with my appetite still barely there, I decide to get changed and head out to the solicitors to sign the paperwork that needs my signature before I leave.

Chapter 31 – Luka, Dubrovnik

On the way back from my chat with the manager at *The Grand Lapad Plaža* I decide to go up into the forests with my camera to clear my head. Whilst I am not working I will make the most of the time and do more photography. I hear Luisa's words of encouragement echoing in my head…perhaps I will try to sell more of my work.

Aleksander is moving in to my spare room tomorrow temporarily so I do not have to use all of my savings to pay for my mortgage. As long as he does not expect me to do everything for him like our mother does at home, we will get along just fine.

Getting back from the forest, I plug my camera into my laptop to take a look at the photos and an email comes through from a name I do not recognise - Jodie Barrett. I am reluctant to open this at first, the only Jodie that I know of…is Luisa's friend. I am too curious to press delete without reading.

It's her, *it is* that Jodie. She is apologising for getting in touch out of the blue and for being so blunt but she is asking me how I feel about Luisa. She says that Luisa claims it was a holiday fling but she knows her too well and can see the depth of her feelings for me. Jodie gives me her number, tells me that as they leave tomorrow for Seville if I reply it might be easier to send a text or I am more than welcome to call her if I want to talk, she says.

She goes on to tell me that Luisa is talking down her feelings when she can tell that it is tearing her apart being away from me.

I have to stand up, to walk away from my computer. I cannot read any more. I walk around my apartment feeling very confused, that is all I do for what seems like hours - circling around my small living room and kitchen.

I go out for a walk, my laptop is still on, my email is still open - email only partially read.

Chapter 32 – Luisa – Seville, Spain

I feel a little guilty in saying that I'm relieved to leave the UK again. Obviously it's where my family and friends live and it's my home, even if I don't technically have a home of my own right now. Going travelling is something exciting, something positive that I'm doing with my life and I know it will open my eyes even more to so many possibilities, not to mention give me more inspiration for my next book.

After disembarking the plane in Malaga, we make the exhilarating walk down the steps to the tarmac - my favourite part. The moment you get your first real glimpse, that first breath of air in the country you're visiting, there's no feeling like it.

As the wonderful intense humid heat of the Spanish sun beams onto our skin, I can't speak for Jodie, but I can certainly feel a peacefulness slowly begin to wash over me. I remove my cropped denim jacket to let the sun onto my arms and feel the very gentle breeze blowing through my hair, seemingly refreshing me of any stresses.

We walk within the designated area towards the terminal building. Staff outside wearing illuminous yellow jackets drive the small trucks over to the plane to begin to offload the hundreds of suitcases, others make their way up the steps to begin the clean-up operation before the next passengers appear for their flight home. I always wonder as I look around out here - how do they cope in the sun all day without their sunglasses? Some of the staff wear them but others don't, it has always puzzled me.

Jodie frantically begins to fan herself with her passport. "Wow, it's so hot, I can't wait for this…" She throws her arm around my waist with restless enthusiasm as I, in turn, lightly drape my arm around her, grateful to have her company for the next couple of days. Her excitement lifts my spirits even further and after just a short wait at the carousel, we're reunited with our luggage.

As Jodie pushes the trolley with my large bag and her small case, I busy myself in trying to locate the car hire paperwork from my bag. We follow the signs directing us to the different hire firms which lead us down a ramp and into the lower level of the terminal where we're greeted by the desks, complete with huge queues, of several different firms.

I study our surroundings further. Despite the hordes of people queuing under the fluorescent lighting of the terminal after their early morning flights, people are still in good spirits - after all this is still part of their holiday.

We follow the signage to the underground car park still hunting for the right company. Hundreds of cars are laid out before us as the humid air wafts in from outside and there in front of us, is the tiny office of 'Lease of Life Car Hire'. Fortunately for us it has no queue whatsoever.

With barely any room inside the office to swing a set of keys, as Jodie is the designated driver she heads inside with the paperwork whilst I wait outside with the luggage.

I see holidaymakers checking their hire cars for any scratches, others are hesitantly leaving the safety of the parking space and heading outside as they attempt to get used to their cars, the sound of the breaks squealing.

I look behind me to see Jodie signing some documents as I hear my phone bursting into life. Three missed calls from Mark followed by a text.

"How can you up and leave for three months, I take it you are contactable?"

Why does this man always have a way of trying to bring me down? I'm so glad to be out of the country and away from him again. I promptly delete the message and block his number. Wow, that feels good.

Hire car checked and we're finally on our way to our hotel in Seville. Our journey from Malaga airport to the heart of the Seville should take just over two hours, providing of course we don't get lost along the way.

It seems rather strange sitting on the right-hand side as a passenger, but it must seem even stranger still for Jodie driving and sitting on the left-hand side, but she seems to be taking it all in her stride.

We head along the A-45 toward Seville before joining the A-92. At first, the area seems quite built-up with shopping centres and the like along the way, but after a few miles the views give way to hills, trees and the odd advertising board. Black wooden bulls sit on the hillsides which, if I remember right, are advertising a type of sherry.

We talk with excitement as we decide what to do first when we arrive.

Jodie changes the subject. "Has he been in touch?"

I assume she means Luka and I get that tug on my emotions at the thought of him. "No, I haven't heard from him since we were out with the girls on Saturday night."

Jodie checks her mirrors and changes lanes on the motorway. "I erm…I was talking about Mark, sorry."

I'm sure I can feel my face begin to flush, I've made it obvious that Luka is firmly on my mind.

"Oh… I had a message when I checked my phone earlier, I've now blocked his number…at least for the time being whilst I'm away."

Jodie doesn't respond, so I occupy myself with reading through some leaflets on Andalusia that I picked up from the airport. Jodie's mobile begins to ring in her bag, which is next to me in the foot well.

"Do you want me to see who that is?"

"No! erm…no sorry, don't worry, it'll just be Darren. I can call him when we get to the hotel."

Sometime later, we're both beginning to feel quite hungry and so we pull into a roadside restaurant called 'Los Viajeros'. As Jodie switches off the engine, we both sit back and relax enjoying a couple of moments of quietness without the car engine and radio. There's just the occasional whizzing noise of a car speeding past the restaurant as it continues on its journey.

The restaurant's fairly large in size with a red awning at the front providing shade for the potted plants. I almost feel like we're in the desert until we hear the sound of cars on the busy road. We decide to sit on the currently empty shaded terrace area, so we can still be outdoors and enjoy the warmth. The terrace is very simply kitted out with small glass topped tables and red plastic chairs and an archway providing an outlook onto the car park and the hills in the distance.

As we take a seat we can hear chatter coming from inside of the restaurant.

Jodie studies the menu. "Why is the English version of the menu always at the back?"

I roll my eyes and giggle at my friend. "Maybe it has something to do with us being in Spain, where they predominantly speak Spanish."

Jodie laughs along with me. "Okay, point taken. I'm absolutely ravenous, I think I'm going to have the chicken and chips. Can you do the honours?"

It's been quite some time since I spoke Spanish to anyone other than my Mom, so as the waiter approaches our table I reopen my menu, just in case I get stuck.

The waiter greets us with a friendly smile. "Hola ¿Para beber?"

"Hola, dos café con leche por favor." I order two coffees before asking for a chicken salad for me and Jodie's chicken and chips.
The waiter smiles and walks away, making me breathe a sigh of relief.

Jodie nudges me. "Technically you have an unfair advantage being half Spanish."

I remove my flip-flops under the table and let my feet relax. "Well, let's see what we end up with before you thank me."

A coach pulls into the car park making an almighty grinding sound, making us turn in our seats to see the passengers scurrying down the steps. There's a smell of car oil and fumes beginning to linger in the air as the driver follows the passengers waving his arms around in frustration. It looks like they might be here for some time. The coach load of tourists head towards us almost filling what was the peaceful terrace area. We certainly eat our food faster than we were intending to.

Another hour of driving later and we arrive in Seville. My first impression is how big and spaced out the city centre seems in comparison to Granada, which is the last Spanish city I visited. Our hotel is quite easy to find with it being just on the outskirts of the centre in the *Remedios* District. As we turn into Calle Virgen de la Victoria, we see our hotel on the left-hand side with the shutters down over the car park. Jodie parks up on the street as I run inside the hotel to enquire about car parking.

Once we're parked up and checked in, we locate our room on the fourth floor. Our room is pretty large, light and airy with whitewashed walls and pine furniture. A fruity aroma tells us that housekeeping has probably just finished preparing the room, and went slightly overboard with the air freshener…it's quite overpowering so we throw open the window.

There's a generous sized bathroom, two single beds and two double wardrobes. We unpack the basics, slather ourselves in sun lotion and I change my maxi dress for a pair of denim shorts and strapless green top. Jodie changes into a flowing yellow vest dress and pulls her hair into a high ponytail.

We step out onto the street from our hotel and consult a map. Jodie's convinced that left is the way to the city centre where as I'm convinced we need to turn right. After a short debate, Jodie wins and we begin walking towards the centre. Our hotel is in a lovely residential area, so all we can hear as we walk is the sound of Spanish chatter as we see people out with their young families and older men sitting on benches talking energetically with their friends, gesticulating with their hands.

We cut through a pedestrian only area where people are enjoying that typical relaxed Spanish way of life as they too sit outside sipping drinks in the late afternoon sun and I'm surprised by how at home I feel here.

We pass small boutiques with mannequins wearing stylish dresses on display in windows, pharmacies with the temperature proudly displayed outside in neon numbers, bakeries with the most delicious smelling bread and cakes and a supermarket, before we are back out onto the main road again.

We cross the San Telmo Bridge, with the view across the Guadalquivir River and we see the Torre del Oro - Gold Tower standing proudly on the left-hand side.

Walking in the direction of the tower, we opt to stroll along the quiet path which runs alongside the river rather than walking along the street. The pathway is lined with pretty pink flowers, palm trees and shrubbery. Joggers run alongside us marvelling at the view as they go and a lady passes by with two little dogs.

Jodie gushes as she watches the dogs. "My three would love walking along here."

"They would love walking anywhere…"

We stop and take a seat on a bench for a few minutes rest overlooking the river. It's really calming sitting here and gazing out, taking a few pictures of the pretty restaurants and cafés on the other side of the river.

I remember to ask Jodie about one of the dog shows I know she has coming up soon. Her passion is so very clear as she tells me about it.

"Zack could qualify for the main championships again next year….here's hoping. He did it this year though so I have complete confidence in my boy. Belle's too old now bless her, but Molly only just missed out this year..."

There's so much work involved in Jodie's hobby but as she's been doing it for so long now it's a way of life for her. She really is dedicated to those beautiful pooches.

I have a flash back of a memory. "Do you remember when we first moved in together and I came along with you to one of the training classes?"

"How can I forget? Little Molly very kindly peed all over the floor - you slipped in it, falling on your backside and stank my car out the whole way home."

We sit in hysterics as we replay the picture in our heads.

"Wasn't that the night you were trying to impress the new teacher as well? What was his name?"

Jodie gasps. "Ohhh, Ryan...I'd forgotten all about him, he was gorgeous."

"Well the next day I seem to remember you met Darren so he really made you forget all about Ryan."

"There so you see, if you hadn't have slipped in dog pee, I wouldn't have had to have gone rushing to the chemist the next morning to get you some pain killers for your back and then I wouldn't have met Darren...at the till...as he was collecting his Mom's bunion cream."

We burst into laughter once again.

The sun is scorching hot even this late in the afternoon, and I can't help but think I should have brought my hat out with me today. We walk back up onto the street for a better unrestricted view of the Torre del Oro.

Reading the signage outside we learn that the tower was built to protect the port of the city and it currently houses a Naval Museum. Looking up at the structure of the tower it looks so smooth, making you want to run your hand over the brickwork, which reminds me of the cobbles in Dubrovnik.

Continuing along the street, we approach the Castle de Alcázar. One of the entrances has a wall painted a deep red in between two castle turrets with a coat of arms on display. We pay our entry fees and begin exploring inside.

The wall designs in the castle interior are really beautiful, with vivid colours of blue mixed with browns and creams. Huge windows do their best to let the light pour inside as we wander through the Hall of the Kings and out into the Alcázar Gardens. Once we're outside, I'm surprised at how tranquil it feels.

Water features are sat amongst the endless greenery, palm trees and various plants which enhance the ambience further still. The gentle curves of archways catch the light as the sun dances on the water below. We sit in the gardens in a shaded area for a while, just taking everything in.

I tilt my head up to the sky and breathing in, I let my cares drift away. "It's so peaceful here."

Jodie pulls her legs up onto the bench, resting her feet on my lap. "Mmmm."

She takes a sip of water from the bottle in her bag before offering it to me. "You can talk about him, you know…"

I swallow hard at her suggestion, screwing the lid back onto the bottle. "What do you mean?"

She takes the bottle from me, chuckling to herself. "Don't play the innocent with me, Luisa, you know who I'm talking about."

I assume she's talking about Mark again, that is until I see her playful grin on her face which, I have to admit, makes me struggle to contain my laughter.

"What is there to talk about?"

She tips her head in my direction and raises her eyebrows questioningly. "Well…I know he gave you the time of your life in Dubrovnik, and I also know you well enough to know that there's more to it than you make out…"

She's right of course, but I don't want to admit that. I snatch the bottle of water out of her hand.

"Well you seem to think you know a lot Jode…but on this occasion, you're wrong."

I smile my best smile at her, but I know she can see through it. This is what will get me over Luka, I need to look at the bigger picture and tell myself every day that it was what it was…past tense.

Chapter 33 – Luka, Dubrovnik

I took some time to think about what to say to Jodie in my reply. I could have lied and told her I was not interested in it being anything more than it was and that would have finished the matter, but if this lie got back to Luisa, I did not want to hurt her, she has already been hurt so much. I am not a liar and I could not just ignore Jodie and so, eventually, I sent her a text.

I told her what happened with Mark and my job and said I did not want Luisa to know about this, it would only cause her more upset. I am hopeful she will not tell her as Luisa does not know that she has been in touch with me.

I was honest in telling her that it would be a risk for both of us and that I did not want to hold her back from living the life she wanted to live.

Melita read Luisa's book on her honeymoon and wasted no time in telling me exactly what it is about. She brought the novel to me, it is still sitting on the table, I am putting off starting this. I want to read it but I feel afraid in some way that it will be even harder to let her go.

I know that Luisa does not want or need the life of her protagonist in her romantic novel – that is of a woman who is married to a millionaire and living the high life but her life is a pretence. It would seem that Mark wanted her to be that way, wanted her to be materialistic and a show off but that is just not her nature.

I know that Luisa wants an honest and fulfilled life living happily with someone who sees her for who she really is and hears her when she speaks, someone who is fully in the room with her in body and mind and that is exactly what she deserves.

Should I leap into this with both feet? Jodie does not know for sure what is going through Luisa's mind. I could be hurt, she could be hurt, there is a lot to lose here and then we will always regret ruining that time we had together on her holiday. A time which was *savršen* – perfect.

Chapter 34 – Luisa, Seville

Back out onto the *avenida* we walk further, alongside the metro with its gentle hum as it glides along advertising different fast foods on the side and soon, we come across the cathedral of Seville.

The vast cathedral is absolutely stunning, photographs just won't do it the justice it deserves. Jodie and I stand outside the main doors as a local man appears, handing out leaflets advertising flamenco shows.

Jodie reads one of his leaflets with interest. "We should go to one of these, what do you think?"

I take the leaflet from her, and take in the pictures of flamenco dancers with the promise of a typical Spanish meal, which is enough to convince me. We buy two tickets for the show the following night. With all of this walking in the heat, we're desperate for a drink, so we visit the café just across the street and order two coffees and two bottles of water.

The Spanish way of life is so relaxing and it's so easy to slip into. It feels good to just sit chatting with Jodie, talking about old times when we worked together and people watching, of course.

Once we're fully re-energised from our caffeine fix, we walk arm in arm through the streets and up to the Barrio Santa Cruz. This is the name given to the area full of cobbled streets and alleyways that wind up and around…which reminds me of you know where.

I start thinking about the night I bumped into Luka with his friends in the old town - him escorting me back to the hotel through the streets, with the pizza stop off.

Jodie nudges me. "You're miles away."

"Sorry, I was just thinking…how about we head back to the hotel, get ready for dinner?"

Jodie looks at her watch. "Good idea its after 6:00 p.m. already…and tonight you can start doing some talking."

Why do I have a feeling that tonight I'm going to be interrogated?

***

After my shower I change back into my maxi dress, adding a chunky bangle borrowed from Jodie (which momentarily makes me think of Pam) and I style my hair into a high ponytail. I can still hear Jodie rifling through the toiletries in the bathroom, so she hasn't even begun to get ready yet. Looking around the room, I spy my trusty notepad sticking out of my hand luggage. Figuring I have about an hour to kill waiting for Jodie, I scribble a note for her and head down to reception to use the *'internet corner'*.

I log onto my email account and as the page slowly loads, I feel restless with wonder. I doubt there will be anything from Luka since I checked my emails on my phone this morning, but it's worth a try. Amongst the mountains of junk mail, I see his name in typeface in front of me but disappointingly, it's just the email he sent to me last week with the photos. I can't resist opening the email to look at the pictures again but as I do so, the realisation hits me that if I keep torturing myself, this will never get easier. I let out a loud breath of exasperation, before logging out of my emails and loading up my online storage facility.

Using my notes, I manage to write a page of my book and I send a short email to Pam and Pete, before Jodie appears next to me in a flowing red maxi skirt and white vest top.

"I'm ready when you are…"

"Wow, you look gorgeous." I tell her as she twirls in front of me to show off her new skirt.

"I can grab a drink in the bar whilst I wait for you if you want more time writing?"

I shut down the computer, taking my bag from the back of the chair. "No, don't be silly, there'll be plenty of time for that over the next few months, we've only got a couple of days before you go home."

We make our way back into town, across the bridge to see the Torre del Oro now bathed in golden light as it's surrounded by darkness. We turn towards the opposite side of the river, taking in the atmosphere that the now illuminated restaurants along the side of the water brings. The humid night air around us is filled with these beautiful lights and they seem to be enough to make the people around us equally light up with happiness, as we hear the sound of laughter echoing in the distance from the restaurants. Luka would absolutely love it here. *Forget him, forget him.*

We walk past the metro station, past the groups of local teenagers as they sit on the steps, chatting amongst themselves, showing off their skills on their bikes and onto the Avenida de la Constitución. We pass by the cathedral, which I have to say, has to be my favourite place in Seville so far.

Now night has fallen, the cathedral - like most of the city, is also immersed in golden light. It looks so warm and welcoming.

The sound of horse shoes clip-clopping against the road makes us turn around and we see a couple of horse and carriages coming towards us carrying tourists. The black carriages have huge yellow wheels and they're pulled along by beautiful white horses.

Jodie links my arm. "They seem to add something to the atmosphere. We should go on one later, how about it?"

"Yeah, why not. But first let's find some food, I'm starving."

You'd think in a city with so many places to eat that deciding where to eat would be simple, yet 20 minutes later we're still walking up and down side streets in an attempt to agree where to go. We pass dozens of perfectly good restaurants but each time, either Jodie thinks there will be a better one around the corner or, there are no available tables. By this time I'm so hungry, I'm tempted to go to the local burger bar, but this would just be criminal when we're surrounded by delicious local Spanish cuisine.

We start our second attempt around the circuit of tapas bars when I spy a couple just about to leave a table. I pull Jodie sharply by the arm linked through mine in that direction.

"Here this will do, I'm in serious danger of collapsing with hunger here."

As we take our seats at the table nestled on the street, the grey haired ponytailed waiter approaches, us taking away the glasses left on the table before wiping the surface with a cloth.

"¡Chicas, bienvenido!" He welcomes us happily, gesturing towards the specials board hung proudly on the wall.

I order two white wines as we cast our eyes over the chalk board to which the waiter suddenly becomes more animated.

"¡Ah, Español! ¿Eres Español o en vacación?"

I can see Jodie staring back and forth at us as though she's watching a tennis match and following every movement of the ball, left and right. I tell him we're on holiday from England.

"You speak Spanish very well. I will get your drinks as you read the menu." He slopes off back inside the restaurant.

Jodie begins to flick through the pages on her menu. "So, what do you fancy?"

"Erm... I'm not sure, it all sounds good to me."

The waiter returns with our huge glasses of wine and waits patiently next to us, ready to take our order. We decide on fresh tuna marinated in soy sauce, mini lamb burgers, cheesy croquettes, asparagus wrapped in *jamon de serrano* and fresh bread rubbed with tomatoes and garlic. As we finish ordering, I hear the distinct noise of my mobile and my heart almost skips a beat. As I hunt under the table for my bag, I hear Jodie utter the words 'yes please'.

I'm half reading a message from my Dad and half listening to Jodie. "What was that you agreed to?"

Jodie sips her wine and coughs heartily. "Ooh, that's strong..." She puts down her glass. "I just said yes to chips, why not, we're on holiday."

I raise my glass in Jodie's direction. "Cheers, here's to an exciting couple of days."

"…and an exciting few months for you!"

The tuna with the soy and the cheesy croquettes are the first to arrive at our table just moments later and we dig in hungrily. The tuna is delicious and goes really well with the sauce. Next, the waiter brings the bread and a massive plate of shrimps. Jodie and I look at each other with confusion.

"Sorry, lo siento…" I call out to the waiter to tell him that we didn't order shrimps.

He looks at Jodie, somewhat puzzled. "You said yes, *las gambas*.…"

Jodie's mouth falls open in realisation. "*Las gambas*… I thought you said *patatas fritas* - chips!"

Jodie begins to guffaw with a look of slight embarrassment, and I join in with her.

"It's okay, we'll eat them." Jodie assures the waiter as he walks away, also in hysterics before returning seconds later with two more glasses of wine.

"Gratis….lo siento." He mutters, before walking away again.

I take a piece of toasted bread from the plate and the scent of garlic and tomatoes mixed with herbs hits my senses.

"See, it was worth the embarrassment for the free glass of wine. I take it we aren't getting the chips then?"

Jodie swallows her food. "Apparently not, who was your message from?"

"It was from my Dad, just saying he hopes we're having a good time." I wash the bread down with another gulp of the rather strong wine.

Jodie clears her throat. "Maybe you should get in touch with Luka again?"

I wasn't expecting that suggestion. "What makes you say that?" I clutch my wine glass to my lips.

"Just an idea, it's obvious every time you hear your phone you're on tenterhooks in the hope that it's him."

Another large gulp of wine finishes my glass and it's on to the next one. "I know…it's silly."

She shakes her head. "How can it be silly?"

"There's no point is there, what exactly can happen between us now? We start a relationship over the phone and on email with the promise of meeting up a few times a year?"

Jodie shifts awkwardly in her seat. "It doesn't have to be like that though. When you get to Zagreb do you honestly mean to tell me you aren't going to get in touch, even then? How long would the flight be from Dubrovnik? An hour, if that."

Hearing this as an option makes excitement begin to brew inside of me. I put my fork down and wipe my mouth with my serviette. "Of course I'd thought about it, but what if that isn't what he wants?"

"Well, there's only one way to find out isn't there? Just think about it, what if you never see him again all because you didn't take the risk of asking?"

I stare at my now empty plate, I know she's right but if he says no, I feel like it will ruin everything that we had. "I know what you're saying makes sense, but…"

"Surely it's worth asking him, if you really believe you will never see him again anyway otherwise, what have you got to lose?"

"I don't want him to think I'm…desperate or something, Jodie."

"Hand on heart, think about it - do you really believe he'll think that? I'm guessing the two of you know each other pretty well by now."

Can I really do this, *should* I really do it? My heart begins to pound in my chest at the thought of seeing him again. "Okay, I'll ask him."

Jodie gasps with delight, and begins to clap like a happy seal. "Yesss…"

"But I haven't spoken to him for a few days, it doesn't feel right just coming straight out with that. I'll send a message now…just general chit chat, asking how he is first." I retrieve my bag from underneath the table again. "I hope you're right about this Jode…"

I compose a text, keeping it simple and friendly, just asking how he is and send it straight away before I can change my mind again. "There, it's done."

"Well done babe, this is so exciting…just think what could happen." Jodie throws back the last of her wine, and we pay the bill.

As we walk back in the direction of the hotel, the streets around us are still just as lively. People around us carry shopping bags from souvenir shops, we see a group of women wandering along enjoying *churros* as they dip into the tasty chocolate sauce.

Again I'm struck by how big Seville actually is. Seeing this many people around at night makes me wonder how many people live in the city itself.

Jodie checks around us. "Oh, how typical, I can't see any free horse and carriages."

"Never mind, we'll try again tomorrow after the flamenco show."

303

We walk slowly as we marvel again at the illuminated buildings around us, until the sound of hysterical laughter catches our attention. We turn around to see a group of men clearly on a stag night, with who we assume is the groom, dressed in a yellow chicken costume. We giggle along as the various people stop to have their photo taken with the chicken.

"Do you think you'll get married again one day, or would you just be happy to 'live in sin' as they say?" Jodie asks unexpectedly.

I think about her question for a second. "I'm not sure really, I'd like to think that Mark hasn't put me off marriage completely, I know not all men are like him. Who knows what the future will hold, eh?"

Jodie squeezes my arm playfully. "Exactly, the man of your dreams could be right around the corner, well across a few countries actually…and in Croatia."

"Yeah, you're right - he's in Croatia and that's the problem."

"What about you? Reckon Darren will make an honest woman of you one day? Or are you happy as you are?"

"Maybe, but I'm not really that bothered about the whole marriage thing."

"You know what Jode, I think that might be the right attitude to have."

Chapter 35 – Luisa, Seville

After the best night's sleep I've had since returning from Dubrovnik, I wake up to the sound of Jodie's gentle snoring in the next bed. We could have almost been the only guests staying at the hotel it was so quiet throughout the night. I creep out of bed and over to the window in the corner of the room. As I do so, I notice my mobile on the dressing table and the sharp spasm of anxiety hits me like a bolt as it dawns on me that after sending another message last night, I've heard nothing from Luka. I suppose there could be something there now, waiting to be read.

Pressing one of the buttons to bring my phone back to life, the empty screen stares back at me and fills me with disappointment. Well, that's that then. I tried at least and now - it's time to get on with things.

I slowly draw the curtain aside and open the shutter. The only view we have is of the hotel next door but as I look skyward, we have the only view we could ever need, the beautiful blue cloudless sky.

I lean my elbows on the window ledge and lean out as far as possible, taking in the early morning aromas of hot coffee and breakfast, and although my stomach's in knots, I'm really hungry.

"Morning." Jodie croaks behind me as she reaches for her watch to check the time.

"How did you sleep?" I walk over to her and perch on the end of her bed.

"Quite well, I think. I take it the sun's out?"

"Yesss, of course. Come on, I don't want to waste another second."

Walking into the breakfast room at the hotel, there are only a couple of tables taken, meaning we can sit wherever we like. I head straight for the tea, pouring a cup for each of us and returning to the table before heading back towards the hot *churros* that have my name written all over them.

Jodie's already tucking into a plate of bacon and eggs when I take my seat opposite her. I have my first bite of a food before stopping suddenly, as I look over at the buffet area and I get a reminder of him again.

"Lu, are you alright?"

I realise I was staring. "Sorry, I was miles away then." I swallow my food. "I've been thinking, maybe it's not such a good idea to ask Luka to meet me in Zagreb."

Jodie stops mid chew. "What, you're joking - you were certain last night…"

"Maybe I was, but…with no reply from him this morning, I think I've just realised I need to leave it be."

"I can't believe this, I really think you should do it."

"I know you do but it's decided now, I need to forget about him Jode, so can we just leave it there?" I smile solemnly and I think she understands as she nods her reply.

Abraham the receptionist waves to us in recognition as we pass through reception on our way out of the hotel a short time later. We round the corner and continue on our walk into town.

"Oh no…" Jodie stops. "I've left my phone in the room, do you mind if I go back for it?"

"It's fine, we'll go back." I turn to walk back in the direction of the hotel.

"I'll run back, it'll only take a minute. You enjoy the sun." She nods in the direction of the bench next to us, and before I can say anything more, she paces off back to the hotel.

I sit down on the bench and retrieve my map from my bag to double check the route to the nearest bus stop where we can buy our tickets for the tourist bus. Reasoning that it should only take a few minutes to get there, I make the most of my relaxation time.

School children are passing by on their way to school, some with their parents and some teenagers walking with their friends. I wonder for a minute what my life would have been like if my parents had settled in Spain where my mother was brought up, rather than in England. I know it's something they discussed before they got married.

I see Jodie turning around the corner towards me, talking away on her phone. Her walking speed seems to slow right down as she almost reaches my side, as though she's biding her time for privacy.

"Okay, speak to you soon, bye." Jodie ends the call. "Sorry about that, just thought I'd give Darren a quick call on my way back. Are we ready?"

"Yep, it's this way."

We reach the street side ticket sellers on the Paseo de Cristóbal Colón, and purchase our tickets for the hop on-hop off bus tour. Jodie buys a one day pass as she's going home tomorrow, but I buy a two day pass for just €6 extra. There's a bus already at the stop so we jump straight on board, climb the stairs up to the open top and take a seat at the front. Plugging in our head set, we hear Spanish guitar music which is the perfect soundtrack to our surroundings.

The early morning sun feels even hotter on the top deck and I think it'll be another glorious day. The traffic is busy already with cars, coaches and numerous bus tours, just like this one. Looking down onto the street, tourists like us are up and out early and people are walking to work in the sunshine. They wait at the traffic lights for that sound - I've noticed since we've been here that plays when the lights change to green for pedestrians. The sound reminders me of baby birds as they chirp in their nests.

Our red bus pulls away and we start the journey to our first point of call for the day, The Plaza de España. Just two bus stops later and we arrive at our destination.

Once were off the bus, we then follow the groups of people towards the landmark and as the *plaza* opens out in front of us, it's exquisite.

The pavilion buildings curve around before us as we stand on the *avenida* next to the stone balcony. We walk across the square itself towards the stunning fountain which throws water up high into the air in the centre and gradually lowers down at each side. We get a few cooling splashes of water on us from the fountain as we get closer.

Jodie spins around in a full circle to take in the sights.

"I really like it here…there's almost something like…a costume drama or a play about it, don't you think?"

"It does feel like that, you're right."

Silence falls between us and we enjoy the sound of the water as it cascades from the fountain before the clatter of horseshoes beckons again and we see a horse trotting past us, carrying a loved up couple along in its carriage.

We walk up the few steps which lead us underneath the archway of the buildings, and go inside the central building to admire the view to the outside from the further steps indoors. Hearing the rippling water of the fountain seems to be really calming as we head back outside on the balcony looking outward. From the intricate beige and brown paving patterns on the floor, to the buildings, the tiling along the walls and the blue and white detailed ceramics - the design of the whole area is nothing short of perfect.

Local people have set up various stalls just outside of the *plaza* selling different goods such as fans, flags and the like as we walk past them and into Maria Luisa Park, which was one of my Mom's favourite places she visited as a child, hence my name. We consider renting a bike to cycle around the park for a while, that is until we realise that neither of us can remember the last time we rode a bike and so rather than humiliating ourselves, we decide to rely on the wheels of the bus as we head back to the bus stop.

I check the map again and realise we need to double back on ourselves to get to where we want to go next, the bullring.

"Why don't we walk back up to the bullring and take in a few shops on the way?"

Jodie leans over my shoulder to take in the map. "Anything involving shopping sounds good to me."

The first shop we come to sells the usual tourist souvenirs and Jodie can't resist the temptation to buy a lovely red and black lace hand-held fan in an attempt to keep her cool for the rest of the day.

Despite the fact that the next shop along the row sells the same sort of goods, we head straight inside continuing our hunt for the unknown. This time, Jodie buys a gorgeous black and pink flamenco dress for her niece.

Not long later we reach the bullring, which looks almost like a large house from the outside. The white building with yellow detail curves around in that tell-tale shape of a ring. We pay our entry fee and take a seat in the cool interior with another 10 or so people as we wait for our guide.

Half an hour later after the visit around the museum inside, we reach the actual bullring itself outside for our free time. We start off up high in the seating area, which is just steps, no real seats. We stare down at the vast arena below us to see people standing, pretending to be bulls with their fingers poised either side of their heads, they run at their 'opponents' as they take their photo. The arena is absolutely enormous, our guide did tell us it holds 14,000 people. I bet the atmosphere is absolutely electric when the arena is full.

My phone sounds the message alert and I'm almost holding my breath. Part of me doesn't want to look so I still have some hope it's Luka... but I need to know. It's Melita and it's so lovely to hear from her. She's telling me she read my book on their honeymoon and she absolutely loved it…I'm shocked to hear that she has now passed her copy onto Luka. I wonder what he will think, will he even read it?

Jodie nudges me. "Is it him?"

I put my phone back in my bag. "Sorry…it was Melita."

"Luka's sister?"

I nod my head. Hearing from Melita…her talking about her brother with such familiarity with me…I just realise even more how much of my heart I left behind in Croatia.

We leave the bullring and begin to walk to the nearest bus stop which should be just a few minutes away.

Jodie links her arm through mine. "I don't know about you but I'm starving…shall we get lunch now before we get back on the bus?"

"I could eat something, what do you fancy?"

We stand at the traffic lights waiting to cross the street, the pavement on the opposite side looking more shaded with huge green trees stretching up and over, creating a natural sunshade. People waiting to cross the street enjoy the few minutes breather from the intense heat of the day.

We cross the road and continue to walk back towards the river.

Jodie points to a nearby restaurant. "Here looks as good a place as any." She heads towards a free table and I pull out the wicker seat next to her to sit down.

"I'm impressed you made a decision on where we should eat so quickly…after last night."

"Ha ha…"

The restaurant's busy and we were lucky to get one of the last couple of tables nestled in the coolness of the shaded patio. A huge grey parasol hangs above us - supported by wooden beams which are covered in delicate fairy lights and artificial greenery.

Jodie takes out her mobile from her bag and I see an intense stare of concentration followed by a mischievous grin then spreading across her face.

I reach for the menu. "What's up with you?"

"Just Darren messing around that's all." She throws her phone back in her bag on the floor. "I quite fancy a drink of something strong."

"Beer for a change?"

"Mmmm, good idea." Jodie stands up and pulls her bag onto her shoulder. "Would you mind ordering for me please, Lu? I'll have what you're having, I just need to nip to the loo."

"Yeah, okay."

Cigarette smoke wafts in my direction from the couple on the next table making me glance their way. It looks like they're having a working lunch as they're both in smart dress, a laptop open on the table in front of them as the guy frantically types notes - the woman's tone serious as she talks at him. He interrupts her mid-sentence and she makes the most of the break to take a drink of her coffee.

I order two beers and two chicken sandwiches and take my phone from my bag to look back at the pics I've taken so far today. I giggle self-consciously at the picture of my bull impersonation, just as Jodie returns to the table.

"I can't believe you're going home tomorrow."

"I know, but we've still got the rest of the day and the flamenco show tonight." Jodie strikes a flamenco pose in her seat, her hands making shapes as she throws them in the air. "...speaking of which, with the long drive back to the airport tomorrow, probably best if I don't drink too much tonight."

"Ha! I'll remind you of that later, shall I?"

The waiter delivers our drinks and I take a sip from my tall glass of refreshing beer.

Jodie studies her glass for a second before taking a sip. "I take it there's still no word from Luka?"

"Nope." Another - *longer* gulp of beer as I sit back in my seat.

"There could be a simple explanation you know, why he hasn't replied. He could be busy..."

I smile, grateful that Jodie's trying to make me feel better. "It's fine. Like I said this morning it's best just forgotten about now."

I do my best to swallow the lump in my throat and ignore the heavy feeling in my heart. The waiter delivers our chicken sandwiches and we sit back and enjoy our food.

***

Back on board the bus after our leisurely lunch, I can already feel the after effects from the two drinks we ended up having. The Spanish guitar music relaxes me again through the earphones as we travel on the bus past the Plaza de España, and into the narrow streets of the *Triana* district. The commentary informs us that *Triana* is a residential and administration district.

Traditionally, the people who live in this area are called *Trianeros*, and some people who live here claim to have never been into the city of Seville. We continue along to the second stop and along past the theme park of Isla Magica, towards the stop for Torre de los Perdigones (the Tower of Pellets).

Getting off the bus, which this time seems to be at a bus station, we follow our map and walk in the direction of the tower. The area is extremely busy with hordes of people walking in every direction, people dipping into the road to overtake the people walking in front of them. There seems to be a lot of shops that are closed down and businesses no longer trading, more than I've noticed in central Seville. Shops are boarded up, some of them just look closed yet they appear to be empty inside.

We see the tower on the right-hand side of the street behind some railings and next to a café, which might be good for a drink afterward. The tower itself has arched windows with a circular pattern built into the brickwork above each window.

Reaching the entrance, we enter the lift which takes us up the 45 metres to the viewing area - according to the poster on the wall. I think we must've come at the right time as other than me and Jodie, there are only two other people in the tower. We look out at the view above the mostly white rooftops and we can see for miles, despite the gridding in front of us. The other couple of tourists catch the lift back down as we walk around the viewing area and see the Puente de la Barqueta, a large

314

suspension bridge which crosses the river. The gleaming white of the structure stands out from the blue sky.

Jodie stands in front of the doors of the lift as I go to press the button, stopping me from calling for the lift.

"We're not going back down onto solid ground until you tell me the truth about how you're feeling…and I mean the honest truth."

I go to speak but she interrupts me. "…I mean the real truth…not just the spiel of how nothing can happen and it was a two week thing. I know you Luisa-Maria!"

"Wow…only my mother calls me that."

She puts her hands on her hips, clearly meaning business. I move around on the spot, looking at the view and taking a breath before looking back at her, holding my hands up in question but staying silent.

"Just admit it Luisa…I know you're in love with him."

What feels like a couple of minutes passes where I wonder how it will feel to say it out loud.

"Okay fine....you win....I'm in love with him. Are you happy now?"

Jodie claps her hands together. "Very happy!" She pulls me into a hug. Doesn't she realise this doesn't change anything?

"Jode…things are still going to be the same, we're still miles apart in distance and maybe even in our feelings I don't even know." I breathe out heavily, I must've been holding my breath and not even realised. "…I never in a million years expected this to happen. How can I have met someone and fallen in love with him so quickly?" Tears fill my eyes as I do my best to hold them in. "Nothing will come of this no matter how much I want it to, I just have to get my head around that."

The look on Jodie's face surprises me as she pulls me in for another comforting hug and exhales in relief to finally hear me speaking openly.

She pulls away, holding onto my shoulders. "I think you're wrong about this, the two of you need to talk."

I look skyward. "Please..." I snap "You're my best friend and I know you're trying to help and you just listening to me is a help and it feels so good to finally say how I feel out loud but...I'm asking you, please, can we leave it there?"

A sombre expression appears on her face. "Oh Luisa...if you really think that's best?"

I smile and nod, squeezing her arm before pressing the call button for the lift.

Back down on ground level, we relax in the small park enjoying the sun as we wait for the next bus back to the centre of town, trying to forget our tense conversation.

As Jodie's struggling a little with the heat of the sun on her pale skin, we do the 15 minute journey back to stop number one on the cooler lower deck of the bus.

Chapter 36 – Luka, Dubrovnik

Melita and I are helping our brother to move his last couple of boxes into my apartment when I receive a message from Jodie. She tells me she is leaving Seville tomorrow and Luisa will be there for another three days staying at the *Hotel Casa de Luna,* before she flies to Madrid – "…if you are willing to take the risk…" she says.

I sit down on the sofa, re-reading this message over and over. Melita asks me what is wrong. I need to make my decision before I tell her because I know what she will say. She will tell me I should be leaving for the airport, but would that be the right thing to do?

Chapter 37 – Luisa, Seville

The atmosphere as we enter *El Tablao* for the flamenco Show that night is a mixture of moodiness and excitement. The restaurant decor is perfect with its bare bricked walls painted in a dark magnolia colour, which reminds me of the colour of wet sand at the beach. We're lucky enough to be seated at one of the slightly elevated tables next to the stage so we have one of the best views in the house.

In front of the stage sit several long tables full of people, eagerly awaiting their food as they chat loudly, taking in the atmosphere around them.

After a few minutes at the table, the waiter approaches us with a bottle of white wine, and begins to pour two glasses, one for each of us.

"Remember what I said..." Jodie flicks her dark hair behind her shoulder as she takes in the good looks of the waiter. "...just one drink for me tonight, you can have the rest of the bottle."

"Okay." I look up at the waiter who seems to have spotted Jodie's rather low cut vest top and roll my eyes in jest.

Our first course of *gazpacho* arrives which is delicious and the slices of boiled egg that sit on its surface really compliments the flavours. I always find it difficult to think of *gazpacho* as soup - being used to eating them hot but it's a very welcome change in the heat. I think of how Pete could have done with this to cool him down that day in Montenegro instead of *rastan*.

The soup is followed by chicken and chorizo *paella* and my taste buds are awoken by the delicious spicy chorizo, the smoky juices giving the subtle flavour to the rice perfectly.

"I made this for Mark once." I continue to chew. "He hated it."

Jodie shakes her head. "Why doesn't that surprise me, did anything please that man?"

"I think the multiple women probably did…" I cover my mouth as we both laugh, so grateful to be finding it funny now.

"It's good to see you making a joke about it…"

I see her looking behind me. "That waiter is clearly checking you out."

I subtly turn my head to the side. "You mean the one that couldn't keep his eyes off your cleavage a few minutes ago?"

"Not him." she giggles. "The one next to him with the black hair…"

As if by magic, he suddenly appears next to us to take away our now empty plates. "Ladies, you are finished?"

Jodie stutters. "Yes, erm…thank you."

"*Gracias.*" I add, to which I receive a wink from the waiter.

The two waiters working on our section stand together repeatedly looking over at our table.

Jodie takes a sip of wine. "They're making it so obvious they're talking about us." She leans towards me, a look of intrigue on her face. "Can you hear what they're saying?"

I look in their direction before turning away again and concentrate on their voices. "It sounds like they're deciding the best way to approach us. The close shaven waiter wants to wait until the end of the night but the dark haired waiter thinks he knows better and wants to come over and make conversation to find out where we're staying…"

"That's so funny…you've got to let them know you understood what they were saying, it'll be hilarious."

I giggle. "Really?"

"Do it…"

I walk towards them asking them in Spanish where the toilets are and as they reply to me in English and point towards them, I go to walk away before walking back to them to let them know in Spanish I heard and fully understood them before continuing on to the toilet. I'm laughing to myself at the look of shock and embarrassment on their faces and as I walk back to Jodie she's almost out of her seat in desperation to know what happened.

"Well? What did you say to them? They looked mortified and both stared at you open mouthed as you walked away."

"I thought I'd tell them it would be better to approach us at the end of the evening just in case it becomes awkward when we tell them you have a boyfriend and I'm going through a divorce…"

Immediately I think of Luka, I wish I didn't but he pops into my head.

After a dessert of a deliciously light caramel tart, two male singers position themselves at the back of the stage. They begin the steady clapping of the rhythm as a third male strums his guitar, whilst the first flamenco dancer begins her routine in front of them. She's wearing the most stunning bright red long dress, with ruffles flowing along the full length of the skirt.

The music is surprisingly powerful and seems to really captivate me, drawing me in to the atmosphere as it tells the story and encourages the audience to clap along to the rhythm. I'm completely drawn in.

I reach for my glass of wine to see it's empty, and only a mouthful remains in the bottle. I catch the attention of the waiter and order another glass of wine for myself and water for Jodie. One of our friendly servers wastes no time in delivering our drinks, telling us there will be no charge for them.

Again, as the next dancer takes to the stage - this time wearing a black and white spotted ruffled dress, I get lost in the story telling.

After the 45 minute show, the whole of the audience is on its feet absolutely enthralled with the performance. We can feel the charged atmosphere in the room after such a powerful and inspiring show.

As I reach for my bag from the floor, my head feels slightly floaty from the wine. The two waiters appear next to us looking rather uncomfortable and begin to speak to us in Spanish until they realise Jodie can't understand them.

"Ladies, we apologise…"

I hold my hand up in dismissal. "There's no need to apologise…"

The dark haired waiter goes to shake my hand. "You speak Spanish very well." He kisses the back of my hand. We chat to them for another couple of minutes before saying good night with the perfunctory kiss on each cheek.

Outside as the night air hits me, the drunkenness really kicks in. Jodie takes hold of my arm as she laughs at my blotto state and gently leads me back out onto the main *avenida* and towards the bridge.

"Lu, that was so much fun."

I have to agree with her as it's been a brilliant night. I pull Jodie to a standstill on the bridge as exhilaration takes over and I stare out at the water and the illuminated Torre del Oro with the restaurants alongside the water.

"Ohhh, its soooo beautiful…" I sing, as I adjust my grip on the railings of the bridge, much to the amusement of Jodie, who's doing her best to get me back to the hotel in one piece.

***

All I can hear are drawers opening and closing and zips being zipped as I force my eyes open to see Jodie packing her trolley case on the bed next to me.

"Morning…sorry about waking you, I should've packed last night really." She picks up her case and wheels it over to the door.

I do my best to sit up in bed, resting my head against the coldness of the wall. "What time is it?"

Jodie brushes her hair. "It's coming up to 10 now. Are you too delicate for breakfast?"

"No, I'll just get dressed." I throw on the first thing I can find, run my fingers through my hair, wash my face and I'm ready.

In the hotel breakfast room, Jodie fills up on sausage and bacon but all I can face is a cup of tea and a slice of toast.

"I hope I wasn't too much of a handful last night, it was a great night though."

Jodie stirs her tea. "Don't be daft. It was a good night, it makes me want to learn flamenco after watching the professionals."

I get a brief recollection of the wonderful displays of traditional Spanish dancing. "What time's your flight?"

"3:50 p.m., I think I'd better get going around 11."

I spread more jam onto my toast. "It'll be weird without you…"

"I wish I could stay longer, I wish I could do the whole three months with you! You're so lucky."

I smile, thinking of the exciting time ahead of me seeing different countries, the places I've always wanted to see.

"I know, it'll be great." I decide I need more tea, offering Jodie a refill.

"Not for me, you carry on. I might just head back to the room to call Darren, if you don't mind?"

"That's fine, I'll meet you in reception."

I savour the taste of my hot milky tea and my mind starts to plan my day ahead. My mobile chirps next to me on the table, it's Jodie letting me know she's in reception and ready to go. I finish my tea and make my way up the stairs from the dining room to see Jodie poised with the car key in hand and her trolley case at her feet.

I pull her in for a hug. "Make sure you let me know when you get to the airport."

"Of course I will…" She squeezes me tightly before letting me go. "…see you in three months, but I want constant updates and photos!"

"I'll speak to you loads..."

"You certainly will." Her face breaks into the biggest grin I think I've ever seen. "Just promise me you'll do everything Lu, just go for it...you deserve to be happy."

***

Unsure of what to do next in Jodie's absence and with my head still pounding, I head back up to bed, intending to have just another hour's sleep, that should be enough to make me feel better. Needless to say, when I wake up to see I have a message from Jodie to say she has arrived safely at the airport and it's just after 3:00 p.m., I'm rather shocked.

I drag myself out of bed and jump straight into the shower, get dressed into my denim shorts and white vest top and head out with my map in the direction of the Museo Del Baile Flamenco. As I walk at a relaxed pace towards the museum enjoying the fresh air rather than catching the bus, I pass the bars and restaurants of Seville. There seems to be a different aroma of food as I pass by each restaurant. There's garlic, paprika, tomatoes and even the sweet scent of chocolate pouring out from a chocolatier. My stomach begins to rumble viciously and it's only then I remember all I've eaten today is one piece of toast.

I pass an eatery with several parasols outside which seem to be squirting water every couple of minutes to cool people off. I take a seat at one of the tables and eagerly order an orange juice with a *jamon de serrano* sandwich which comes with chips. I'm absolutely famished.

As I'm adjusting the hem of my shorts - they seem to be riding up and currently feel more like hot pants, rather embarrassingly this is the moment the waiter chooses to arrive with my lunch.

"*Jamon de serrano, señorita...*"

I clear my throat with shame. "*Gracias...*"

The huge *bocadillo* that sits in front of me looks delicious. I wait until the waiter's out of view so I don't look like I've been starving myself for the last two weeks before I take a bite. I've barely swallowed my first mouthful and I'm onto the second, I must look like a vulture.

Whilst I eat, it's no surprise to find that my mind drifts over to Dubrovnik. As much as I'm hurt that he's ignored my last two messages, I really do wish Luka well and I know whoever is fortunate enough to be with him in the future, they'll be extremely lucky. An unwelcome image of Luka in an embrace with another woman enters my head, which is enough to slow down my eating, bringing it to a complete stop. I've suddenly lost my appetite.

I sit back in my chair with my orange juice and watch as people walk by and force myself to realise that this is a new start for me. I'm taking all the lessons I've learnt and moving on, my journey well and truly starts here. I know how lucky I am to be travelling and to have my family and friends behind me, but that physical ache is what distracts me...*no I have to stop this.*

I look at my phone and I'm chuffed to see an email reply from Pam and Pete. They tell me how they've already booked to go back to the *Sun Elegance Hotel* for two weeks next year and are wondering if there's anyone that could tempt me to go back. They're clearly asking about me and Luka which makes me smile for a second as I picture Pam giving me one of her winks. I'll reply in a few days.

After lunch I turn the corner and arrive outside of the Museo del Baile Flamenco. The receptionist inside greets me in Spanish and asks me to complete the visitor's book before I pay for my entry ticket. It seems a lot smaller and more modern inside than I imagined, not the image that springs to mind when you think of a typical museum.

I'm directed into the lift and when I arrive on the first floor I enter a darkened room with screens which automatically begin to play a short video of the history of flamenco dancing.

I wonder through into the next room to find large stands giving various facts about the different types of the dance. Up until this point I had absolutely no idea there were different variations, I thought flamenco dancing was simply flamenco dancing, but it seems that there are over 50 different types which all vary in the rhythm of the *palmas* (the clapping). Some are solely for men and some for women, some are accompanied by guitar and some are not.

Another large room displays many typical outfits. Gorgeous red dresses with white spots, complete with ruffles up to the hips and on the shoulders, plain red dresses, again with ruffles a plenty, beautiful bright coloured dresses, I could have hours of fun trying these on - if only.

After picturing myself wearing every dress on show, I continue through the exhibition, back to the ground floor where I see the rooms in which the dancing is taught.

I now enter a room which feels almost like a tunnel, where the brickwork is painted cream and subtle side lighting shows images from various local photographers of the dance in action. Photography…another reminder.

With typical guitar music playing in my head for the rest of the day, it's back outside and into the sun. I follow the back streets noticing it's pretty quiet out here this afternoon. I think I probably chose the wrong time of day to have my *siesta* earlier as I fan myself with my museum leaflet.

I near the bus stop and see a bus approaching so with a bit of fast paced walking, I make it to the stop in the nick of time and secure a seat downstairs near the front in the coolness of the air conditioning. I'm not the only one to have chosen to sit downstairs as I take one of the last few seats.

The streets as we drive through them on the bus have that lovely relaxed end of the day feel despite there being more traffic around now and us stopping at more red lights.

Out of the window I see a group of three elderly men gathered on the corner. One of them singing, one playing guitar and one playing an accordion. I remove my earphones to hear the cheery rhythm as it floats in and I'm reminded of my *Tito* and the times he used to sing to us. I can't help but smile before the bus pulls off in the direction of the hotel.

Getting off the bus, I notice a sign at one of the street side ticket sellers offering a day trip to Ronda. As I enquire at the desk, I'm told there are tickets left for the bus tomorrow leaving at 7:00 a.m. priced at €22. Opening my purse, I see that I annoyingly only have €14 left of what I've brought out for the day and purposely haven't been carrying my cards around with me. With only half an hour until the ticket desk closes for the day, I rush back to the hotel to pick up some more money from my room safe to secure my place on tomorrow's trip. I cross the bridge, picking up the pace and feeling my face begin to flush in the heat and my vest top sticking ever so slightly to my skin. Nice.

I reach the doors to the hotel, smoothing my hair back from my face and almost throw myself through reception in the rush, opting for the stairs rather than the lift. I'm just about to begin climbing the stairs to my room when the sound of someone calling my name stops me momentarily. I turn around and my heart skips a beat. It's Luka.

Chapter 38 – Luisa and Luka, Seville

I think I'm in shock. The man I've missed so much for the past week, the man who keeps occupying my thoughts - who I thought I would never see again is standing in front of me.

I walk slowly towards him, unsure of what to do or what to say as he stands before me looking as delicious as ever in his cropped khaki combats and a white T-shirt, his dark hair looking slightly shorter and a little ruffled, his hands firmly in his pockets. I want to throw my arms around him but at the same time, I'm confused as to how I should greet him.

He speaks first. "It is hot out there..." He smirks, making me very aware of my red face and the sweat I can feel on my skin.

"L-Luka..."

He closes the gap between us by reaching his hand out toward my face and lifting my hair away, I feel my body quiver beneath his touch. I'm no longer worrying about the heat on my skin, now feeling a different type of heat. I look deep into his eyes and as he presses his lips to mine I'm in heaven. He pulls away a few seconds later, his arms still around me and mine around him.

He begins to laugh. "You have lost your voice?"

"I... I think I'm in shock, how are you here?"

He looks around us. "Can we go up to your room? I will explain."

We walk up the stairs to the fourth floor and the whole time I'm shaking with anticipation, wondering how this could be and questioning if I'm actually awake…or maybe I'm dreaming.

I open the door to my room and Luka follows me inside, throwing his gigantic backpack down next to the door. As I notice his bag - the sheer size of it, my stomach flips with excitement. He's obviously planning on staying for a while, but even thinking this makes me afraid of jinxing it.

"So…how did you know where I was? What are you doing here?" Luka pulls the chair out from the dressing table and sits down, I sit on the edge of the bed opposite him.

"Jodie - she emailed me last week before you left."

I'm filled with dread as I wonder what she said to him. "Jodie, what did she say? How did she even get your address?"

"She said that you sent her an email from me…with the photographs?" It suddenly makes sense, but I'm desperate to know what she's said.

"…she asked me how I felt about you…"

My hands fly up to my face with awkwardness. ".. I'm so sorry, just wait until I speak to her…"

Luka laughs, his perfect teeth showing as he grins through his goatee. "Luisa, I am here now, what do you think that tells you?"

I smile, realising what he's saying but at the same time, I remember how I've felt with him not replying to me. "I hadn't heard from you for a few days…you didn't reply…I thought maybe…"

"…I had changed my mind about you?"

I nod with honesty as he stands up and sits next to me on the bed. "Never."

I dissolve into his arms as he kisses me again and we're filled with passion for one another. He pulls at my vest top, which still feels damp from the heat of the day but at this moment, I really don't care…I only hope he doesn't.

As we lie back on the bed tangled together afterward, things just feel so right. I watch the rise and fall of his chest as my head rests on his shoulder and his hand rests on my lower back. We lie like this for a while, I'd be happy enough to lie like this forever, but being in desperate need of a drink, I peel myself away to pick up a bottle of water from the fridge.

I throw on his T-shirt…which is apparently now a habit of mine, and sit down next to him on the bed, gulping back half the bottle of water in one go. Luka lies on the bed watching me before sitting up and kissing me on the lips and taking the water from me. Questions run through my mind as I watch him drinking.

"I've got to ask, how long are you here for?"

He catches his breath after drinking. "Are you bored of me already?"

I playfully punch his arm and he hooks his arm around my shoulders, pulling me into him.

"Erm… a few days."

I snuggle back into his chest. Knowing I have him here for a few days is fantastic, but the thought of then saying goodbye to him all over again makes me feel sick. I'll definitely make the most of every second we have together.

I have a sudden thought. "How did you manage to swing the time off work at this time of year?"

"I can be very persuasive. Anyone would think you were not pleased I was here."

"I think you know how pleased I am you're here…I was just wondering, that's all…"

"Well, stop wondering." He kisses me on the head. "I think we both need a shower after that, and then I am desperate for food." He leads the way into the bathroom and I follow him, giggling all the way.

***

A message comes through on my phone from Jodie, asking *"If my surprise has arrived yet."* I type out my response telling her how grateful I am to have an interfering best friend and that my surprise was the best surprise I've ever had.

I learn that after she received the email with the photos, she contacted Luka. When she was trying to persuade me ask him to meet me in Zagreb and then I changed my mind, that's when she took matters into her own hands. She told him where we were and how she could see the depth of my feelings for him and the rest, as she said, was up to him.

Later Luka and I stroll hand in hand towards the San Telmo Bridge as darkness falls around us. The surroundings and of course the company, are wonderful. The buildings around us begin to light up and the humidity of the day is still as strong as ever. I can't believe that just last night I was standing in this very spot in awe of the view, with Luka never far away from my thoughts and now here I am, 24 hours later with him by my side. I feel like I need to pinch myself.

I steer him by the hand over to the railings on the bridge and he casually leans his arms on the side and casts his gaze in the direction of the Torre del Oro.

I watch him taking in the stunning sight before us, asking him what he thinks of the view.

"It is very beautiful...I am glad I came." He leans one arm on the railing and passes his other hand on to the small of my back. "It is not just these views I want to look at though..."

I giggle contentedly as he pulls me toward him before he carries on.

"What I want to know is...that night with your friends, the male attention you were getting...."

I feel a smirk begin to appear whilst at the same time, I try desperately to keep a straight face.

"What about it?" I can feel him watching me but, I purposely continue to stare across the water.

I hear the infectious sound of his playful laughter and I practically have to bite my cheeks to hold my laughter inside.

I admit defeat and the laughter rushes out of me. Luka puts both of his arms around my waist, making me feel serious again as the strength of his intent look almost hypnotises me. We stand like this just for a few moments drinking each other in and then I untangle myself before I end up saying something to him that I've wanted to say for weeks, but I'm afraid of what will happen if I do.

I pull Luka along beside me. "Come on, I thought you were hungry…" I notice he has a look of confusion on his face.

Chapter 39

My mind starts working overtime as we walk along the *avenida*. I'm absolutely ecstatic to have Luka here with me and now I know he definitely feels something for me and we weren't just a 'two-week thing' in his eyes either. It's fantastic. I'm buoyed by knowing something's possible between us, but the fact of the matter is that in a few days when he goes home again, I still don't know what happens next.

Luka's chatting away beside me, telling me about Melita and Patrik and how much they loved their honeymoon, but the whole time he's talking my mind is elsewhere, trying to answer the questions I have going around in my head.

We choose '*La Comida Tapas Restaurant*' for dinner, a cosy place with the terrace filled with outdoor floor lamps on the corner of the *avenida*. We take a seat outside and order food but I'm struggling to fight away the questions that continuously run through my mind.

Sensing something isn't quite right he places his hand softly on my arm that rests on the table.

"Are you okay?...You are glad that I came to Seville?"

"Of course I am..." I move my hand towards his and hold it on the table. "...I'm just thinking about things, that's all..."

"What things?"

Why did I have to say that?! "Just, about how things were between us... after I left Dubrovnik and was back at home."

Luka leans back in his seat and takes a deep breath, the material of his black shirt seemingly tightening across his broad chest as he does so. He clears his throat as he releases his hold of my hand.

"After you left, I did not know what to do or how you felt - not for certain. I knew that you wanted to know how I felt...but with everything you had going on with Mark, I did not want to make things more difficult for you, so I tried to give you some space..." He looks down at the table before making eye contact with me again.

"...that night you told me you had booked your flights...I knew that if I told you how I was starting to feel I did not want you to cancel your trip, I know this means very much to you."

The waitress delivers our first dishes of cheese and potato *tortilla* and smoky paprika chicken skewers, meaning an awkward silence as the conversation stops between us briefly.

"*Gracias...*" I utter gratefully as the waitress pauses to top up our glasses of wine, before walking away again.

"But you must have known how I felt? I clearly wanted to keep in touch."

"I know you did, but I had to do a lot of thinking myself there is always a risk involved."

I can tell Luka's finding it difficult to explain how he feels. He's always so matter-of-fact about everything, but when it comes to feelings, it's certainly different.

He continues talking, playing with the stem of his wine glass. "There has been no one I felt this way about before..."

Hearing him say that about me makes me feel like I could explode with happiness. "What about Amra?"

"Not even her…things are different with you, so different."

My smile grows wider. "I'm so glad to hear that."

"Seeing you around my family and friends at the wedding…you were yourself and you seemed so… content…" he shakes his head as he smiles. "… it made me so happy to see you this way."

He meets my eyes properly for the first time since he began talking about the situation. I squeeze his hand, feeling such a rush of love for him.

I realise I hadn't even thought about the possibility that maybe Luka was scared of being hurt too. I didn't think about things from his point of view. Now I'm doing so, I can understand a bit more of why he went quiet on me before I left for travelling.

We both start to pick at the food in front of us before it goes completely cold, the natural change in the subject of conversation making things feel easier again.

We chat about my meeting with the solicitor about my divorce and Luka tells me a little more about his divorce before we move on to the topic of Seville. I tell him about the previous night at the flamenco show, how good the performances were, how good the wine was, but how bad the hangover was this morning. We decide that we'll do the day trip to Rhonda the day after tomorrow before we fly off to Madrid the following day. It appears that Jodie has also been a travel agent for Luka in getting him on the same flights as me.

After some further food of *empandillas* and *aceitunas*, we decide to ask for the bill.

I catch the attention of the waitress. "La cuenta, por favor." She nods her head and rushes back inside the restaurant, returning 15 minutes later - in typical Spanish relaxed style, with the bill. After the usual squabble about me paying half towards the bill and Luka not letting me, I drink back the last of my wine as the waitress collects our payment.

Luka moves closer toward me, his hands resting on the table. "There's something I haven't told you, Luisa…"

A flutter of anxiety rushes into my stomach. "Go on…"

"When you wondered how I got time off work earlier? I have lost my job."

Just for a second, I think he's joking until I take in his humourless expression. "What, why?" And then realisation hits me like a slap in the face. "Not Mark?"

He raises his eyebrows. "Afraid so."

I close my eyes and rest my head in my hands. Anger boils inside of me, just when I thought Mark couldn't get any lower, it seems he can. "I'm so sorry, Luka…" Tears fill my eyes.

Luka walks around the table and stoops down next to me, lightly rubbing my leg. "Come on, let's walk."

He wraps his arm around my shoulders, giving me a couple of minutes to get my head around what he's just told me. We walk in the direction of the cathedral.

I'm desperate to know the full story. "What happened exactly?"

"The day you were leaving - after my breakfast shift, I found out he had made a complaint against me. He said I was harassing his wife, it is probably the only time he has told the truth in his life." Luka laughs softly.

I'm glad to see him laughing about it, but this is serious. "It was hardly harassing though was it and that's beside the point, why can't he just leave things alone?"

"I was, how you say… suspended?" I nod my head. "…but I knew I could be sacked so, I resigned."

"I'm so angry… I just…ugghh!" I can hardly talk, I'm so annoyed.

Luka continues to laugh, which completely baffles me. How can he not be worried about losing his job?

"How can you find this funny?"

He stops walking and pulls me to one side out of the way of the flow of people. "You cannot see he has done us a favour?" He holds both of my hands with his as they hang loosely by my sides.

I frown as I try to take in what he's telling me.

"Without my job, I knew there was nothing really stopping me coming out here to find you. Luisa, I am not just here for a few days, I want to come travelling with you…"

My mouth falls open with shock. "That's amazing!"

I throw my arms around him and he squeezes me tightly, I feel like all of my Christmases have come at once. I pull away, keeping a hold of his arms. "What about your apartment, your mortgage?"

"Aleksander is staying there whilst I am away, and before you ask about a job, there is a job coming up in November - the head chef at the *The Grand Lapad Plaža...*" He holds me tightly around my waist. "It is more money and I will be helping to design the á la carte menu, it is a great opportunity for me."

"Melita's hotel?"

"Yes, I know the right people." he grins. "I have spoken to the manager and the job - it is mine if I want it."

It's clear to me then that Luka knows me completely inside and out as he stuns me once again by knowing what I'm thinking. "...but I will only accept the job if you will come back to Dubrovnik with me?"

Exhilaration kicks in as I listen to him, I can hardly wipe the smile off my face.

He stares at me, waiting for me to speak. "Do I take the silence with the grin as a yes?"

I begin to giggle blissfully as I attempt to get my words out. "Y-you want me to live with you in Dubrovnik?"

"Preferably Dubrovnik or if you would rather stay at home, I could come to be with you? Luisa, that week I had away from you was the longest week of my life. I love you and I do not want to be away from you again."

His hand works its way up to the back of my neck as my eyes fill with tears of complete joy and happiness and I can see he actually looks quite choked up himself.

"I love you too..." I'm shaking, I feel like the luckiest girl in the world. Luka smiles and right now, I know I've never been happier. He kisses me and a stray tear finds its way down my cheek and as Luka pulls away, still holding me tightly, he shakes his head and sniggers, wiping the tear from my cheek.

I see him look over my left shoulder and hold his arm up as though he's hailing a taxi and I turn around to see an empty horse and carriage come to a halt behind us. I hadn't even heard the horse shoes sound I was so absorbed in that wonderful moment.

"Let's go…" Luka leads me to the carriage, holding my hand as I climb the two steps up and into the seats and he pulls me into his embrace.

As we're pulled along by the white horse through the beautiful streets of Seville with the world going on around us, in my head we're the only two people in the world. I know that with this man by my side I don't have anything to fear. I rest my head on his shoulder in pure contentment and as he tells me he loves me all over again, I know that our future together will be nothing short of perfect.

Epilogue

As I reach the beginning of the aisle, scattered with rose petals which leads down past the carefully laid out white chairs and into the shade of two huge trees, our families are patiently awaiting the arrival of the bridal party. I feel the tell-tale signs of nerves takeover me as my turquoise knee length dress blows lightly in the gentle breeze. I follow Georgia as she holds her father's arm and walks slowly down the aisle towards my emotional looking brother.

We walk towards Luka, who stands at the front next to the registrar, clearly enjoying his job as the wedding photographer for the day. Just looking at Luka is still enough to make my legs weak, even after nine months together.

Once the short ceremony is completed, in the spacious gardens of the gorgeous *Hotel Lujo*, in Córdoba, Ben and Georgia are now the new Mr and Mrs Summers. They look an absolute picture of joy as they pose for their wedding photographs underneath an archway of cream flowers and green foliage. Georgia's simple cut ivory dress being absolutely spot-on for the location and the day and with her long blonde hair hanging loosely in gentle waves, she looks flawless.

I continue to watch Luka, happy at work as Jodie and Darren appear beside me. Jodie fully immersed in the surroundings it would seem.

"Ohhh, what a lovely ceremony, so romantic…"

"I know, isn't this place just so picturesque…" I glance around at the landscaped gardens with the sound of laughter from the wedding guests echoing in the background against the peacefulness of the location. My parents stand with their arms around each other, sipping fizz and mingling with the other guests.

After the three months travelling I went home for a week taking Luka with me to introduce him to my parents. To say they were shocked at me bringing someone home is an understatement but, within a couple of days, they could see how happy he made me and so when I announced I would be moving to Dubrovnik to be with Luka they understood, well…eventually.

It's hard to believe I've been living in Dubrovnik for almost 6 months already. My second book is about to be published and I'm working as an events and excursions assistant three days a week at the *Sun Elegance Hotel…* right back where our story began. Pam and Pete have booked their usual two weeks at the hotel so I'll be seeing them again very soon.

Luka got the job as Head chef at *The Grand Lapad Plaža* and has started selling even more of his photographs.

I do miss my family and friends but Mom and Dad have been to see us a couple of times, and with Jodie's discounted flights, it feels like her and Darren are never away from us for longer than a month at a time, which is really nice especially as Darren and Luka seem to have struck up a genuine friendship. With my divorce almost complete, I'm planning to celebrate by changing my name back to my maiden name, completely putting Mark firmly in my past.

With the bride and groom having finished their photos, we're all called to take our seats inside the marquee for the barbecue wedding breakfast.

I meet Luka next to the floral archway as he changes his camera lens. His grey suit shows off his physique wonderfully, he looks so attractive and a complete natural with his camera. He sees me walking towards him, and holds out a glass of fizz and a gorgeous smile in my direction.

"Are you trying to ply me with drink?"

He kisses me on the lips. "I might be."

"Thanks again for doing this for Ben and Georgia, it's such a lovely wedding present for them."

"You know I will do anything to help family, it is no problem."

It's so nice to hear Luka treating my family as though they're his family too, he has a heart of gold.

We walk slowly hand in hand to the marquee entrance, before stopping to take in the fresh air and exquisite surroundings.

I can see my Dad laughing heartily with my Uncle Eladio and my Mom and Auntie Nina, fussing around my brother - my Mom straightening his tie and brushing the shoulders of his jacket with her hands.

Luka squeezes my hand. "I have been thinking, maybe you do not change your name when your divorce is final?"

"Oh?" I frown.

We walk on past the marquee, the quietness hanging in the air.

Luka then continues. "I just thought that, well, maybe you could keep the name just a while longer, until...maybe we get married?" Luka looks at me, almost wearily.

"Luka, is the fact that we're at a wedding going to your head?"

He laughs. "Of course not, it is just something I have been thinking about for a couple of months."

The seriousness of what he's saying gradually sinks in as I meet his eyes. "I could just change my name to Domitrovik instead?" I guffaw, making a joke about the situation to hide my nerves.

"I am being serious. I know we have not spoken before about us getting married but, one day…soon…maybe you would like to?"

I laugh again, feeling myself begin to light up. I pull him to a standstill, reaching my arms up and around his neck, looking deep into his eyes.

"One day soon…very soon…I would *love* to marry you."

Luka gives me a long kiss on the lips. I hook my arm around his waist, feeling the familiar warmness of his skin beneath his jacket and his arm slung around my shoulders as we continue walking.

"At least now I know…" He smirks.

"I'm surprised you didn't already."

Also by Jayne May:

Hola Madrid

Please read on….

Thank you!

I cannot thank you enough for reading my book and I really hope you enjoyed Luisa and Luka's story. This story was inspired by a holiday in Dubrovnik back in 2013, it really is such a beautiful and interesting place with so much to see.

It would mean so much to me if you could write a review of my book on Amazon, as we all rely on reviews so much for everything nowadays.

I would like to thank as always my husband Paul for listening to me blabbering on about my writing and the characters but most of all, for supporting my dream of writing and being an author.

I'd like to also thank my parents for their support, my Mom for reading this book many many times and reducing herself to tears frequently as she got so involved with the story. I think she's a little bit in love with Luka herself!

Thank you to my friends for encouraging me, caring and just always being there to listen.

Also thank you to Julie my old school friend who gave me some background information on dog shows and dog handling when I decided that Jodie needed some more characterisation.

If you would like to follow me on social media…

X : @JayneMay_Author

Instagram : @Jaynemayauthor

Hola Madrid

*****

"Intriguing and Engaging"

*****

"So well written - combating mental health as well as love at its finest!"

*****

"Truly captivating. It's so pure and realistic."

*****

"At times I genuinely forgot that I was reading a book - I was fully immersed in the story."

Read on for a sneaky peek of the blurb and first chapter....

Hola Madrid

Imagine finding out your twin sister has betrayed you in the worst possible way…would you stick around for the aftermath, or would you run away and start the new life you always dreamt of? A shocking confession from Nicole's sister Annie threatens to tear the sisters apart as Nicole runs away to Madrid.

Meeting local policeman, Jesé is a welcome distraction but she soon discovers he's hiding a secret – his girlfriend.

Say 'Hola Madrid' as Nicole throws herself into speaking Spanish, salsa dancing and begins her journey of self-discovery. Can her new life heal her past heart break? Will the irresistible Jesé make her learn to trust again?

Chapter 1

I rest my head against the window of the plane, that familiar scent of reheated aeroplane food lingering in the air. Closing my eyes, I at last drift off into a much needed deep sleep but it doesn't take long…I'm back there, I'm reliving it.

The darkness of the outside feels heavy and oppressive…my heart pounds loudly in my chest. I feel as though the world is closing in around me. I lean against the lamp post next to me, desperately trying to steady my breathing. I feel disorientated as ringing begins in my ears.

I concentrate on my breathing, slowly taking a deep breath in as I count to five before releasing as I count to five.

I hear her footsteps as she slowly reaches my side. "Nic are you okay, are you having a panic attack?" She reaches out toward me but I push her arm away, concentrating on my breathing.

Who is this woman? I thought I knew her better than anyone but why do I get the feeling that this is the first time in 29 years I'm seeing her for who she really is? The sense of dread washes over me again and again. I feel dizzy, like I can't control my body or anything around me...

I wake with a jolt, quickly realising my surroundings and looking cautiously around me, trying to catch my breath.

"Are you okay, dear?" The lady in the seat beside me asks, her hand on my arm in concern.

I exhale waiting for my breathing to steady back to normal, that familiar clammy feel on my skin.

"I'm okay thanks, bit of a bad dream..." I smile nervously as she turns her attention back to her magazine.

It's less than 24 hours since that happened to me and every time I close my eyes it's like I'm back there, finding out all over again.

I look out the window of the plane and focus on the positives of this situation. I'm almost there, my dream is in touching distance.

The view as I come in to land at Madrid Barajas Airport isn't how I expected it to be. Views of field after field, I wonder if it could be a national park, or maybe just farmland? There's certainly more greenery than I was expecting which is lovely to see.

The huge expanses of green grass with the roads running in between remind me of veins as they stretch up and around, connecting everything together. There's a lake or maybe a reservoir, the water looks so still and peaceful almost like a pane of glass, the sun reflecting its' rays against it.

The closer to the airport we get, the more built up it becomes, which is more in line with the image I'd painted in my head. Motorways with the cars driving along appearing tiny from our altitude and huge apartment blocks. I see another tower which looks as though it's made of crystal as it protrudes up into the skyline sitting amongst three other towers. They make me think of trophies sitting on display in their grandeur.

We come into land and as the plane comes to a halt I feel some relief already, relief at being far away from her.

Once I'm off the plane, I follow the signs and reach the luggage carousel. Waiting for my enormous overloaded suitcase, I text my parents to let them know I've arrived safely and that I'll call them in a couple of days. I can't face any more questions at the moment. Judging by my Dad's attitude before I left this morning, he can't accept my decision to be here. If only he knew…

When the luggage carousel starts to move, my suitcase is surprisingly and to my relief one of the first to be off-loaded. I heave the weight of my case onto the floor and exhale, feeling liberated. I'm here and better still, without a return ticket and that's a great feeling.

So many people are scared of flying but believe it or not it's actually one of the few things I'm not afraid of. If I'm on a flight and turbulence starts

I'm fine at first, I know it's to be expected. As long as the captain speaks to us to reassure us, I'm back to enjoying the flight. If it lasts too long, and the captain doesn't speak to us, I start to get horrible images.

I imagine the pilot panicking in the flight deck pushing all of those buttons and I have to do something to distract myself, so out comes the book. I do love flying though because, for me, flying always means I'm on my way to a time where I know that I'll feel safer, more settled and calm. More in control of my mind. Whenever I go on holiday my anxiety eases off, I don't worry about every single thing and my mind is just focused on the here and now, not three weeks into the future, not two months away but all on the present moment and those times are so few and far between.

When I'm on holiday or travelling I feel like I'm a completely different person, like I'm the person that I should always be and I feel like I'm the same as everybody else and I fit in.

Getting here today didn't exactly happen according to a carefully laid out plan which is usually more my style. Things happened in rather a rush, which is something that would normally cause me a massive amount of anxiety but in the end, I felt like this was the only option. I just had to get away from there, away from her. I know I've made the right decision.

I follow the crowds out into the busy arrivals hall. There, people stand waiting for friends and family to arrive. I see drivers holding signs as they wait for their clients. I spot a sign for Doctor Rosá and who looks like a Chauffeur waiting for her in his smart grey suit and hat. A casual looking driver holds a sign for Mr and Mrs Corbett, another for Mark Palmer...I wonder what their stories are, why they're here?

I make my way through the noise of echoed excited chatter from the people around me and outside to the taxi rank.

The heat hits me as I step outdoors, the bright sunshine reminds of where I am and what I've been missing since I was last here, in Spain. I get that feeling as though I've just opened a steaming hot oven door and it's wonderful. I can't help but take a deep breath, needing to let some fresh air into my lungs.

Armed with Laura's address written on a scrap of paper I approach a taxi driver, feeling nervous as the palms of my hands begin to sweat. I attempt my first conversation.

"Hola, necesito ir a este dirección por favor."

I show him the piece of paper, keeping my fingers crossed he can read my writing as well as understand me. My heart pounds loudly in my chest as I nervously await his response. He glances down at the paper, seems to do a double take at the size of my suitcase before finally he replies.

"Sí, por supuesto." He reaches down to take the handle of my suitcase from my grasp and taking that as a good sign, I climb into the back of the taxi.

As I sit down, the leather seats feel scalding hot from the intense heat of the day, even through my jeans. The shock of the temperature makes me move my hand sharply away from the seat beside me.

I type out a short text letting Laura know I'm on my way.

Laura - my best friend, lives and works here in Madrid teaching English as a Foreign Language. She made the move out here just a couple of months ago and promises me it's the best thing she ever did and now here I am, suitcase in tow following in her footsteps, only I'll be sleeping in her spare room.

Leaving the airport and heading for the city, the traffic is heavy. Cars, taxis, vans and buses are backed up bumper to bumper along the street as motorbikes do their best to cut through the lanes. Drivers are getting irate, horns are being blasted, people are shouting out of their windows. It's quite a shock to the system.

The taxi driver puts his window further down, muttering away, apparently rather annoyed as he leans his head out of the window. A couple of minutes later we begin to move forward again at a slow pace, passing shops I know from back home, banks, restaurants and bars. I notice to my left on the other side of the road, the Gran Via metro station where we seem to come to a standstill once more. I know this is the nearest station to Laura's apartment and so feeling brave, I tell the driver that I can walk from here.

"*¿Aquí?*" He asks me, pointing to the kerb. He indicates to pull over. When the driver lifts my case from the boot of the taxi I start to have second thoughts. Dragging my luggage around in this heat along with my huge handbag may not be the best idea I've ever had, but it's time to start living now, not panicking. Heaven knows I've done enough of that over the years. This is my new life. MY new life.

I move away from the edge of the kerb and into the shade of a shop awning to check where I am on the map on my phone. Apparently it's a five-minute walk from here, but 10 minutes later I'm completely lost and really regretting wearing jeans to travel, I feel like my legs are suffocating. I take another breather and after catching sight of myself in a shop window, I smooth my hair down. It's starting to frizz slightly already. I rest my sunglasses on my head and it's then that I notice how red and puffy my eyes seem to look. I'm reminded all over again of what happened.

A sudden yapping at my feet snaps me out of my thoughts and I can't help but smile as I bend down to pet the adorable Yorkshire Terrier sitting beside my feet. Her owner rounds the corner holding an empty lead looking rather flustered and muttering his apologies. Noticing the grin that's now appeared on my face, I could do with a distraction like that every time I start to dwell on things.

I look back down at my phone map before scanning my surroundings, looking for street names, anything that can help me. What I wasn't expecting was to see two policemen walking towards me, one of which catches my eye and I think I actually make a tiny gasp under my breath.

They're both dressed in the uniform of navy blue short-sleeved shirts with navy blue trousers, cap and black boots. They have a gun held in a holster on their belts and a silver whistle which the sun reflects off. They walk with such authority but the slightly taller one of the two, I can't take my eyes off him. They're chatting between themselves but I can't stop looking. It's like there's a magnet between us, some kind of force that pulls me in his direction. I feel like I need to make contact somehow, but obviously I don't.

As they draw closer to me I notice his dark brown eyes, his smattering of stubble clearly defining his jaw and that's when it happens, we lock eyes. I hold my breath for a split second, excitement filling my body. As they get closer still I can feel the heat radiating from him. Moments later, they've passed me, they've carried on and so I look back to my phone, only I can't help myself. I have to look over my shoulder and as I do so, I see him doing the same. Dare I think he could be looking at me?

I feel embarrassed and turn my attention back to directions, trying to steady my breathing down back to normal and then suddenly he appears at my side. I'm so shocked that I appear to have forgotten how to speak at first, but I certainly haven't forgotten how to blush and I do so, profusely.

"¿Hola, estás perdido?" He asks me, as he points to my map, his alluring voice in that beautiful language. Think Nicole think, '*perdido*' he said, *perdido*…lost?

"Hola, sí, necesito…erm…ayudarme?"

"You are *Inglés*? English?" he asks.

I smile, feeling partly pleased because now the pressure will be off as I can get directions in English, but also annoyed because I should be speaking Spanish.

"Yes, I'm lost… I think."

I show him where I need to get to, and as he moves his fingers on my phone screen to show me how far away I am on the map, I can't stop looking at his beautiful hands. My eyes travel along to his arms. A silver watch sits on his left wrist, I notice how the watch face is rather scratched.

His very well-toned arms, his biceps hiding underneath the sleeves of his shirt, the sleeves rolled up slightly higher.

He gestures that I need to take the next left and walk just a few minutes down the street, at least I think that's what he's saying. I'm struggling to take it in as I can't help but study him some more. His skin has that lovely olive tone which comes from walking around in the sun protecting the public and fighting crime. I bet he's no stranger to admiring glances.

Fully equipped with my directions, I smile my thanks to him. It must be so obvious that I'm attracted to him, but I'm making the most of every second being in close proximity to this man.

"I hope that you enjoy Madrid, how long you stay?" He asks me, the scent of whatever he's wearing filling the air between us. He smells very masculine yet not overpowering. His stance as he talks to me tells me he's confident and completely comfortable in his own skin. He turns the volume down on his radio as it sits against his shirt pocket, the rapid Spanish now becoming just a background hum.

"Well…I've sort of just moved here today…" I take my sunglasses from my head as I talk and attempt to self-consciously tidy up my hair, hoping that it's behaving itself. If anytime I need it to, it's now.

He seems surprised at my response. "Well….enjoy."

On that, he seems to cast his eyes over me once more as he pulls his sunglasses from his shirt pocket and slides them on. He gives me a cheeky smile and off he jogs to catch up with his colleague. Welcome to Madrid, Nicole….

I'm brought out of my trancelike state by the sound of my mobile ringing. It's Laura.

"Hi, I was completely lost, but I think I know where I am now…"

I start to push my case along, pressing my bodyweight against it.

Laura laughs. "I guessed that. Are you sure you know where you are?"

I turn around and stare up at the shop behind me.

"I'm on a corner standing outside a make up shop I think…" I lean back, struggling to see the name with the glare of the sun "…a policeman just gave me directions from here."

"Did he?" She giggles. "I'll wait outside the restaurant called Mio's, it has a green sign you should see it and we're two floors up from there."

"Right okay…"

"If you're not here in five minutes, I'll call you again. I know what you're like with directions and I also know how flustered you get around a good looking man."

Surprisingly, a few minutes later I take the next corner and I see the restaurant a few metres away. I walk past a chemist and a couple of shops that look like they've recently gone out of business. The metal shutters are pulled down and some have graffiti on them. I recognise some of the Spanish slang words sprayed across the shutters. A couple of taxis are parked on one side of the street and a driver stands on the pavement, leaning through into one of the cars impatiently pressing his horn as he stares up at the apartments next to him. I get closer to the restaurant and I see Laura.

She's wearing cut-off denim shorts and a black vest top, her dark hair pulled up into a high ponytail. She chats away with an elderly man with an apron tied around his waist. Seeing me walking towards her she grins with excitement, running towards me. She grabs me so tightly I feel like she'll leave me distorted.

"It's so good to see you."

"Laura….." I sigh, returning her embrace.

Emotion takes over as we continue to hug and I try my hardest to stay strong. She releases me, holding both of my hands in hers and looks at me solemnly, tilting her head like she's trying to look into my soul.

"You're here now Nic…" She tries compose herself, looking emotional. "…put her out of your mind…"

I nod my head, pressing my lips together to stop me from crying yet again. I take a breath as she leads me towards the elderly man who stands hands on hips, outside the restaurant next to us.

"Nic, Nicole, I'd like you to meet Mio."

She motions proudly towards the man. I reach out my hand to shake his.

"*Encantada…*" I tell him I'm pleased to meet him, to which he grins as he shakes my hand placing his other hand on top of mine.

"Guapa…Encantado. I have heard a lot about you, I feel that I…I know you already."

He speaks in a rather husky voice with a very strong accent. Mio has a familiar quality about him, maybe it's because Laura talks about him so much.

Laura gestures proudly. "Mio's the owner of this restaurant, it's one of the best restaurants around." She gives his arm a friendly squeeze.

Mio nods. "This is true…" Which makes the three of us laugh.

Laura turns to me. "Right, I'll take you upstairs get you unpacked and maybe later we could eat here?"

"Sounds good."

We slowly edge away from the restaurant towards the door to the side, which leads up to the apartments above.

"Hasta Luego Mio." Laura calls as we walk away.

Mio waves to us, as he greets some diners into his restaurant. We walk up the two flights of stairs, both of us attempting to haul my case behind us.

"Mio's lovely." Laura starts. "…Diego has known him for years and I call him our 'surrogate Uncle'. He's almost 70 but he still insists on working…." She pauses to catch her breath. "He used to do all the cooking but he's started to slow down a little now, just serving drinks and mostly chats to the customers, they're all regulars."

We reach the top of the stairs, both out of breath from the lugging of my suitcase and Laura opens the seemingly traditional brown Spanish front door and leads me inside. A compact living room houses a burgundy sofa and armchair. Behind the sofa is a dining table, which is home to Laura's laptop. There's a large open window behind the table which a soothing breeze floats through, the people and the sound of the outside on the street now barely audible.

The scene of the window with the laptop on the table is so familiar to me from our numerous video calls. I recognise the wooden blinds as they sit partially pulled up against the window. It feels strange to be here for the first time and yet in some ways, I feel like it isn't the first time because I've seen that image before so often.

A comforting arm is thrown around my shoulders and I look at Laura.

"I can't face talking about it anymore yet…" I tell her.

"Let's get you settled in tonight and relaxed and then tomorrow…we'll talk properly if you feel like you want to. I want your first night in Madrid to be a happy one."

"I like the sound of that." Trying to forget about things for a few hours certainly sounds good.

Laura knows exactly what happened. She found out in the early hours of this morning when I called her in hysterics from the back of the taxi on my way home. I told her I'd booked a flight and she immediately agreed it was the right thing. She even told me that she'd pull a sickie from work to meet me at the airport but I told her no, that I'd find my way…and I will find my way - through this…wont I?

Printed in Great Britain
by Amazon

36413847R00205